SIX STEPS TO SALVATION

ANOTHER SATIRE

P.J. MURPHY

ISBN: 978-1-0683815-0-8 (eBook)

ISBN: 978-1-0683815-1-5 (Paperback)

For everyone who has encouraged and supported me along the way. I keep writing, and Trent Argent lives on.

CONTENTS

STEP 1 – BROADEN YOUR HORIZONS

CHAPTER 1

THE CAMPMATES

It was easy enough for Trent to identify the exact moment he hit rock bottom. It happened while he was vomiting his guts out beneath Geneva's Pont Butin bridge, his sleeping bag clinging to his legs like a drowsy lover. He had never been able to hold down his beer, but the Coop's *Prix Garantie Lager Bier* was the cheapest alcohol he could find in Switzerland's overpriced supermarkets.

Trent was on his hands and knees, looking down at the vomit. As it soaked into the soil, he regarded it as a fortune-teller might divine tea leaves. The former contents of his stomach swirled, heralding a scathing message from beyond: *'How the mighty have fallen!'*

How did the great Trent Argent, celebrated entrepreneur and self-styled Community Troubleshooter, come to this?

'You need a permit to camp here, mate.'

Trent glanced behind him. *'Je ne comprends pas le français,'* he said by rote before realising that the stranger had spoken in English. The words had been drenched with a heavy Australian accent, but by most people's interpretation, they were still English.

'Just playing with you, mate. Welcome.' The fair-headed young man standing above him thrust out a hand. 'I'm Hobbs.'

Trent turned over and wriggled out of his sleeping bag, knocking aside discarded beer cans. He was a pale, skeletal thing, a consequence not just of the life he'd led during the previous five years but also of a general lack of interest in health and exercise. In another world, where he had a different personality, he might have been considered handsome, especially in that business suit he used to wear. But in jogging bottoms and a frayed T-shirt, every one of his forty-two years was evident, plus an advance instalment of others he had yet to live.

Trent wiped away the vomit from the corner of his mouth and proceeded to shake Hobbs' hand. Then, he paused to contemplate whether he had used the same hand both times.

Hobbs didn't blink. No disgust. No judgement.

'Need a boost?' Hobbs pulled Trent to his feet. 'We noticed you pitch up yesterday. Came to say hello, but you were out. Important business?' He glanced at the cans.

'I was meeting my employment adviser,' Trent mumbled.

Hobbs grinned. 'Ah, you're one of us, then? The great unwashed unemployed! Care to join us for breakfast?'

Trent was wary of company, but he needed a drink badly. To be more precise, he needed a non-alcoholic drink badly. He followed Hobbs to a collection of tents surrounding the embers of a campfire. He had seen figures crowded around it when sneaking back the previous night, but he hadn't approached.

Above them towered Geneva's Pont Butin, which spanned the gulley the Rhône had carved through the crumbling land. This river valley was a world away from the rest of the city, a haven of nature sandwiched between apartment buildings, tightly packed villas and endless construction sites. A footpath accompanied the river out of the city, squeezing between the water and the near-vertical slopes. In certain places, such as under the bridge, the gap was large enough for a small campsite. The relative privacy it afforded, and the shelter from the elements, meant this was precisely what had sprung up there.

The bridge was an impressive sight, connecting the two clifftops so traffic could travel seamlessly across one of Geneva's few river crossings. Further into town, closer to the lake, there were more opportunities to get from one bank to the other, but the circulation there was clogged with spiteful traffic lights and incomprehensible one-way systems. The next crossing further out of town was the frequently gridlocked autoroute. The Pont Butin appeared quite aware of its importance. It was two bridges in one, a grand arch spanning the river, with a layer of smaller ones on top of it, supporting the road.

About fifty metres above Trent, traffic zipped by. Cars, trucks, bicycles and the dreaded e-bike, with which he had already suffered one near-death experience. There was even a decent amount of foot traffic, thanks in part to the view the bridge afforded of the city centre. The cathedral, old town and the lake were visible from there, as though someone had assembled them for a postcard photo. This wasn't a prime tourist spot, though: it was far too busy with traffic, and to get an unimpeded view, you had to press your nose between closely spaced three-metre-high bars erected to stop people jumping. When the sun was low at the beginning or end of the day, it flickered between the bars like an old-style picture box. The suicide rate had plummeted since the fencing had been put in place, but Geneva was now a contender for the coveted title of "European capital of epileptic seizures".

In the calm of the campsite, Trent could almost forget all that was above him.

Another young man was hunched over a gas stove. He had broad shoulders and wore an oversized puffer jacket, traffic-cone orange. All around him lay a collection of broken matchsticks, scattered as though he had dived into a vat of them. The air shimmered with whispered expletives. As Hobbs and Trent approached, he looked up. His face was covered in clumps of stubble, like a sun-parched lawn, but that wasn't the first thing Trent noticed. No, it was the desperation in his eyes. Perhaps this was someone with whom he could find common ground.

'Every morning!' Hobbs cried. 'Why do you put yourself through it, man?'

'Why do *you* put me through it?' the stubbled man replied. 'That lighter only cost three francs. I still don't get why you wouldn't let me buy it.'

'It would have meant three francs less for food.'

Another voice came from a nearby tent. 'For heaven's sake!' The zipper unzipped aggressively, and a woman with wild hair in striped pastel pyjamas crawled out. 'Why do you *both* put me through it?'

In one seamless motion, she snatched the box, grabbed one of the remaining matches and lit the flame on the gas stove. Then she disappeared into her tent, uttering, 'Mine's a coffee. And it had better be strong this time!'

The three men waited a few seconds until they were sure the storm had passed. Trent regarded Hobbs, trying to work him out. He had an honest-looking face, but Trent was well aware that this could not be relied upon in character assessment. His skin was tanned dark, not just from the Geneva summer, but with a depth that suggested a great many more spent outdoors.

'This is Bong,' Hobbs said, gesturing to his friend, who was now busy balancing a kettle on the stove.

'Nice to meet you, Bong,' Trent said.

Hobbs and Bong immediately keeled over in hysterics. Hobbs' laugh was hearty; Bong's was more of a snigger, but they both went on longer than Trent judged necessary. He waited patiently until they had settled down.

'Your name's not Bong, is it?' he said.

Bong winked at Hobbs. 'Absolutely, it's Bong. That's the truth.'

Trent had too much of a headache for such nonsense, but that cup of tea was tantalisingly close, so he bit his tongue.

'And the other member of our group is Amara,' Hobbs continued. 'But we just call her A.'

'No, we bloody don't!' Amara shouted from her tent.

'You'll have to excuse her,' Hobbs said. 'Wrong side of the bed, and all that.'

'If I *had* a bed, I'd be a different woman!'

Hobbs sat down on an upturned crate and gestured towards a moss-ridden log. 'Pull up a stump.'

Trent did as invited. They waited quietly for a few minutes while Bong made the drinks. There was such a look of concentration on his face that no one dared distract him. Besides, Trent wasn't about to complain about a bit of peace and calm.

At the same moment that the drinks were ready, Amara emerged from the tent, a woman transformed. Whatever equipment she had in there had tamed that wild hair into a pristine plait. Trent guessed that she was of Indian heritage, and she carried it proudly, with ornate chandelier earrings and a long burgundy dress patterned with gold. She grabbed her coffee and perched on a tree stump on the other side of the small clearing from Trent without acknowledging him.

Trent regarded his tea with dispassionate interest. To call it "tea" was a bit of a stretch. The lukewarm water appeared supremely disinterested in being infused, and it didn't help that they had shared one teabag between three cups. He didn't bother asking for milk. One thing he'd learned since leaving the UK was that having milk in one's tea was not just unusual on the continent, it was positively frowned upon – in the same vein as baked beans and *Cadbury* chocolate. Not that he would have been hugely confident about drinking milk left out on that campsite overnight anyway, not in July.

Slightly-brown-tinted water it was, then.

'So,' Hobbs said to Trent. 'Are you interning here, too?'

Trent wasn't sure whether to find that flattering. Even on his best day, he looked at least a decade over internship age – and his "best day" was years behind him. But this was an opportunity. He had travelled to Geneva seeking new beginnings, with the nonprofit organisations clustered around the UN headquarters like limpets to a ship's hull. Time to start building his new identity.

'Not exactly,' Trent said. 'I'm looking for work. I've got a few interviews lined up. I was a big deal back in the UK. I've come here to give something back.'

"A big deal". Listen to yourself, man!

Trent battled the urge to tell them he used to be a millionaire. Back in the day, he hid this for professional and personal reasons, avoiding the scrutiny it brought with it. But now, he was ready to wave it around because it offered him... he wasn't sure... a certain level of legitimacy, perhaps? In reality, it wouldn't have offered him even that. If he'd have told these people about it, they would just have laughed at him, this drunk, sleeping rough under a bridge. Even if they'd believed him, what would it have proven? That he was stupid enough to lose a fortune. What legitimacy did that give anyone?

'Too old, I guess,' Hobbs said.

Trent failed to hide his flash of disappointment. He had a good two decades on these kids, although not everything that had happened in that period had been "good". He had begun to warm to the idea of pretending they hadn't happened.

'We're here interning,' Hobbs continued. 'Various gigs. At the moment, we're doing a stint with the IRA.'

Trent coughed out his murky water.

'International Refugee Agency,' Hobbs said slowly. 'Don't tell me you haven't heard of them. They do good work.'

Trent reflected that some acronyms apparently didn't have as much international meaning as he might have thought.

'I'll add them to my list to look up,' he said. 'And you?'

He addressed Amara, not out of any particular interest in where she was interning but because she was glaring at him. In his experience, it was essential to involve the silent people in any group. It was the best way to influence what they might say after he'd gone, when they would start speaking their minds.

'Reporters Everywhere,' Amara said.

Trent almost spit out his tea again. *Reporters Everywhere,* that sounded like a fever dream. His experiences over the years with journalists had been – what was the word? – complicated. He certainly didn't want to relive them right then, even for a fraction of a second.

'She's on the other side,' Bong said. 'Just reporting on things. She doesn't get involved.'

Amara scoffed at that. 'I'll have you know that journalists have more impact on the world than any of your international organisations. We change minds. We mobilise people. All your people do is bureaucracy, bureaucracy, bureaucracy.'

These were Trent's new neighbours, the first he'd had since childhood – unless you counted the fellow residents of the motorway hotels he used to frequent. Trent had rarely stayed in one place long enough to make roots. Anyone he had met had always been related to the job, and it had been critical to avoid getting too close to any of them. It was much harder to screw people over if you liked them, not if you wanted to keep any part of your soul. So, Trent had connected with no one.

Apart from the reporter.

Trent shook himself. He couldn't let himself go there, not in front of others. Besides, he had just remembered about his job interview later that morning. He was still only halfway back to full consciousness. Just one thing would take him the rest of the way.

'Thanks for the...' Trent forced himself to say the next word, 'tea. Where's the best place for a shower around here?'

Bong pointed towards the river. 'Shower, tap, toilet – all our needs in one!'

Trent sighed inwardly but feigned a smile. He thanked

them again and made his excuses, backing away with a bow of his head.

He fished a shirt and trousers from his tent and descended to the river, stopping behind a bush to strip down to his underpants. The water glowed fluorescent turquoise, where the clear water from Lac Leman met the sediment from the Arve. Back in the UK, he would have assumed nuclear contamination; here, he accepted nature at work. Still, his body was ill-prepared for the cold.

As Trent tiptoed into the water, his calf muscles tensed. He gritted his teeth and forced himself to paddle deeper. He couldn't turn up at a job interview smelling of beer, sweat and vomit. It was one of many trials he would endure on his path to redemption.

Anton Fredevich watched, and he waited. And he drank Aperol Spritz.

The cafés of Geneva did not fully uphold the legend of European café culture. These were not the boulevards of Paris, with their chic names, fascinating history and general haughtiness. This terrace was little more than a collection of tables blocking half of the pavement, with a fine view of traffic waiting impatiently at one of Geneva's perpetually red traffic lights. But this would do. He could go unnoticed out there, sipping cocktails with the international workers taking an early lunch break, and trying to ignore their self-involved conversation.

How he hated them. Their institution was their world. They spoke about going into "the field" like it was some game. It was his reality. He had fought his way to the top, clambering out of the mud. It had taken determination, strength and blood. More of other people's blood, perhaps, than he cared to admit. But it certainly hadn't taken paperwork.

That was the difference between him and them, not the label they had given him, which pursued him from country to country. Achievement, in his world, was something tangible, not just words on a screen.

Fredevich gulped his drink. He was used to stronger, so it did little to mute the interminable chatter from the next table.

He stared at the building across the street, as though that alone would liberate the object from its prison. He needed to find a weak point.

Trent checked himself in the pizzeria window. Not bad, he thought, given the state he had been in an hour earlier. It hadn't been the best of ideas to get inebriated the night before an interview, but it had felt necessary at the time. It was almost as though the old Trent, who thought this whole venture was a complete waste of time and money, was repeatedly pressing the self-destruct button. There was no point in trying to redeem himself; it wasn't worth the effort.

Not that going back to the UK was really an option, either. He was a pariah there now, with his questionable business dealings exposed. This had been as big a reason for him leaving the country as the lure of Geneva's nonprofits.

The man at the nearest table scowled at him. It was an intense stare from little eyes, which appeared to have sunken back into the face, recoiling from the things they had seen. He looked like a brawler, this one, with a square head, close-cropped hair and sturdy elbows. Trent didn't wait around to find out what currency was funding that glare.

This part of town was known as Nations. It was dominated by the villa where the League of Nations had met between the First and Second World Wars. These days, this housed the European headquarters of the United Nations. The site was known for the array of flags out front, the three-legged chair sculpture outside (a victim of landmines or a carpentry mishap, no one was certain), the peacocks that roamed free on the grounds and the extensive queues for security. At the front lay a concrete square where fountains of water spurted up periodically from the ground, providing a diverting water feature / a nice game for the kids / a deterrent for crowds gathering to protest.

Trent's interview was not with such a prestigious organisation. He was there to meet one of the NGOs scattered about town, above carpet stores, bakeries and homeware outlets. This one had the good sense or good fortune to be positioned at the heart of the action, opposite a pizzeria that served as an additional cafeteria for the UN workers. What better way to ensure you're on the agenda of the international organisations that fund you than to be there during lunch? Accordingly, their front windows were covered with posters advertising their cause.

Sheltering from the glare of the man at the pizzeria, Trent crossed the road towards the Geneva headquarters of Halitosis International.

≈

Trent didn't wear his best suit to the interview; he kept it in a vacuum-packed bag at one end of his tent. It had been a pain to bus across France carrying it, but he wouldn't leave it behind. Back in his heyday, it had been his armour. Crisp, finely cut and expensive, it had a scuff on the knee from the last time he wore it. He'd tripped while making a hasty exit from a village that had turned against him – his final scheme turned bad. He hadn't had it repaired, hadn't considered replacing the trousers. Sometimes, armour can protect you subtly, by reminding you of your mistakes.

Its replacement was a cheap department store suit, which he would never have been caught dead wearing back in the UK. Then again, he would never have been caught doing most of the things he now spent his time doing: busking his way to Geneva on a tourist visa; sleeping rough under a bridge with a bunch of interns; trying to do something positive for the world...

He wasn't the only one pursuing lofty goals. The reception of Halitosis International was decorated with photographs of their various projects, but at its centrepiece was a photo of an African community. All the village had come out to hold up letters that together spelt "Thank you, Halitosis Int." A plaque to one side boasted that the organisation had donated to Mapeto Village as part of its "Giving Back" programme. Trent looked at their happy faces and wondered what these people's lives were like thousands of miles away – the village elder with the tangled beard, the girl with the bright pink T-shirt, the men in their *Adidas* trainers.

'Mr Argent?'

Trent turned to see a man in a tracksuit beaming at him. The man thrust his hand towards Trent with the precision of someone moving in for the kill. Trent did his best to intercept it and ended up grabbing him by the wrist, like some gangland handshake. Still, his would-be assassin looked satisfied.

'I'm François. We spoke on the phone.'

That was an age ago, when Trent was back in the UK, pretending to be in Geneva, grasping for any lead.

'Nice to meet you,' Trent replied.

François led him to the interview room, making small talk, which inevitably strayed to the state of the weather. Trent suspected he did this due to the prevalent view that this was the only thing the English knew how to talk about, but he humoured him anyway, hoping his reward would be tea with fresh milk in it.

It was a nice enough room, well-lit, and sliced in half by a long wooden table. On the other side of the table sat his three-person jury. They introduced themselves and shook his hand before directing him to his designated seat. Trent forgot who they were as soon as they said their names. One was Victoria, Ella or Vanessa, Head of Fundraising; then there was Stefanos or Steven from HR; and finally, an older man with grey, bushy eyebrows, whose role was unclear. A volunteer, perhaps.

A few years earlier, he would have remembered every detail about them. Names have power, and titles have meaning; all those things are threads at which one can tug. What had happened to him? Had he lost those powers around the time he hit the bottle? Or was it earlier than that, when he had started to grow a conscience?

'Mr Argent,' said the Head of Fundraising. 'Thank you for applying for the role of Fundraising Assistant. I want to start by giving you an opportunity to outline your experience and why you think you are a good match for the role.'

That's when it hit Trent. Fundraising Assistant.

Assistant. It would be his job to beg people for money. And he wouldn't even be head of the department: he'd be taking instruction, running around like a dog. Was that honestly something he could lower himself to? It hadn't bothered him when he'd sent in his application – he had been scrambling about looking for anything back then – but reality struck home.

Then he remembered his sales training, from his unenviable first job flogging life insurance to the clueless. Working in sales wasn't about getting people to buy stuff, but giving them opportunities. If they wanted something but weren't sure how to get it, you were there to explain to them the options. Perhaps they didn't even know they wanted something, in which case you were there to coax out that hidden need. And if they weren't sure they could afford it, you were there to reassure them that it was a worthy investment. Fundraising couldn't be too far removed from all that, could it? There were people out there who wanted to make a difference in the world; they had the money but didn't know how to use it. His role would be to facilitate that.

And so, Trent dug deep, and he played the game, for the love of the sport, if not the end result. He talked about his skills and the fantastic ways he had applied them. He told them about his career and his long list of successes. As he spoke, he realised he had been dancing the same dance, in one form or another, his whole life; he just hadn't necessarily been aware of it. Life was a sales pitch.

He also recognised that he had given an almost identical speech when meeting with his employment adviser a day before. It had probably been more convincing that time around because he hadn't anticipated the response. Both times, he talked at length about his experience with communities across the UK and how he had helped people get a better quality of life. Both times, he left off the more sordid details of the business empire he'd built off the back of it. His resumé was impressive: rejuvenation of the Dogshon area in Liverpool; an increase in life expectancy in a community in East Sussex; reduction of STDs in Brighton, even.

The Head of Fundraising listened to all of this attentively before summarising it, just as Trent's employment advisor had done the previous day, with four words: 'So, no international experience?' It was this that had driven Trent to his alcohol-related lapse. But he was prepared this time around:

'The UK is a highly diverse country. I've been working with communities the width and breadth of the country in partnership with some of the country's most prestigious and innovative actors.'

As he spoke, he could read his interviewer's thoughts as though they were tattooed across her forehead. One word: "provincial".

'You used the word "country" three times, there,' she said.

She regarded him stone-faced for a few seconds. Then, a smile cracked, and Trent thought he detected pity in her eyes. He was wrong.

'Let me tell you a story,' she said. 'When I was a kid, I thought I was the nimblest of them all. I'd duck, dive, and run as fast as my little legs carried me. When we were in a crowded place – a supermarket or an event or whatever – and needed to get somewhere, I'd run ahead of my parents, weaving between trolleys or pensioners. I'd squeeze through the smallest gap, and as soon as I was there, I was gone. I thought I was the fastest. These days, when I see little kids doing that, I just see them getting in the way. People trip over them or spill their drinks and curse under their breath. I didn't realise that then, but now it's clear as day.'

Trent wasn't sure what he had done to offend this woman. He was supposed to be selling himself, wasn't he? Dancing the dance, making a convincing case, just as he'd do on behalf of the organisation when he got the job. This was what they expected, wasn't it? Still, it was clear he had put her back up somehow. Maybe she was tired of watching people perform for her; more likely, she objected to him being him. She had only just met him, but she already believed she had the measure of him. And she didn't even know how deep the depths went.

'This is a little direct for an interview, isn't it?' Trent said.

'At Halitosis International, we believe in the gift of feedback. Direct, unfettered feedback.'

'Thank you for your gift. I will treasure it forever.'

The old Trent would have reprimanded himself for such a mistake. Humour was the last respite of the powerless.

'At Halitosis International,' the HR guy chipped in, 'we believe sarcasm is a blight on society.'

Trent kept quiet.

'So, you tell us,' the third panellist – the older one – said, in a softer tone, 'that you have relevant experience from, where is it, Eastbottom?'

'Eastshire.'

'Why did you move to Geneva?'

'I want to do something for the greater good. I want to make a difference. There's so much going on here, what with the UN and all the nonprofits. It's the place to be.'

The interviewer grunted and marked something on his paper that looked suspiciously like a cross.

The next question came from the HR guy. Trent's hopes that this might signal the turn of a new page were quickly crushed.

'You advertise yourself as a Community Troubleshooter,' he said. 'What exactly does that mean? When there's trouble in a community, you go in and... shoot it?'

'Yes,' Trent replied wearily.

'How quaint.'

Once upon a time, Trent had been proud of that title. He would dive in and sort out an area's problems, connecting things to make them work like he was rewiring a circuit board. Yes, he had amassed a fortune off the back of it, but that didn't make his impact any less valid. If only people could see beyond their juvenile accusations that he had taken advantage of others' misfortune.

Trent might have tried to represent his old job better if he thought it might get him anywhere, but it wasn't worth the energy.

The interrogation continued in a similar vein for another twenty minutes, with each panellist going through the motions, even though they'd all known the outcome from two minutes in. They had to follow a fixed set of questions. That way, it was fair to all the candidates. It didn't feel at all fair to Trent, though. It felt like a horrendous waste of everybody's time.

The interview ended with a question from the volunteer about Trent's interest in halitosis. Trent presumed this was supposed to be the crowning glory of a candidate's interview time, an opportunity for them to shine with examples of how much the cause meant to them. It completely blindsided him. He had spent all his time preparing different ways to convince them of how great he was and sell them the value of his experience. He hadn't even considered such an obvious question.

He knew what was expected of him, though: he had to manufacture on the spot a deep-rooted desire to work for an organisation he had never heard of a few weeks before. He was vaguely aware that bad breath could signal more significant health problems, but that was about the extent of his knowledge.

They watched with detached curiosity as he writhed.

'Halitosis is very important to me,' he mumbled. 'Some of my best friends have it... it can be debilitating.'

With a bit more time, he'd probably have come up with a better response – but not much.

The ordeal was over not long after that. The volunteer escorted him from the building. Trent wasn't worth investing more of the paid staff's time. He had a kind smile that one; wise, a little patronising, perhaps, but that seemed to be par for the course.

'Let me give you a little piece of free advice,' he said to Trent as they passed through the open-plan office. 'You need to work on your motivation. Think about it: organisations like ours can look all across the world for someone who's passionate about what we do. You can't fake that. If you don't have a special reason to work somewhere, don't bother applying. Look at Simon over there. He lost his mother to halitosis.'

Trent suppressed a smirk. The old Trent started hammering at the "abort" button with no effect.

'Really?' he said.

The volunteer stared him down. 'Really.'

'Hers or someone else's?'

~

Just next door, in the headquarters of a more prestigious international organisation (i.e. one with a bigger office), Hobbs examined a photo of an African community. It seemed like all the village had turned out, beaming and happy, holding up letters that together spelt, "Thank you, IRA." A plaque to one side boasted that the organisation had donated to Masepo Village as part of its "Giving Back" programme. Hobbs studied their happy faces and wondered what these people's lives were like a thousand miles away – the village elder with the tangled beard, the girl with the bright pink T-shirt, the men in their *Adidas* trainers.

This was a good place to work, helping somewhere like that.

He and Bong were on their way from an "ironic cigarette break". The term was Bong's, and he was as pleased about it as the idea itself. Hobbs couldn't bring himself to tell his friend that he had misused the word "ironic", but anyway, the fact remained that it was not a bog-standard cigarette break because neither of them smoked. They took it because they performed their regular duties in the heart of the building, which was not nearly as vital as it had sounded when this had first been sold to them. They were confined in a box room without access to natural light for the best part of the day. It hadn't taken long for claustrophobia to develop from being a slight buzz on the edge of hearing to a full-blown panic attack. Or it would have done had Bong not brandished a packet of *Marlboroughs* on the third day, just when Hobbs was on the verge of scratching on the walls. Since then, their "ironic cigarette breaks" had taken place every hour, on the hour, with Bong brandishing the packet as though it was a torch protecting them from a smothering mist, until they were outside, around the corner, and able to breathe again, with the cigarettes safely pocketed.

Hobbs didn't enjoy the guile, but it was necessary. He just wished Bong didn't take so much satisfaction from the deception.

The building's security was tight, so the security guards manning the scanners got to know them well. They were good enough not to point out that Hobbs and Bong didn't stink of smoke when they returned. These were interns. What they were doing couldn't be important enough that they shouldn't be allowed a bit of skiving off every so often.

He was a nice guy, today's security guard. Tracey was his name, which made Bong snigger, even after the internet informed them that Tracey was a man's name just as much as a woman's. Not that they would have laughed in Tracey's presence, anyway. Tracey had a baton and a taser on his belt. Hobbs conjectured that his primary motivation for the choice of profession was that it forced people to treat him respectfully.

He wondered how much of people's lives were dictated by their names. It was a pertinent question for Hobbs, whose full name was Michael Hobson. But why call him Michael or Mike when they could call him Hobnob or – even better – just Nob? It was Australian humour at its finest, and he'd had more than enough of it. Moving to Geneva had been a chance to reset. He had considered rebranding himself "Hobson", but he had no desire to present as being anyone's son, least of all his own father's.

He was Hobbs. Serious, professional, Hobbs.

He had invested a good part of his inheritance in this. After his mother passed away, his father sent him off to a boot camp to "knock some sense into him". The fact that Hobbs had never formally come out as gay, even though it was evident to them both, had made it somehow acceptable for his dad to talk about "making a man of him". They had both known what it was really about.

Hobbs shook away those thoughts. Somehow, they were still preferable to what awaited him in the room where they had been stationed. But he had procrastinated enough. It was time to return to the cube.

Bong had headed back several minutes earlier while Hobbs visited the toilets. Hobbs found him staring fixedly at a computer monitor. He had seen Bong exhibit a similar level of concentration when attempting to light the campfire, but his lips curled with a curious pleasure this time.

'Look at this,' Bong said.

Stupidly, Hobbs obeyed. Something about the boot camp had rubbed off on him. Obedience came as second nature to him now. He squeezed around the large table, with its two computer stations, and stood behind Bong, just in time to watch someone get murdered.

'I never realised that the human body just crumples like that,' Bong said. 'In the movies, you always see people fall back with the force of the blow when they're shot. Maybe yes, for a shotgun blast to the head, but a pistol to the guts makes people fall like a sack of potatoes.' He rewound the footage and played it again to emphasise his point. 'That's the way you do it.'

Hobbs wondered about the origin of the comparison with a sack of potatoes. He didn't think he had ever been in the presence of one big enough to be considered similar to a human body. Then he realised that he was dissociating and should really have been asking what the hell Bong was doing watching that stuff on replay.

Hobbs already knew part of the answer: it was their job to watch this footage, not for the kind of forensic detail that Bong seemed interested in, but to see if they could spot details that might help identify people. All the footage stored there was horrific. This was the refugee agency's war crimes project, which gathered footage of atrocities that refugees had taken with their phones. It had to be tagged and catalogued. Most importantly, they were looking for faces. Their work could help lay the foundations for future war crime prosecutions.

Hobbs retreated quickly. He sat at his own terminal and regarded distastefully the list of files he needed to review that day. His stomach turned at the very thought of it.

Why had the International Refugee Agency entrusted this horrendous task to two interns? Such work could be achieved with AI, surely, but that would require the agency to have the funds and general technical willingness to invest in it. No, it made more sense to set the interns on it. Hobbs wagered that their rationale for selecting him and Bong was that they figured two men in their twenties would be so desensitised to violence by movies and video games that they could handle it. This was definitely the case for Bong, who watched the footage with a morbid interest because he wanted to work in special effects when he got out of there.

Hobbs didn't get it. He had watched probably as many action movies as Bong, and he really, honestly, couldn't understand the narrative purpose of getting the blood spatter pattern right when someone got shot in the head.

The result was the same: the guy was dead, and the movie moved on.

It was then that Hobbs noticed the mobile phone in a transparent plastic pouch next to his keyboard. It looked well-used, but it was a recent model – although the technology moved so fast that it might as well have been a *Betamax* tape.

'What's this?' he said.

Bong struggled to tear his eyes away from the screen. 'They brought it in while you were taking a piss.'

That was unusual. They had only been working there a few weeks, but it was very much Hobbs' understanding that all the footage they reviewed was stored securely on the local server. While most of it had been recorded on mobile devices, these were returned to the witnesses after the offending files were uploaded.

Still, whatever this was, it was a distraction from the task ahead of him.

He picked up the phone and pressed the power button. Nothing. It was completely dead. He checked the bottom. It had the same port as his own. He always brought his mobile charger in with him. Makeshift campsites under major traffic routes were notoriously bereft of power sockets, so he usually charged his phone using the IRA's power supply. It was one of the few perks of working there.

He wondered why the phone was in a pouch. Maybe they were trying to preserve DNA or fingerprints or something. Bong was not at all forthcoming about whether their supervisor had provided any instructions to this effect, so Hobbs decided to take the middle path and punch a hole in the bottom to feed the power cord through.

After a few seconds, he tried the power button again.

The phone told him to wait while it charged. When it finally illuminated, he was surprised to discover it wasn't locked with a pin code. He wondered what to do next. This felt like that time he'd picked up a wallet dropped in the street. Even though his intentions had been good, and he'd just been trying to identify the owner, he'd still feel like someone would turn up at any moment and accuse him of theft.

Hobbs decided to navigate straight to the photos. He assumed that this was why the device had been given to him. There were no photos and just one video. Unusual. He went ahead and played it.

He soon wished he hadn't.

The room was dark. A warehouse, perhaps, or a cellar. In its centre, a man was tied to a chair. Hobbs couldn't make out his face, but he could hear him whimpering.

'The only thing we're wasting here is time,' came a voice off-camera. The words were English, but the accent was heavy – Eastern European, perhaps, although Hobbs was no expert. 'No one knows you're here. No one who cares, anyway.'

Bong must have noticed Hobbs' forehead furrow because he said, 'What have you got there?'

When Hobbs didn't reply, Bong abandoned his work-station to look over his shoulder.

Shortly afterwards, the screaming began.

'This is really something,' Bong said.

Hobbs let the phone slip through his fingers and onto the desk. Bong picked it up eagerly.

Hobbs grabbed Bong's headphones and tossed them towards him. 'Put them on.'

He paced the room, stretching out his arms as though the motion would make the corruption slide off him. No, no, he was tainted now. He looked at his friend, whose eyes were glued to the phone screen.

'Hobbs,' Bong said eventually, 'you have to listen to this.'

'No,' Hobbs said. 'I really don't.'

But Bong was right.

CHAPTER 2

THE CAMPMATES

Trent slurped at the remains of his milkshake. It had a brand-oriented name, which he rejected completely – to him, it was just a milkshake. It was enough that he had gone into that fast food restaurant at all, to that haven of those who have given up on life. That wasn't the brand's strapline, of course. All around the world, people looked to those restaurants for stability on which they could rely. You knew what you were getting when you ordered a meal there. It was a universal taste, with a few local variants tacked on for good measure. For Trent, it was the taste of defeat.

As a child, he used to look forward to his parents taking him. It was a treat, presented as a reward for good (i.e. conformist) behaviour, although, in reality, it was more likely an inexpensive option when they didn't feel like cooking. No matter, for pre-adolescent Trent, it was a wonderous experience: eating out, eating with his fingers, and getting given a tacky plastic toy to remember it by.

He wondered how many other activities he enjoyed as a

child now seemed like the depths of tedium: parties, art, football; team sports in general.

Trent looked around and realised that little had changed. This was one of the few memories from childhood that remained relatively untouched. Maybe the toys had become more elaborate, but they were no more robust. There were a few more options on the menu, too, and some even pretended to be healthy. But the clientele was the same. This was the week's big outing for the family at the table next to him. The father put his arm around the mother while she stuffed herself with fries. Trent would have looked down his nose at them, but he was in no position to judge anyone.

He had gone there because it was the cheapest meal within a 50-mile radius. The sauces made the food taste like it might have actual nutritional value, so long as he didn't think too closely about what he was eating. Most importantly, they served milk with their tea.

He had taken up a seat at the window, a bar looking out on Plainpalais, a diamond of terracotta concrete which played host to a market at weekends to the market, a fairground during the school holidays, and a skatepark all year round. This place had history, although Trent doubted it would have been quite the same back in the day. It was mentioned in Mary Shelley's *Frankenstein* as one of the sites where the monster would prowl. It had been recreated as a bronze statue at the nearest corner of the plain. A couple of kids were taking out their frustration on it, kicking and stamping on its foot, as though that would achieve something. Secretly, Trent wished it would animate and rip them limb from limb, not because he was particularly protective of national monuments but because it would have given him a laugh. He counted every time the world kicked back at someone other than him as a small victory.

It had been five years since the world kicked his way. Since then, he had been on the receiving end. And it hadn't been just one kick, either. Again and again, it had taken revenge on him for all the people he had screwed over in his business dealings.

Trent reckoned that if he were to do a straw poll of everyone he'd met in his life, the vast majority would say he'd had it coming. He had been complicit in his downfall, too, and still was every time he picked up a bottle.

As if to illustrate that point, he began drinking. Not a milkshake this time, but something more intoxicating, purchased from the kiosk down the road. This time, he splashed out on a liqueur as he couldn't face the thought of another beer. The next few hours were a blur. When he regained control, it was the evening. He was beside the campfire.

It was not the first time he had skipped a chunk of the day.

Not that he actually lost consciousness. He had been there all along, a passenger coaxing his body to make its meandering way back home – or the closest thing he had to it, that campsite under Pont Butin. Some part of him had participated in the pleasantries when he got there, a part that was oblivious to the sideway glances of his camp-mates. It had agreed to join them for dinner, and now it spoke up, indifferent to all but the most sacred of boundaries.

As the fog cleared in different parts of Trent's mind, he found himself in the middle of telling an anecdote.

'I saw a man standing there. He had a black hoodie over

his head and a plastic bag in his hand.' Trent was pleased to discover that he wasn't slurring (although what drunk person realises when they are?), but his judgement must definitely have been off if he had chosen that story. 'He was just standing outside a car showroom, not looking at the cars, not looking at anything. Just staring into space.'

Bong leaned forward. His face flickered in the flames of the cooking fire, and there was a wild enthusiasm in his eyes. 'Was he a zombie? Sniffing for the scent of human flesh?'

Trent lacked the mental bandwidth to process such a change in direction. 'I never did find out what his story was,' he said, 'because I caught a glimpse of myself in the bus shelter glass. I realised I was the same as him. I was walking the slow, aimless walk of the unemployed. I had no appointment to keep, no office to get to. There was nothing to do any more. I had been leading my life all wrong. That's when I decided to come to Geneva.'

It was partly true, and in his inebriated state, Trent half believed it himself. The reality was more complex, a mixture of push and pull factors. Yes, he had been out of work, and he did have a revelation of sorts (as much as anyone as cynical as Trent can), but that was not his only reason to flee the country. One could not discount the exposure of his more morally ambiguous business dealings. Working in the UK was no longer viable. His empire had crumbled. He had no credibility there anymore.

Trent noticed Bong wink indiscreetly at Amara. Despite the fire and the remnants of the summer day's heat, he was still wearing his orange bomber jacket; some kind of statement, apparently, but Trent couldn't begin to guess about what. Amara had changed out of her Indian dress and was now wearing jeans and a long-sleeved T-shirt to protect her from the mosquitos. Neither she nor Bong said anything.

It was Hobbs who spoke over Bong's snigger. Kind, honest Hobbs.

'My story's a bit different,' he said. 'I always wanted to help people. The problem was finding the right way to do so. I looked into doing a stint with an African orphanage. Then, I saw they demanded a contribution to the upkeep of the orphanage, and I realised it was a business. Us volunteers were just an income stream for them. Those children and their suffering were a commodity, just there to lure us in.'

On any other day, he might have tried to sugarcoat it a bit more.

'Every industry has its victims,' Trent said. 'Some are hidden in plain sight; others are half the world away.'

Trent didn't mention that he, too, had considered volunteering in Africa. He hadn't been particularly discouraged by the voluntourism aspect, nor that it supported a business model that kept children in orphanages, lining the pockets of those who managed them. That niche needed filling, and a few years ago, Trent would have had few qualms about doing so himself. He hoped he was different now but didn't want to test it too closely. After all, the real reason he turned down that opportunity was because it was unpaid; worse still, he would have had to fork out cash to work there. He hadn't been ready for that yet. No, he would end up in Geneva instead.

'It was the pictures in the brochures that got me,' Hobbs continued. 'People watching these dramatic sunsets and playing football with the kids. It was too slick. Everyone was smiling. It wasn't real. So, I decided to come here. Somewhere less sexy.'

'One of the richest cities in the world,' Amara said. At Hobbs' injured look, she added, 'This is where all the do-gooders start. It's such a male thing, wanting to save the world. So selfish.'

Hobbs coughed. 'How can trying to help people be selfish?'

'Because it's all about you. Whether you're some mega-lomanic trying to take over the world or save it, it's about you being at its centre – doing to others. Actually, I think you may be worse than the megalomaniac. At least they don't expect everyone to thank them for it.'

Hobbs spluttered. An awkward silence followed, broken only by Bong uttering, 'Controversial.'

Even inebriated, Trent was sensitive enough to the situation to realise that it would be best if they moved on. 'What brought you here, Bong?' he said.

Bong snorted. Apparently, the teenage prank about his name was continuing. Trent resolved to find out Bong's real name and not be the butt of the jokes forever, but for now, he just ignored the hilarity and waited for an answer.

'Just trying to stop the world from burning,' Bong said eventually.

'What does that mean?' Trent said. 'Climate change? Nuclear war?'

'Either/or.'

There seemed to be limited value in exploring further. The hypnotic effect of fire had returned them to their primitive nature, making them want to expose their souls. All the complexity the modern world piled on them, all the guile and politesse, had just fallen away. Bong's most basic nature was, evidently, quite basic.

Trent turned to the final member of the group.

'And you, Amara?'

Trent had worked for years cultivating the habit of keeping the conversation going. It now came as second nature to him, even in his debilitated state. He avoided dead air at all costs because it allowed people time to reflect on what he'd said. But there was more to it that evening, perhaps. These were his new neighbours. They had welcomed him (to some extent). And the new Trent needed all the friends he could get.

'I just wanted to do something with my life, plain and simple,' Amara said. 'They say India's a thriving country, but most of us are stuck in a rut. I looked at my mother, my father, and my grandparents. They were clever people. Motivated. So much potential. So much they could have done with their lives. They took on crappy jobs to keep food on the table. It was only supposed to be temporary, to bide them over until they moved on to better things. But unless you push against it, these situations become long-term, and a job defines who you are. They ended up as factory workers, helpdesk technicians, cash tillers. That's who they became to their very being. By the time they realised, it was too late. Their window to do something different had passed. The part of their life where they could choose their path was over. For me, the time is now. This is the one chance I have to break free.'

'That's very noble of you,' Hobbs said sulkily, 'doing that for yourself.'

'Thank you,' Amara replied.

Trent wondered if he might grow to like Amara. She was quite possibly as self-serving as him, only more honest about it. She certainly shared his cynical outlook on the world. Trent, too, had looked down on his parents when he was younger.

Still, he wanted to ask, 'What about the tram driver

who takes you to the office? Is he not worthy? You wouldn't be able to do your world-changing work without him.' He didn't bother because he realised it would make him a hypocrite. These were the same people he used to take advantage of. At the time, of course, he wouldn't have described it that way, reasoning that it was the system he was exploiting, not the people. Now, he saw the truth: you can't separate people from the system they labour in.

This time, it was Bong that broke the silence:

'If it makes you feel better,' he said, 'I think we can do something selfish.'

He pulled out a mobile phone in a plastic pocket.

Hobbs jumped to his feet. 'You sneaked it out! That's reprehensible!'

'What is it?' Trent said.

'It's the key to our changing fortunes,' Bong said. 'This phone contains the passcode for a vault in a Geneva bank.'

'To be more specific,' Hobbs interjected, 'it contains a video of someone being tortured until they reveal the code to a bank vault.'

'Can I see?' Trent said.

It had been a close contest, in Trent's mind, between the reactions caused by the words "bank vault" and "tortured". For most people, the word "tortured" would likely have won out, and they would not have ventured to watch Bong's video. Trent counted it a small victory that it had been a tight contest. There was hope for him yet.

Amara turned away at the first sight of blood. She went over to Hobbs and got him to fill her in on the backstory. Hobbs had retreated to the far side of the clearing, where he set about unpegging his washing from a line they had hung between two trees. Trent, usually squeamish, gulped down his initial reaction to what he saw and focused on the goal.

When he could bear it no more, he closed his eyes and listened.

'Now, would you be good enough to tell Mr Fredevich where you hid his jewels?' the torturer said once the first round of screaming had diminished. In all the footage Trent saw, his face was never revealed.

Trent did see the victim's blood-spattered face, though, even after he closed his eyes. He heard the torturer's foot-steps and then more screaming. It was so blood-curdling that even the phone's speakers objected, crackling and distorting the sound.

Then followed several seconds of panting and sputtering:

'Vault 45.2, Swiss Cantonal Bank, code 6-8-9-4-0.'

The video cut off shortly afterwards.

'Where did you get this?' Trent said with difficulty. His lips were numb, and it wasn't from the alcohol anymore.

'It's our job to watch this stuff,' Bong explained. 'They send us footage of human rights atrocities. We check it for signs of authenticity, keywords, names – like this Mr Frede-vich – and catalogue it.'

Trent was incredulous. 'How much do they pay you for that?'

'A big fat zeeerooo,' Bong said. 'Why do you think we're camping out here?'

'Nothing? Are you serious?'

'Nobody gets paid for interning at these organisations. Equality and all.'

'There's nothing fairer than everyone getting nothing,' Trent mused.

'It's very fair,' Amara said. 'If you can't afford to work for nothing, don't come here. Internships are a tax on middle-class do-gooders that can afford to take a gap year.'

'That's why we shouldn't feel bad about taking full advantage of this situation,' Bong said.

Trent reflected briefly on how readily they had moved from watching a brutal scene of torture to considering the inequalities of the Western world. Perhaps it was a defence mechanism, or maybe they had all become desensitised to violence. Yes, it had been difficult to watch, but the only difference between that video and some of the hideous things they had all seen in films was that this was real. Or was it? Nothing could be trusted anymore.

Amara set that question to bed quickly when she asked, 'You do know who you're dealing with, don't you?'

They looked at her. She got out her phone, and for a moment, Trent worried she might show them another video.

'Do you guys never follow the news?' she said.

Bong snorted. 'What did the news ever do for us?'

'Well, for one, it tells us about crime lords spotted in the vicinity. Anton Fredevich is wanted for racketeering, and he's been associated with several high-profile hit jobs.' She waved her phone at them but didn't keep it still enough for anyone to read a word. 'They've frozen his assets. He's public enemy number one right now.'

'Do they still use that term?' Bong asked.

Before Amara could answer, Hobbs swiped the old mobile phone, still in its plastic bag, out of Bong's hands.

'We've got to hand this over to the authorities.'

Quicker still, Bong snatched it back.

'For them to seize his stolen jewels? I don't think so. They'll just use the money to destroy the world like they always do.'

'Who says there is any money? We have no idea how old

that video is. For all we know, Fredevich got his jewels years ago. This could be evidence for his trial.'

'Look at the timestamp,' said Bong. 'This thing is only a few weeks old. We're in with a chance of getting there before Fredevich. Don't you see, this is a gift? This is Geneva thanking us for our service.'

'It's too dangerous,' Hobbs insisted. 'Supposing you're right and he hasn't got his jewels, why do you think he's here?'

'We just have to be careful, that's all,' said Bong. 'Unless we do something stupid, there's no way he'll find us.'

∼

There are plenty of places to hide in Geneva for criminal masterminds on the run. Few choose the campsite-under-a-bridge option. Most choose five-star hotels with lake views.

Anton Fredevich kicked back on his king-sized bed and regarded his slippers, embossed with the hotel's branding. He wondered how much longer it would last, this plush life of his. How long would it be before hotel-issued became prison-issued? They were after him. Someone needed to pay for the things he did when working his way up the food chain. The powers that be didn't understand how business worked, that he was no worse than those they deemed "respectable". They needed a scapegoat. Someone had to go down, and they had decided it should be him.

They had to catch him first.

Fredevich had always suspected his career would end like this. He had tried on occasion to curb his violent tendencies. After a heart scare, his doctor advised him to see a therapist to work through his anger issues, and the therapist suggested he try his hand at arts and crafts. It hadn't been for him. No one had dared tell him that "wonky swan" was not a legitimate origami design, but he wasn't blind. He'd shredded the paper, and the nearest convenient hired hand had wound up with a black eye. And crochet, he failed to understand why anyone would put themselves through that. After an hour spent twiddling around with a ball of wool and a misshapen needle, he'd been the proud owner of a knotted mess and an even higher blood pressure. No, Fredevich's hobby was violence. It was his therapy.

He had taken a risk going to Geneva but had made the mistake of trusting hired help for the last time. Sometimes, they did the most intelligent things, like not uploading an incriminating video in which his name was mentioned and instead electing to hand it over in person. Then they did something stupid, like letting their phone get mixed up with the affairs of a relative fleeing a war-torn country.

A knock at the door. Fredevich rolled out of bed and rearranged his nightgown to cover his chest. The handgun in one pocket deformed the robe so that it hung lower on one side, but that was less of an issue if he gripped it tight.

'Who is it?' he growled.

'It's Mallory, sir. We have something.'

Fredevich unlatched the door and stepped back, gun still in hand. He recognised Mallory's voice but couldn't be too careful. Mallory pushed the door open and noted the telltale signs of someone concealing a gun in their pocket, but that didn't bother her. This was all in a day's work.

MI5 had let go of Mallory due to a certain moral ambiguity, which Fredevich viewed as an asset. Their loss, his gain. She had certainly been efficient in dispatching his former right-hand man, the one responsible for the phone debacle. But sooner or later, she would fail. They always did.

'We picked up the signal again,' she reported. Her steady voice betrayed no hint of emotion. It matched the way she dressed and carried herself: standard office attire. Her dark hair was brushed back neatly behind her ears.

Fredevich looked away to hide his grin.

'Where?'

'In the building at first. Looks like they brought it up from storage. Then it went dark again. And then...'

Fredevich willed every muscle in his face not to move. In this game, it was best to avoid showing enthusiasm. It was a fine line between enthusiasm and desperation. And giving out even a whiff of desperation was the beginning of the end. He focused the full force of his stare on Mallory as she continued her account.

'We picked it up a few kilometres away. But we're not sure it's right. It was moving; then it just stopped on a bridge. Hasn't moved since.'

'You went to check it out.' It wasn't a question.

'Yes, sir. Nothing, just traffic.'

'You'll return in the morning and do a thorough search. Manhole covers, drains, everything.'

Just as crime lords do not consider staying in anything less than a five-star hotel, Fredevich could not conceive that someone with his phone would be living on a makeshift campsite under a bridge. And so, Bong and his companions were safe. For a time.

'I didn't expect you'd be up for this,' Trent said to Amara.

They were sitting on a strategically placed bench opposite the Swiss Cantonal Bank. It was strategic in the sense that it gave them a good meeting point from which to conduct their reconnaissance, but it was certainly not strategic when it came to its view of beauty spots. Laid out before them were tram tracks, paving slabs and concrete walls.

'Are you kidding me?' Amara replied. 'Do you have any idea how much Swiss currency is worth back home? Of course I'm in! What about you? Aren't you too old and wise for this sort of thing?'

Trent had asked himself the same question earlier that morning (minus the "old" bit) when cancelling an appointment with his employment advisor. It was true that this wasn't exactly his plan for Geneva, but it would do. The likelihood of this venture succeeding was extremely low, but such was the case with most make-or-break business ventures. You just had to be out there, trying things, waiting for something to stick. He thought of it as "the startup approach", only involving bank vaults, jewels, and crime lords on the run.

'I just couldn't help but get swept up with the enthusiasm of youth,' Trent said.

Bong came back across the street to them a little while later. He was concentrating so much on stuffing his oversized wallet into his trouser pocket that he almost got hit by a cyclist.

'There are three lifts,' he said, 'each programmable by security. You get in, and they send you to the relevant floor. Upstairs for the new clients or down to the vaults. I think they can be reprogrammed, but I need a distraction.'

'What, are you a hacker now?' Amara said.

'Do you have a better idea?' Bong snapped, but his heart wasn't in it. He was still struggling with his wallet. He opened it up and started playing around with the brightly coloured paper that passed for Swiss currency, folding and arranging it carefully.

'Hey, big spender,' Amara said.

Bong looked at her helplessly. 'This is all the money I've got in the entire world. I had to keep drawing some out every time I went in there. How many's that been now?'

'Four or five.'

'Well, that's how far my money gets me. I'm done. If I go in there again, that security guard will grab me, I'm sure of it. They seem like nice enough people – they've got this *Giving Back* scheme in Africa – but when it comes to security, they're not joking.'

'No one's asking you to go in again,' Amara said. 'You've done enough.' She spoke those last words in a tone that could have been interpreted as both congratulations or disdain.

'What next, then?'

'My turn.'

Bong grunted with amazement. 'What, *you*?'

'Yes, *me*.'

Amara and Bong spent the next few minutes arguing about what strategy she might employ. Bong proposed that she might distract the guards by posing as a lost Indian girl and asking lots of questions. Amara objected vehemently to the stereotype.

'I'm going to go in there and open an account,' she insisted. 'A Valley girl visiting her daddy and wanting somewhere to store her pocket money.'

'Ah, so it's okay to be racist if it's against white Americans?'

Amara rolled her eyes. 'Well, like, duh.'

Bong shook his head in bewilderment.

Trent watched the exchange passively. Was this how the new generation worked? If so, the world was doomed, whether or not they tried to help it. Especially, perhaps, if they tried.

Then again, he was there with them. He couldn't pretend he wasn't implicated. It served his purpose to retain some distance, to observe and buy himself some thinking time. A bit of quiet would have helped, too, but that wasn't to be.

Amara was on her feet now. She had a determined expression on her face and appeared fixated on proving she could pass as a spoilt rich kid that she had lost sight of what they were there to achieve. Trent couldn't blame her. This was all so removed from reality. Perhaps this was what real life was like outside of "provincial" England, but he could scarcely believe it.

'Wait, wait,' Trent said.

Bong and Amara looked at him as though they had forgotten he was there.

'I think we may be making things a little more complicated than they need be,' he said. 'We know who's renting that vault and we know the code. How about we make use of that information?'

Bong and Amara looked at each other.

'I suppose we could do that,' Bong said.

'Actually, I suppose *you* could do that,' Amara said. 'Bong's already blown his cover, and I don't think I'd pass as a Mr Fredevich.'

'Good to see you've not completely lost your grip on reality,' Bong muttered.

'Ah, no, no,' Trent sighed.

He had invited this, but it wasn't what he had signed up for. He was always there in the background. This was too big a risk.

While it was possible that the safe hadn't yet been emptied, that was just one of the risks. Fredevich was a wanted man. What if there was an alert on that account? Trent would have to explain to the authorities that he wasn't actually who they were looking for, and he didn't think they'd be thrilled when they found out how he'd got hold of the code. He doubted they'd let him stay in the country much longer after that.

'Who else do you think is going to do it?' Amara demanded. 'What did you think? We wanted you here just for your "wisdom"? I thought we were in this together.'

'We are,' Trent said, 'it's just...'

He couldn't finish the sentence. Where were all his clever arguments? He wasn't intoxicated, but some spark was missing from Trent. Life had dulled him.

'I told you he couldn't be trusted.' Amara muttered to Bong.

And it was true: Trent couldn't be trusted. He usually hid it better. Amara might be sharp, but he had fooled people far more astute than her. He was off his game. Admittedly, this was partly because he was trying to give up that game and lead a straight life. Only the prospect of a vault full of jewels had been enough to tempt him back for one last hurrah. One last betrayal.

The truth was that he had already made an appointment to access the vault. He would be going there the following morning. The die was already cast; the betrayal was done. All that was left was the execution.

In the back of his brain, a name came back to him: Dean. He'd not thought about Brian in a long while and wasn't about to then. He buried that name into his subconscious along with all the associations it brought back with it.

He owed these kids nothing. They were just using each other. He suspected that they had only involved him because he looked old enough for it to be credible that he stored valuables in a vault. What a laugh! He still doubted that they believed he had once been – how had he put it? – a "big deal back in the UK."

It didn't matter what they thought. All that mattered was whether the bank's staff would find him convincing. Did he still have it in him? If Amara could see through him, a bank employee trained to know what to look out for would undoubtedly do so.

But that was tomorrow's problem. Right then, he needed to defend his honour – or whatever projection of it he was trying to cast. At times like these, he needed someone straight to hide behind, to manipulate into defending him. This would have gone a whole lot smoother if Hobbs had been there.

'We'll do it tomorrow,' he said. 'I'll make an appointment, get some documents together and do this thing like a normal person. We're in this together.'

Why am I so straight? Hobbs asked himself.

No, "straight" wasn't the right word – more like "square" – but it had stuck. They'd laughed at him, Bong and Amara, when he had walked for thirty minutes to hand over to the police a twenty franc note he'd found. 'He's so straight,' they'd said, 'that he once followed the bike lane into a lamppost'.

It wasn't true. He had seen the lamppost at the last minute and swerved to miss it. He'd wrecked his bike, that was true, but he hadn't collided with the obstacle straight on. That was an important clarification.

Anyway, a more relevant point was, "Who put a lamp-post in the middle of a cycle lane?" It very much defeated the object of cycle lanes if you're going to plonk lampposts right in them. Why was nobody asking that question?

Still, "straight", "square", or whatever, the fact was that trying to steal a dangerous crime boss' jewels from a bank vault just wasn't Hobbs' bag. Now he thought of it like that, he couldn't imagine how it could be anybody's bag.

Be that as it may, the fact remained that he was once again the butt of the group's jokes.

And their new campmate, Trent, was somehow in the group. Not that Hobbs could bring himself to resent Trent. There was so much pitiable about the man. No, it was himself he was growing tired of, more than anything.

Hobbs clicked open another video in the safe room at the heart of the International Refugee Agency. He knew it wouldn't bring him relief. The best he could hope for was that the footage of some human rights abuse might distract him for a few seconds. It was not an optimistic thought.

Yes, Hobbs had returned to work. While his friends were pursuing their get-rich or get-arrested-quick scheme, he had locked himself away from sunlight, giving up his time to labour for nothing. Was it for the greater good? He didn't know. The worst had already happened to the people he watched on his screen. For many, the justice they sought was from beyond the grave. It seemed awfully like revenge. What about the living? Didn't he have a right to be selfish for a minute?

For every one of those points, there was a counterargument, much more persuasive. Was he honestly countenancing that the dead had no rights? That seemed like a sure-fire path to people murdering everyone they did a small wrong to, to make sure they had no comeback. Okay, so justice would come too late, and punishment was a mere token gesture when weighed against human suffering, but it was still something. He owed it to them to help them get it. The living owed a debt to the dead.

So, Hobbs blinked away his doubts and concentrated on the terrors.

'I'm sorry, sir,' Mallory said. She looked tired, having been doing her boss' bidding all day.

Fredevich drew a deep breath and placed his soup spoon beside the bowl. He would have flipped the table if he hadn't been in a posh restaurant and at pains not to draw attention to himself. In a former life, he would have also dismissed Mallory on the spot. It did not do to let word get out that he accepted failure. It was important to have standards.

But he needed her. She was one of the few employees who still held on and was the only one with brains. Surely, she must have known he couldn't afford to pay her. In that sense, getting their hands on the phone was as vital to her as to him. He considered for a moment whether she would betray him when they succeeded. He wouldn't blame her for it – he would have done the same – and he would be prepared.

Still, the fact remained that she had failed.

'We spent several hours there,' Mallory said. 'We combed the footpaths and the gutters, working from one end of the bridge to the other. I had Jones stick his head down the drains. Then, the police moved us on.'

Jones was the thug who followed Mallory around. He didn't care about money; he just did whatever Mallory told him to, no matter how depraved. It must have been easier that way. Fredevich wished he had someone following him with such blind obedience. He wouldn't have to keep watching his back all the time.

'No more signal from the phone?'

'Whoever's got it must be keeping it off. Or it's out of battery.'

Fredevich supposed that whoever had the phone didn't need to turn it on again. They must have already watched the video. Where he had initially approved that his underling hadn't sent it to him – you don't upload that sort of thing to the cloud – more recently, it had occurred to him that it would have been much easier if he had just texted the code. Not the video, just the code. It had been chaos in the country where they had tracked down the thief. It had been a grave mistake to entrust that knowledge to a device that could go missing in an exodus.

The underling in question was no longer in Fredevich's employment. He would not be working for anyone ever again.

'You checked under the bridge?' he said.

The crazy thing about maps is that they make one see everything in two dimensions. That's why the machines could never become the dominant life form on planet Earth. That's why Fredevich was growing increasingly convinced that if he wanted something done, he had to do it himself.

'Yes,' Mallory replied without expression. 'There's some kind of campsite there. No one was present. We searched every tent but found nothing.'

As Fredevich suspected, she had brains. That showdown between the two of them seemed increasingly inevitable. Still, they would use each other up until then.

'We go back,' Fredevich said, emphasising the "we". The days of trusting this to his hired hands were over. 'First thing tomorrow.'

He called over the waiter to cancel the rest of his meal. He had lost his appetite.

CHAPTER 3
UNDER THE BRIDGE

'Have you been going through my stuff, Bong?' Amara demanded.

Bong snorted. 'How could I? We've been together all day.'

Trent felt certain he would have been the next to be accused were it not for the fact that he'd been with Amara, too. Instead, her glare turned to Hobbs.

'It's happened to all of us,' Hobbs said before she had a chance to say anything.

Somebody had rifled through all their things while they were out. They hadn't been discreet about it, either, leaving clothing strewn across their tents. Trent discovered later that this wasn't the first time this had happened. Sleeping rough wasn't conducive to privacy. Some people are able to overcome their innate aversion to going through someone else's property, lured by the riches that might nestle amongst dirty socks and underpants. He didn't understand it. What great treasure could possibly be possessed by someone sleeping under a bridge? Still, it happened.

Then and there, though, it seemed too much of a coincidence.

'I told you that phone was trouble,' Hobbs said. 'You've kicked the hornet's nest now.'

'Come on!' Bong said. 'How on earth could anyone know it's here?'

'We turned it on, didn't we? Have you never heard of phone tracking?'

Bong paled.

'We should move,' Amara said.

'Where to?' Hobbs replied. 'It's not like there are loads of free spots around the city, just waiting for us to pitch up. No, we're screwed, thank you very much.'

Bong threw his hands in the air. 'Whatever! You've been against this from the start. I bet this feels good for you, doesn't it?'

'No,' Hobbs said. 'Actually, it really doesn't.'

'Well, grow a pair!' Bong continued, oblivious, although he did pause to say, 'Sorry, Amara.'

'Apology not accepted,' Amara muttered.

Bong turned back to Hobbs. 'We're about to pull off the heist of the century. Campsites will be a thing of the past. Get with the program!'

'Get with reality!' Hobbs retorted.

Trent had lost count of the times he had observed his campmates bicker. He usually took advantage of it as an opportunity to assess how they responded to pressure, but then and there, it seemed so pointless. They would be better off debating a course of action than who was at fault.

Still, he let them fight. It made what he would do the following morning feel more forgivable. It wasn't as if he was about to betray a harmonious collective – they were tearing at each other's throats. Maybe their hatred of him would bind them together. Maybe in time, they'd thank him for it...

Maybe in time, Trent could push back down the part of him that cared.

They eventually resolved to move out the next day, agreeing that it would be better if they made themselves scarce after they got the jewels, anyway.

So, they built a fire and gathered around it as the sun set and the day's warmth escaped to the stars. They shared their food with Trent. It would be their last meal together. It wasn't much, just a light stew, but it still counted for something. Trent ate with them and tried not to think too much about what he was preparing to do.

He took a break halfway through to retire to his tent. There, he uncovered his old suit, still vacuum-packed. He knelt and regarded it for a while. He fingered the transparent plastic above the hole in the trouser leg, contemplating the lesson it recounted. Depending on how he chose to interpret it, it was a warning not to go back to the life he once led or not to stick around long enough to get found out. He tried his best to read it the second way, but it wasn't easy.

He drew in a deep breath before heading back to the others.

When they had finished eating, Hobbs (never one to let a point slide) informed them about the research he had conducted that day. While they had been plotting to defraud a crime boss, Hobbs had been looking up who exactly they were dealing with.

'They call him "The Butcher",' he said. 'His business strategies are, shall we say, rather direct.'

'Don't tell me,' Bong said. 'If anyone crosses him, he cuts their limbs off.'

'If you're lucky,' Hobbs said. 'He prefers another part of the anatomy. They say if you were to line up all the appendages chopped off at his order, you could make a trail from one end of the Champs-Elysées to the other.'

Bong, whose vocabulary lacked the word "inference", scoffed at that. 'That's a lot of penises!'

'Depends on their length,' Amara said.

They contemplated that for a few moments until Bong asked. 'Why do they have to have names like that? Being a butcher is a fine profession. Nobody complains about having a well-cut steak.'

Coincidentally, Bong's family had made their name in the business. This went a good way towards explaining his lack of squeamishness.

They went on to discuss which other professions would make a good nickname for a killer – The Milkman, the Baker, the Hairdresser – and come up with scenarios where these were actually quite frightening. The Florist, growing plants in the skulls of his victims, with blooms spouting out of the eye sockets, was a highlight from Amara's suggestions.

That was how they closed out the night. Anyone who's told ghost stories around a campfire knows well that the flames make the darkness darker and the terror absolute. Consequently, no one slept that night.

The next morning, they gathered around the stove while the water heated from cold to lukewarm. With haunted eyes above puffed, darkened skin, they recounted their ordeals.

'She was chasing me,' Hobbs said in a hushed voice. 'The Librarian. I was late returning a book and didn't have the money for the fine. She reached under her desk and got out one of those date stamps they used. Only it had all these spikes on it, and it was covered in blood. I ran. Tried to hide in one of the aisles, but she kept finding me. I ran and ran, but the shelves kept going on and on. I couldn't find a way out. And then I got to the culinary section, and it was a dead end. I turned around, and there she was, closing in on me with her murder stamp. That's when I woke up.'

'I don't think we need Freud to help us with this one,' Amara said.

Trent stood before Bong had an opportunity to recount his own horrors – which were likely twice as terrifying. 'Come on. We've got some packing to do.'

'It's here, sir,' Mallory said.

The staircase was metal. It was tacked onto one side of the bridge like an afterthought, a mere hole in the rails. It was easy enough to miss. Fredevich had already walked past it by the time Mallory pointed it out.

He glanced over the rail and realised they weren't over water. There was a whole woodland down there, sloping down to the river. He put one foot on the top step. It was sturdy enough, but the holes in the metal grill were wide enough to offer a clear view of the drop. He had a thing about heights. He couldn't show that, though, so he adopted his usual strategy of getting angrier.

'It's down there?' he growled.

'Yes, sir.' Mallory seemed unfazed by her boss' rage. 'The path leads back under the bridge. That's where we found the site.

'Well, we'd better get on with it!'

Fredevich started down the steps. He gestured for Mallory and Jones to follow.

Hobbs was putting out the fire when Fredevich arrived.

At first, he ignored the footsteps. It was not unusual for people to pass by that time of morning. Runners, mostly, and the occasional dog walker. They kept their distance as they went about their business, doubtless reluctant to engage with whoever they might find camping under the bridge.

These footsteps grew closer. He realised that they were from more than one person. His campmates might have accused him of having an overly active imagination, but you're not paranoid if it's true. He knew it was Fredevich before he set eyes on him. He knew the moment the footsteps stopped.

There weren't many photographs of Fredevich online. This was a man who weighed power not in social media hits but in hard currency, and who knew the value of keeping a low profile. The scraps of security camera footage didn't do him justice. The real, three-dimensional Fredevich was infinitely more terrifying.

His eyes were cold, and he was squat and in body, giving the impression of having more innate strength than Hobbs had gained even after months at the boot camp in Australia. He was flanked by a woman with a piercing stare and a man with a shaven head and a scar that ran down his brow and across his cheek. To an outside observer, Fredevich might have appeared as a villain straight from one of Bong's movies, but at that moment, that mattered little to Hobbs. It was hardly as though he would be able to press pause in between being fed his own testicles to complain that this man was a walking, talking cliché.

'You have something that belongs to me,' Fredevich said.

And the way he spoke, too. There was no subtlety there. This man knew what he wanted and would take the most direct way there.

They were in trouble.

'Excuse me?' Hobbs tried. 'Do I know you?'

'You will.'

Hobbs' next thought was of his companions. They hadn't got far with their packing, not that this mattered anymore. Amara was getting changed in her tent, and Bong was urinating down at the river. With luck, neither had been spotted. If they stayed hidden, they might be safe. Where was Trent? The last Hobbs remembered, he had been packing his things in his tent, but that was a while ago, as it wasn't as if there was much to pack, was it?

No matter. The important thing was to warn them.

'Whatever you want, you can have it,' Hobbs said loudly enough that he hoped his companions would hear. 'We don't want any trouble.'

'It's a bit late for that,' said Fredevich, gesturing to his goons.

Trent fought his way through the bushes up the embankment towards the staircase. There were much easier ways to get there, but he wanted to make sure his campmates didn't spot him. They couldn't know he was leaving ahead of time. He had told them his appointment at the bank was two hours later than it actually was.

He tried his best not to think of anything, to do this on autopilot. If he'd have engaged his brain, it might have reminded him of the risk he was taking, presenting himself to a bank, posing as a known criminal. Fortunately, he had grown used to disengaging that part of his brain over the past few years. Had it been fully operational throughout, he wouldn't have squandered his fortune. It had been consigned to a corner of his skull, making space for the part of his personality that sought oblivion.

Trent was well aware that his loss of fortune was a symptom rather than the cause of the problem. Still, he reasoned that if he had another chance, he wouldn't fritter his money away like he had done before. He no longer had anything to prove. He would stay away from gambling, and maybe, maybe, he could make something of himself again.

Another part of his brain was tugging away at him, too, a part he had tried to foster in the months since he had resolved to live a better life. Had he given it the opportunity, it would have reminded him that this was a betrayal. It didn't matter that he didn't know his campmates well enough to call them acquaintances, never mind friends (and he was unpractised with that notion anyway). It was a betrayal, regardless of all that.

Trent's activities in the UK had never had a victim – at least, not that he recognised. He had just been taking advantage of a situation. This was not a victimless crime. He knew exactly who he was screwing over: he knew their names and even something of their aspirations.

It was this thought that made him glance back.

From the bottom steps of the staircase, he looked down into the valley and the better life he had tried to live; the friends he'd almost had. There they were: Hobbs, Bong and Amara. They were not alone.

They had been joined by three others, two men and a woman. Trent couldn't see them well enough to make out who they were, but he didn't need to. He could sense the panic in Hobbs' jagged movement as he scrabbled around the campsite, searching for something. Amara was there, too, as still as anything, and Bong was looking at the ground like a scolded schoolchild.

The crows had come home to roost. And these crows allegedly enjoyed chopping off body parts and laying them out along the Champs-Elysées.

Every part of Trent's brain started working then. It had been a while since it had done that. He grabbed the metal barrier to steady himself.

They hadn't seen him yet. All options were still open to him. He could continue up the stairs and walk away from this. Fredevich and his cronies would tear the campsite apart in search of the phone. They would then set upon Hobbs, Bong, and Amara in rage when they found it was not there. For Trent had taken the phone with him. He didn't need it, having memorised the vault's code, but he'd taken it as a precaution.

Now that he thought of it, it had been a stupid thing to do. Were he to get detained at the bank, it was probably best that he wasn't found in possession of a torture video.

What else could he do? Call for help? Who knew how long it would take the police to get there? And then there would follow all sorts of complicated questions.

And if he were to try to lure Fredevich and his cronies away, might that work? They would chase him up the stairs and onto the bridge, where, hopefully, some passers-by would intervene. With luck, he'd be greeted soon after by the sound of police sirens. Same outcome for Trent and Fredevich, but at least it kept the others out of it.

No, that wouldn't work. They'd catch him long before the police arrived. The nearest of them looked sturdily built, the type whose job it was to provide "security", in whatever guise that might mean. These people were in peak condition. Trent was a wreck. He'd attained peak physical form at the age of seven. Ever since then, his body had been in decline.

No, there was only one real choice. He headed back down the slope.

Things had turned nasty by the time he got back to the campsite. The squat-looking one had Amara by the hair.

'If you won't do this for yourselves, do it for your girl-friend,' the leader, whom Trent identified as Fredevich, said. 'Such a pretty one. It would be a shame to mess that up for an old phone.'

Amara was struggling, but she had no hope of getting free.

Trent whistled. Six pairs of eyes settled on him.

'Is this what you're looking for?' He held the phone aloft. It was still sheathed in its plastic packaging.

'Finally,' Fredevich said. 'Someone sees sense.'

'Let her go,' Trent said.

Fredevich nodded, and Amara was released. She fell to her knees but was too proud to cry. Hobbs and Bong displayed noticeable signs of relief.

'What now?' Fredevich said. 'You just played your only card.'

And it was true. He had gone from having many options available to him to almost none. He considered threatening to throw the phone in the river. He discounted that idea quickly. It was the only thing that was keeping them alive. Were he to destroy it, the vault's code would exist only in their heads. And he didn't need to imagine what methods Fredevich would employ to extract that information: he had seen them recorded live on the very phone he was holding.

At this point, Trent realised he had chosen the scenario where they pulled out guns and shot him.

He threw the phone to the ground and prayed for mercy.

The woman stepped forward and picked it up without taking her eyes off him. She turned it on and waited for it to boot up, still fixing him with that glare. She was not the only one watching him. Hobbs, Bong and Amara were all gazing at him with a mix of surprise and bewilderment.

The video played. The tinny sound of someone being tortured filled the clearing. The woman nodded to Fredevich.

Fredevich regarded the campmates victoriously. 'You might hate him for giving it up, but he's your saviour.' He turned to the woman. 'Beat him within an inch of his life. Have his friends watch. An inch, mind. I have enough complications without a murder charge pursuing me.'

Trent had made enemies before. He had been on the wrong side of whole communities but never felt under physical threat, not like this. He may have been chased out of villages by mobs with pitchforks, but there had never been any real risk that they would impale him if they caught him. Notwithstanding the scuff on his trouser knee, he hadn't been made to suffer for his actions, not physically.

This was different.

The thug stepped forward with a smile on his face.

The first blow, square in Trent's stomach, put him on the ground. Then, he felt a boot hit his ribs, then his side, then his head. Fredevich's goon knew what he was doing. He was well-practised at the art of roughing someone up without attracting the attention of the authorities: nothing broken but plenty of pain.

Hobbs, Bong and Amara just watched. There was nothing else they could do.

There was something cathartic about being beaten to a pulp. Trent took it as a signal that he was on the right path. They were knocking something out of him, a part of him he'd been wanting to see the back of for some time. So, he endured the beating (not that he had much choice in the matter). After a while, he stopped feeling the blows. It was like they were happening to someone else.

He wished he'd done this years ago. However, like many things that feel good at the time, he would regret it later.

At some point, Trent blacked out.

'We should call an ambulance,' Hobbs said.

'You've got to be joking!' Bong said. 'They'll bring the police with them. Do you really want them crawling over this place, asking questions?'

'Okay, so do you want to carry him to hospital? You get his legs, and I get his shoulders. I don't think so!'

Their voices were above Trent. They were standing over the mess that was his body. Amara's voice was closer. She must have been crouching beside him.

'We've got to help him,' she said.

Trent felt her touch his arm.

'It's okay,' he groaned. He wasn't sure the words were intelligible because he could barely move his lips.

'He's awake,' Amara said. 'Trent, are you alright?'

'Wonderful.' Trent spat out a bloody laugh. His chest seared in complaint.

They started the fire again and warmed the drinking water. After ascertaining that Trent had no broken bones (at least, that they could tell), they propped him up on rolled up sleeping bags, and Amara set about cleaning his wounds with a blanket torn into pieces. Bong went to the pharmacy to get painkillers.

'I'm sorry,' Trent said when he summoned the strength to speak again. Everything was swelling up now. He felt like a pufferfish that had remembered to inflate only after it had been attacked.

'Don't be sorry,' Amara said. 'You had to give it to them. You had no choice.'

That wasn't what Trent had meant.

The next few hours passed in a blur. Hobbs insisted the others went to work, but he took the day off to nurse him. He even re-pitched Trent's tent closer to theirs. That way, they could keep an eye on him while he recovered.

As evening fell, Amara and Bong returned. Amara had a satisfied expression on her face. As their food cooked, she explained why:

'They got him. It's all over the news. One of the bank staff recognised him. When he came up from his vault, the police were waiting.'

'Stupid risk,' Trent said. 'Why would he go there himself?'

'I suppose that when you're in that sort of position, you trust no one.'

And Trent knew why.

After they had eaten, Bong got out his guitar. It was one of their little rituals before they settled in for the night. That evening, he shared his version of Bob Marley's *Redemption Song* with them. Hobbs joined in as he reached the chorus, adopting an exaggerated Jamaican accent. They sang with the shameless naivety of white men trying to sing reggae. In other circumstances, it would have been comical; in still others, offensive. Trent just wished they had chosen a different song. He considered himself far from redeemed.

He remembered Dean, his first betrayal. He had followed through on that one.

Trent could still picture Dean's face clearly at the point of realisation: the vacant look in his eyes, with his mouth ajar, as though someone had only explained the game's rules to him just as he was about to lose. That image came to Trent like the ghost of Christmas past, a ghost whose chains had been jangling in the background throughout his career, even though he'd been deaf to them until recently.

A younger, less damaged Trent would have highly recommended partnering with anyone called Dean. They tended to be hard-working, dependable, and – best of all – they didn't recognise duplicity until it was too late.

They were colleagues, Brian and Trent, during Trent's first job in life insurance sales. They'd worked long hours, and the pressure had been constant. The company had invested in their training, and it expected a return. Brian and Trent had spent their days searching for people they affectionately referred to as "marks", cultivating relationships with them in the build-up to a sale. It had been an exciting life, with the threat of being fired rarely far from mind. In such an environment, a strong camaraderie developed. Trent wouldn't have referred to Brian as his friend, but he was as close to one as he ever had.

In those days, they had still worked off paper. Their notepads were precious, for they recorded all their potential leads in them. That's why Trent could barely believe it when Brian went home one night, leaving his on his desk.

Despite his bond with Dean, Trent hadn't hesitated before slipping the notepad into his bag. As soon as he got out of the office and away from prying eyes, he began flicking through it. Brian had been a highly successful salesman. He had the sort of face people could trust, and his voice betrayed no guile. His "marks" just lapped it up. He barely needed to nudge them to make the sale. Trent had been labouring in his shadow for months.

He copied down names and numbers. The following day, as soon as the hour was decent, he began making calls. It hadn't taken much to identify the fruit ripe for picking: Brian had done him the favour of underlining his key marks, people he'd been softening up for the sale. All Trent had needed to do was give them a final push.

The company tracked its employees' progress against targets every week. That week, Trent's sales went through the roof, and Brian floundered like a lost child. He'd been forced to start from scratch, and building leads takes time.

Dean had been suspicious, of course. He had accused pretty much everybody of swiping his precious notepad. Even the cleaner hadn't got away unscathed, accused of binning it. Only Trent avoided Dean's wrath.

When that week's results were announced, there was little doubt about the culprit. Trent felt sure he would get fired when Brian complained to their boss. He was summoned to his office shortly afterwards. When it came to it, it didn't matter at all.

'It's all about sealing the deal,' the greasy man told Brian in his gravelly voice. 'You snooze, you lose.'

Trent just stood by, expressionless.

And there it was: employee of the month for Trent, bottom of the class for Dean, and a trust forever severed. Brian hadn't lasted much longer in the company.

The ruthless Trent Argent had been born, one that would cheat, lie and manipulate for almost two decades until finally, in a little village in the middle of nowhere, he met his downfall.

In all the years that had passed, he had never really thought about Dean. He had no idea what had become of him and had never made any attempt to find out. But he thought about him then. He hoped the experience had prompted Brian to take up a profession that didn't reward people who shafted their colleagues; that he'd gone on to lead a happy, fulfilled life, keep fit and eat healthily. If the alternative was true, and he'd ended up in the gutter like Trent, he didn't want to know.

Trent remembered that first betrayal feeling like second nature. Some people are born to it, driven by a hunger that consumes morality. But Trent had since learned that this hunger could never be sated, no matter what he tried. There had to be another way.

It had been a split-second decision, going back to the campsite and putting himself in harm's way. He hadn't thought through the consequences and couldn't say with his hand on his heart that he would make the same choice again. Self-sacrifice just wasn't in his makeup. Still, buried deep in the pain from his injuries, there was hope...

Trent fell asleep with the fire warm on his skin. Despite his misgivings, he felt more confident than ever about who he wanted to be.

STEP 2 – BETTER YOURSELF

CHAPTER 4

LE LANGAGE DE L'AMOUR

The first time Trent set eyes on Serena, he would never have imagined that within a few weeks he would sleep with her.

First, there was the issue of type. Trent had never considered himself to have a "type", but even if he had, she wouldn't have been it. She was too attractive – in an obvious, mainstream way. And Trent prided himself on never doing the obvious thing.

That wasn't the whole story, not by a long way. The main reason Trent didn't have a "type" was that many years earlier, he had made a conscious decision not to let anyone get close. Deciding on a "type" was to open himself up to the possibility that something might come to pass at some point, and he couldn't allow that to happen. Intimacy meant vulnerability, which couldn't be allowed in his line of business. Opening himself up to the pleasures of sex was to reveal a real, genuine part of himself that he strove to keep hidden. Let someone access that, and they might find a backdoor they could use on any occasion to get to the true Trent. It was too risky.

Not that he had never been tempted. Once, in a backward corner of rural England, someone had pierced through the shell. But he had been trying for five years to put that behind him.

Serena, though, she was a temptation. Even falls from grace can have their perks.

Trent reflected on this as he entered a stranger's bedroom in Geneva's "billionaires" quarter, Cologny. He didn't reflect on it for long because there were other things to consider. Were his eyes drawn to the collection of fine Swiss watches gleaming in a briefcase on the luxurious bed or the stunning views across the lake? No, his gaze was fixed on the woman who had invited him up there, who was waiting for him expectantly in her revealing swimsuit. This vision of glamour had eyes only for him, and she had made her intentions clear. She took him in with her gaze, both alluring and terrifying.

Oh, yes, Trent was tempted.

Who would have imagined that this tale began with a French lesson?

Trent's employment advisor looked bored. This wasn't easy to tell because a greying beard dominated his face, but his body language made it clear enough. He was lounging back in his chair as though hoping it would recline for a long-haul flight and he could take a doze. His eyes strayed around the room, from the framed diplomas on the walls to the executive toys that lined his antique desk.

Trent didn't blame him. He had, after all, just finished recounting his series of failed job interviews from the comfort of his employment advisor's felt-lined sofa. It hardly made for riveting listening.

'Well, grade "A" for effort,' Edouard said, for Edouard was his name. Edouard Boucher, as though his parents had made a slapdash effort to Gallicize his name.

'Thank you, I think,' Trent said. He hadn't gone there in search of a gold star. He was looking for pointers, for inside information, for something more than the vague messages of support he had received to date. 'Do you have any suggestions about what I should do next?'

Edouard looked up to the heavens as though God would offer him the answer. Trent wondered whether the Almighty also charged by the hour, at Geneva rates, which were far from heavenly.

'You need to check your expectations,' Edouard said. 'You can't just come in and expect to be swept up. Think of it this way: if you were one of those international organisations, would you rather take on someone young, who you can mould and who'll do anything just to get a start in their career, or would you go for someone with certain expectations and set ways of working?'

'I have years of experience behind me,' Trent said firmly.

'And yet you're only now deciding this is what you want to do. Hardly an advertisement for good judgement, is it?'

Is this what I pay him for? Trent asked himself. When he had first contacted Edouard, it was under the pretext that he had plenty of connections in Geneva that could help him find employment. He certainly hadn't been looking for someone to tell him he was old and past it. On the other hand, Trent respected the guy's business acumen. He had capitalised on an opportunity. Everyone wanted to work in Geneva, be it for the salaries, the quality of life, or the feeling of being part of an organisation doing something positive for the world. There was a niche for a whole coaching industry. In 99% of cases, all efforts would ultimately result in failure, but only after the coaches had lined their pockets.

Still, Trent needed all the help he could get. If there was just the slimmest chance that Edouard might help him unlock something, it was worth the money.

Ninety days. He had ninety days to make it work. Then, his permit to remain in Switzerland would expire, and he'd have to return home penniless.

Edouard's face lit up like the dawn rising. Divine inspiration had arrived.

'Let's try this,' he said. 'How would you go about buying a fine bottle of wine here?'

Trent had his doubts about his new direction, but he elected to play along for a while. 'I suppose I'd go to the supermarket and choose one.'

Edouard regarded him as though he had tasted something unpleasant. 'We do not purchase fine wine at a *supermarket*. We go to a wine merchant.'

'Okay,' Trent said patiently. 'I'd go up the counter and ask for one.'

'What would you say?'

'I don't know. Can I have a bottle of red, please?'

'You English have no understanding of wine!' Edouard stormed. 'Red and white, that's all you see! And before you say it, rosé isn't proper wine!'

Trent was beginning to think Edouard might have chosen the wrong subject for his example.

After taking a moment to compose himself, Edouard continued in a hushed voice, 'What if the wine merchant doesn't speak English?'

'I'd just point and read out the name on the label, I suppose.'

Edouard breathed in deep. The air whistled between his teeth. When he spoke again, his voice quivered. 'And here we arrive at the crux of the issue. If you had someone come up to you, point at something and grunt a few words, you'd probably think they were very rude. You certainly wouldn't hire them. What you've just described, a two-year-old could do.'

Trent wondered what sort of country this was where a two-year-old could purchase wine.

Edouard was now on his feet. It was the most energetic Trent had seen him in the past hour. He went to his desk and rummaged in a drawer, pulling out a pamphlet and handing it to Trent.

'What's this?' Trent was inherently indisposed to respond favourably to something handed to him like a prescription. He'd had enough of those recently, mainly for painkillers and anti-inflammatories after his encounter with Fredevich's cronies.

'It's details of an association that does free French classes for expats. It's run by volunteers. I think it will be right up your street.'

'Ah, I see,' Trent said. 'Instead of being mocked because I can't speak French, they'll mock me for speaking French badly.'

For the first time that session, Edouard looked him straight in the eye. 'In my profession, we call that progress.'

They came together in a converted warehouse near Geneva's central train station. The volunteers arrived first, some earlier than others, to have a chat outside before getting started. This was their social centre. For many, it was their way of giving back, of sharing some of the fortune Geneva had brought them by delivering French lessons in the same way that they might hand out soup in a night shelter.

Trent took the desk in the corner, hoping it would make the teacher less likely to single him out. He remembered the tortuous French lessons he'd sat through at school. Speaking another language had been like someone had put on the brakes, slowing not just his ability to express himself but his entire thought process. Everyone would be much happier if they found a way to implant a language directly in the brain, sparing them the grammatical traps linguists had set out for them centuries before.

The lesson had its perks. At one point, they were asked to pair off and introduce themselves to the person sitting next to them. His partner was a blonde-haired woman with a bright smile. Trent barely managed to formulate the words, '*Bonjour, je m'appelle Trent.*' He probably wouldn't have fared much better in English. He had never been one for small talk, especially with women.

'*Je m'appelle Serena,*' she said, brushing back a strand of hair. '*Vous êtes anglais?*'

'*Oui,*' Trent said.

'*Vous habitez içi?*'

'*Oui,*' Trent said.

She looked at him expectantly.

Trent smiled helplessly. '*Sous le Pont Butin.*' He hoped she'd take it as a joke, doubting that she'd be impressed by him sleeping under a bridge.

'First lesson?'

She had a strong American accent. Trent couldn't place it, but it was somewhere southern.

'Yes,' Trent said, glancing at the teacher to make sure she hadn't heard they'd switched to English. 'How could you tell?'

'Just a little inkling. Listen, I'll tell you a trick.' Serena moved in closer. 'Learning a new language is all about confidence. You've got to be okay to make mistakes.'

Trent considered this for a moment. He was not at all okay with making mistakes in any part of his life. He had spent decades punishing himself for them, in fact.

'How many languages do you know?' he asked.

'Three,' she said. 'I've moved around a lot. Learning a language is a fantastic way to get the feel of a place. And it's great for meeting new people. It's very nice to meet you, Trent.'

At that point, the teacher, who was doing her rounds, hovered behind them. Trent reverted to the classic, '*Ça va?*'

'*Oui, ça va,*' Serena said. '*Et toi, ça va?*'

'*Ça va,*' Trent said.

He had a long way to go.

By the end of the lesson. Trent was able to conduct the most banal of introductory conversations in French. He doubted that this was likely to win him a job.

On the plus side, the lesson turned out to be a different experience from those at school. For one, there was less singing. He remembered having to learn a song about a national highway, *la route nationale*, a propaganda coup for whichever government department was responsible for its maintenance. The tune still rang in his head whenever he tried to curl his tongue around a French word.

Trent's campsite neighbours were waiting for him when he came out – at least, Bong and Amara were. They loitered at the bottom of the steps at the front of the building. He had discovered earlier that morning that they were taking lessons at the same site. They were in more advanced classes, but everyone had to start somewhere.

'It's how we met,' Amara had explained. 'We were couch surfing or sleeping rough in different parts of Geneva, but we were all in the same class. We decided to band together and form a little camping club.'

'You don't need French for your internships, though, do you?' Trent had asked.

'Well, no. But some of us are here to improve ourselves.'

Trent couldn't argue with the concept that learning a new language held more benefits than simply enhancing one's employability. During his recuperation, he had spent considerable time with Hobbs, who'd suspended his internship to look after him. They'd done a lot of talking; well, specifically, Hobbs had done a lot of talking. For someone who'd spent half as much time on earth as Trent, he certainly had plenty to say for himself. He'd told Trent about growing up in Australia, his college experiences, and his eventual move to another continent to join "the civilised world". In among all that were pearls of wisdom, such as when he had pointed out that the French word for bridge was *pont*. This had made Trent realise that whenever he spoke of the "Pont Butin bridge", he had been saying "Bridge Butin bridge", or "Butin Bridge bridge", or something equally nonsensical.

It could have been worse. Bong, allegedly, had decided it was high time to brush up on his French only after walking into *La Maison de Pain* and asking for a dominatrix. They'd chased him out of there, waving their baguettes like pitchforks. He had since been fully converted to the cause:

'Languages are important,' he'd declared that morning. 'They help you communicate with the *flora and fauna*.'

Amara had rolled her eyes. 'Once you've finished with French, you definitely need to work on your Latin.'

Since the incident with Fredevich, Trent's campmates had welcomed him into the fold. They had relocated his tent closer to theirs so that they could tend to him more easily while he recovered from his injuries, and they hadn't moved it back after he was up and about. They shopped together, ate together and treated him as one of their own. He had put himself on the line to protect them and had suffered for it. There was a debt to be repaid.

If only they had known the truth. Yes, Trent could take pride in having sacrificed himself for others, but there was a less noble reason why he hadn't been there when Fredevich arrived.

Only Amara maintained her distance. Initially, Trent had attributed it to her character: she was never the warmest of personalities. But recently, he had come to suspect it was more than that. She would look at him as though she could see right through him, to the guilt buried within.

She regarded him that way as he descended the steps to the street. Fortunately, Bong spoke up, breaking the tension.

'How did it go?' he said.

'Well, it went,' Trent replied. 'That's the best that can be said about it.'

'*Petit à petit, l'oiseau fait son nid.*'

'What?'

Trent never received an answer to that question because Amara wolf-whistled in admiration of her campmates' progress. 'Showing off are we now, Bong?'

Bong polished his nails on his bomber jacket. 'You know me.'

They made to head off sooner than Trent expected. Hobbs hadn't yet joined them. Trent imagined that he was still inside, discussing the finer points of French grammar with one of the tutors. Now, there was someone for whom the term "teacher's pet" had been coined.

'He's gone on ahead,' Amara explained. 'He doesn't like to leave the campsite unattended too long.'

Trent realised why at once. 'Vincent?'

'Vincent.'

Hobbs got the fire going quickly. The long summer evenings were still warm, but he didn't do it for heat. It was a beacon signal to indicate that someone was home.

He's done something similar back in Australia. He had spent weeks in various properties, turning on the lights and opening and closing curtains. It had been a great source of pocket money in his teens, housesitting while family friends were on holiday. He'd stayed in the grandest of properties in the most beautiful locations, whose owners were perpetually afraid that someone who'd gone "walka-bout" would select their house as a prime location for "squatabout".

He had never imagined having to do similar at a camp-site. Of late, he had come to accept that he'd once had a rose-tinted view of what sleeping rough was like. That might seem a strange thing to say, as no one believed it was a walk in the park, but he hadn't anticipated a key element. Just as nature is cruel, and animals living in the wild must fight for survival day by day, so was homelessness about territory. Territory that no one owned but to which people could claim rights, nevertheless.

When they'd met Vincent, he had made it crystal clear that the space beneath the grand arches of the Pont Butin was his.

Hobbs had heard people less charitable than himself refer to the likes of Vincent as "career homeless", suggesting that the root cause of his situation was buried so deep in the past that it no longer mattered. Vincent was homeless in his very being. He no longer dreamed of better. Hobbs rejected such conclusions. He knew nothing about Vincent; it wasn't his place to him. It would have been much easier to maintain his open mind had Vincent held off insulting them for more than a few seconds.

'Va-t'en, c'est le mien!' That had been his opening gambit. Then, realising that they were foreigners, he had spelt it out, 'Piss off, this is mine!'

It was then that Hobbs understood that certain niches of the city were highly desired. This spot of theirs might as well have been a mansion. The bridge offered shelter, and the river provided fresh water nearby. It was relatively quiet and not far from town. All things considered, it was a wonder they had found it unoccupied. He discovered later that Vincent migrated with the seasons like the nomadic tribes of old. There were richer pickings in the city centre in summer.

Vincent called them "fair-weather homeless". This was a reasonable point. However uncomfortable Hobbs might have found living out of a tent, they were doing it during the summer. Their experience would have been very different in December.

And so, Hobbs occupied the campsite with the stead-fastness of a guard dog. He had already quit his internship with the International Refugee Agency to look after Trent, so he spent most of his days there, leaving only for French lessons or to recharge his mobile phone at a nearby café. He did this daily, as he got through the battery quickly with all the internship applications he was completing.

Hobbs could see Vincent's site a little further down in the valley. It wasn't as organised as theirs. He had no tent, and had instead erected a lean-to from leaves and branches, covering an old, muddy mattress scavenged from a rubbish heap.

Hobbs drew breath and descended to meet him. It was high time he put his negotiation skills to the test.

Trent hadn't been entirely truthful with Edouard. He'd told his employment advisor that none of his interviews had come to anything, yet there he was, entering the reception of Fundraising Services AG for the first day at his new job. It was a temporary assignment, very casual, the sort of thing that gets advertised on less reputable social media outlets. It wasn't shame that had made him keep quiet about it, though: he just hadn't wanted Edouard to count it as an excuse to stop helping him look for something better.

This was not where Trent intended to end up.

He had seen grander receptions in backstreet clinics (not that he had visited any). It was just a small room with a waist-high reception desk, behind which a tired-looking man was checking his Facebook profile. The textured wallpaper was tobacco yellow and probably hadn't been redone since the days before the smoking ban. The plastic chairs had faded to a dull cream or mauve, and they looked uncomfortable, with a ridge halfway up the back.

The receptionist ushered Trent into an adjacent room, where a group of new starters were about to be onboarded. There, an energetic young woman named Jenny greeted him, taking note of his suit.

'Fantastic!' she said. 'It screams professionalism. And it's visibly a cheap polyester one, too. Nothing too fancy. Can't have that.'

Trent smiled thinly. He hadn't imagined that turning up in a suit would be viewed as a statement. It was out of the question for him to turn up to work in anything else. His suit was his armour; that was his motto – or, at least, it had been where his old, expensive suit was concerned. This new one felt more like a Halloween costume.

All the other inductees had turned up in jeans and T-shirts. There were eight of them, and none appeared enthusiastic about being there.

'Our number is complete,' Jenny said. 'Let's start with the equipment.'

She began distributing clipboards from a pile on a nearby table. 'These are company property. When you leave, it's down to you to return them. Otherwise, the cost will be deducted from your pay cheque.'

'Well, isn't this all very 1995?' one of the trainees declared, regarding his clipboard disdainfully.

Jenny cast a withering glare at the young man who'd been stupid enough to pipe up. 'Well, technically, of course, we could provide all our fundraisers with tablets. How do you think that would go down? Yes, it would look like we represent a professional organisation, great, but it would also look like it could afford to give expensive gadgets to its fundraisers. And, if that's the case, why do they need more money?'

'For more tablets,' the smart-arse said.

'Any other questions?' Jenny said to the rest of the group, ignoring his remark She didn't wait for an answer. 'This month, we have a contract with Friends of the Disappeared. We've emailed you their dossier and a link to their website. Before your first shift, you're expected to read up on them thoroughly. You'll be an expert on their work. If needed, you'll be able to write an essay on why they're the most vital yet criminally underfunded NGO in the country.'

'What do they do?' the same hapless young man asked. Trent doubted he would last long in this job. Perhaps he didn't intend to.

Again, Jenny gave him that glare. 'Well, that should be obvious from the name. They find missing people and shit.' Jenny turned to a map behind her. 'Now, let me take you through Geneva's main fundraising spots. You'll be assigned in pairs to each of them. Check the number on the back of your clipboard.'

Trent turned over his clipboard. Number two. That meant he would be stationed by the bus stop outside the Coop on the Rue du Rhône. It was shopping central. He would have to grab the attention of people who had already spent more than they should in Geneva's luxury shops. If there was one thing he knew for sure, it was that it would be supremely challenging to get someone already suffering from shoppers' guilt to part with more of their money.

To make matters worse, Jenny declared, 'We'll start you on a Saturday afternoon. That's our peak time. Be ready.'

This was not going to be fun.

'Ça va, Trent?'

It was Trent's second French lesson that week, and he

had taken up residence at the same desk at the back of the room. He was markedly less enthusiastic about being there than before. Even though it had gone relatively well, that first lesson had brought home how much he had to learn. He was no quitter, but sometimes he wished he could bring himself to give up on things a little easier.

He perked up a bit when Serena made a beeline for the desk next to him and greeted him with a brilliant smile. He had seen people with whitened teeth before, but rarely had it looked so good. He remembered the beginnings of a connection that had formed in the previous lesson, only to be rudely cut short by the imposition of having to speak in French. Perhaps this session wouldn't be as tortuous as he'd imagined.

'*Ça va,*' Trent said. '*Et toi, ça va?*'

'*Ça va.*'

It seemed clear that this relationship was set to go far.

As the lesson progressed, Serena kept talking to him, even outside the occasional pair-up-and-try-with-a-partner exercise. She augmented the tutor's instruction with little asides, sharing secrets about others in the class. At the front was Veronica, who was there because she wanted to communicate with her boyfriend, who couldn't speak a word of English.

'That'll be the beginning of the end,' Serena said, 'the moment they start understanding what the other one's saying.'

She pointed out John, too, a househusband who was there as an escape from the kitchen.

'He told me once he'd always wanted to be a stay-at-home dad,' Serena said. 'But then he discovered that the highlight of his week was cleaning out the oven. So, here he is.'

As Trent discovered more about his classmates, he realised that this place was a haven for the other-halfs: partners who had followed expat husbands or wives to Switzerland. These people had no need to work because their partner had a cushy deal. Working was actually illegal for many, as they lacked the necessary permits. The room was full of people with far too much time on their hands and a diminishing sense of their own worth.

The tutor seemed aware of this and didn't miss an opportunity to rub it in. She demanded a few times, '*Vous cherchez du travail?*' (Are you looking for work?)

'*Ça ne sert à rien,*' came the response, pretty much uniformly. '*Nous allons bientôt partir.*' (It's not worth it. We'll be leaving soon.)

The tutor smiled. It wasn't clear whether this was because she was pleased with their French or that she felt confirmed in her superiority over them.

Trent himself wasn't spared such interrogation. '*Je suis içi pour sauver le monde,*' he explained. ("I'm here to save the world." It sounded so naïve. He was a child in French).

His comment was greeted by knowing nods.

At the end of the lesson, Serena laid her hand on his arm. 'Come with me.'

Trent didn't question her. He got his things together quickly, and they raced out of the door, hot on the tail of Veronica, the one with the French boyfriend, whose relationship extended as far as '*bonjour*' and '*ça va?*'

'I want to see him,' Serena said as they hurried. At Trent's perplexed expression, she asked, 'Aren't you curious? I certainly am!'

Trent wasn't nearly as curious as Bong and Amara were when they saw him and Serena leave together. Bong appeared over the moon to see Trent with a woman. He shouted 'Oye, oye, oye!' as they passed. Amara frowned.

Trent smiled to himself smugly.

They followed Veronica to the tram stop and hopped onto the number 15 a few doors down. The tram was busy, so there was a chance they hadn't been spotted. They held their breath until the doors closed, anticipating that Veronica might step off at the last minute, like a chase scene from a movie. She didn't.

She got off the tram a few stops later at Stand, where the line connected with the 14 and various bus routes. She walked from there. They followed her into one of the local bars, busy with the after-work crowd. The prices were high, but Serena brought them both cocktails, and they watched from the bar as Veronica found a spot in a small alcove.

Then, nothing happened.

'I've always thought it very rude when a man makes a woman wait,' Serena commented. 'I know some girls like a bad boy, but there are limits.'

'Do you think she's dating a bad boy?' Trent said. 'She doesn't seem the type.'

Veronica had a mousy, twitchy way of moving. She had the air of the librarian about her, but who knew what lay beneath?

Fifteen minutes later, a man sporting a leather jacket and a general sense of importance slipped into the booth. He was wearing dark glasses, like a celebrity who didn't want to be spotted. For all Trent knew, he could have been exactly that. His knowledge of Swiss popular culture was limited.

Any sense of intrigue evaporated when Veronica leaned across the table, lips pouted. It was a long kiss, and it was certainly not subtle. Trent thought he could hear the moist noises from across the room – but that was probably just his imagination.

'It's him!' Serena enthused.

'Well, I hope so,' Trent said,' and she doesn't do this with everyone she meets in a bar.'

He had been quite content to follow Serena like a puppy, but it felt now like she was subjecting him to a soft porn movie.

'You brought me here to watch this?' he said.

'Well, I think it's romantic! In a rather obvious way, maybe, but we take what we can get!'

Trent had never been able to understand why people got themselves so worked up about romance. It was a ritual, that was all, an adherence to a series of norms dreamt up centuries earlier in a very different world. What place did it have in the here and now? The concept that there was one person out there for everyone seemed positively archaic. Every ounce of evidence pointed to the contrary: that there was a limit to what human beings could do. They were interchangeable and replaceable.

And yet, Trent understood longing. He understood unfulfilled desire. He knew it only too well. There was one woman he thought of now and then when he let his guard down. One woman whose smile he saw on others' faces, but they were never, never hers.

Serena seemed to read his thoughts. 'Have you ever felt like that about someone?'

Trent chuckled. 'Oh, no, you're not going to get that out of me so easily!' He felt now like she was studying him in the same way they'd done earlier to others in class. How long would it be before she came up with an entertaining backstory for him? And how accurate would it be?

'It was bad, then?'

'No, it wasn't bad,' he said carefully. 'It just never happened. I made a choice. It seemed like the right one at the time.'

'Ah, one of those! Nothing gets us like a story never written. Fertile ground for the imagination. It all stays rose-tinted; you never got to see the downside.'

'Oh, I saw it, right enough. We used each other. That was the basis of our relationship.'

Serena grinned. 'That's the basis of most marriages. The ones that last, they're where you're each using the other more-or-less equally.'

'That's a very cynical view of marriage.'

'Call it insider knowledge.'

Trent took a sip from his cocktail, buying himself a moment to digest that latest piece of information. 'You're married?'

'You seem surprised. It's hardly as if I've been trying to hide it. I mean, look at this thing!'

Serena held up her left hand. Her ring finger was adorned with a rather substantial diamond.

Trent laughed to hide a twinge of disappointment. 'I just thought that was part of the bling.'

'Bling? You can't call this bling! You're talking about it like it's a tooth jewel.'

'I didn't mean offence.'

Serena took his hand. 'That's okay. Can we still be f-wends?'

Trent found himself laughing again. He couldn't help himself around her. 'Yes, we can be friends.'

He took a drink to break eye contact because he suspected that neither of them would allow it to stay that way.

CHAPTER 5
THE URINE THICKENS

Hobbs wanted to break the news to his campmates right away that evening, but they were preoccupied with gossip. He knew better than to get in the way of that. And it was about Trent, of all people. He couldn't pretend he wasn't curious.

'So, who's the bit of stuff?' Bong demanded, poking the campfire as though that would make it cook their meal faster.

'"Bit of stuff?"' Trent said. 'I didn't think people still used that term.'

'They shouldn't,' Amara said. 'Although perhaps I'll make an exception for Serena.'

'You know her?' Trent said.

Amara nodded. 'She used to be in my class. You know, she swaps classes all the time, like she's going on some grand tour. She's the only person I've seen go down a level. Must be something caught her eye.'

'What exactly are you trying to imply?'

'Just look at the way she dresses. And her lipstick. Does

anyone wear bright red who's not on the lookout for male attention?'

'Now, just hang on one second.' Trent had apparently located the chivalrous bone in his body. It must have been the smallest of inner ear bones, but it was there. 'You shouldn't judge a book by its cover.'

Amara sniggered. 'She positively *invites* you to judge her by her cover!'

Hobbs grinned and immediately felt guilty about it. The last thing he wanted to see was tension in the group, but he had found himself growing jealous of Trent. He couldn't discount the fact that Trent had saved all their skins, but it would have been nice if he'd done it without endangering Hobbs' place at the heart of the group.

Perhaps now was a good time to make his announcement. Nothing like a change of subject to clear the air. Plus, he was conscious of the rustling in the bushes.

'We have a visitor tonight,' he said.

'Not a crime lord this time, I hope,' Bong said.

Amara was more on the ball about where this was leading. 'No!'

Moments later, the creature emerged from the bushes. The branches had clawed at its clothes and hair, making it look wilder than usual. It wasn't the entrance Hobbs had hoped for, but if he knew one thing for sure, it was that Vincent was no fan of living up to other people's expectations.

'*Bonsoir, mes amis!*' Vincent announced.

'*Bonsoir,*' they replied in chorus as though they were back in French lessons.

Vincent had dressed up for the evening. He was wearing a suede jacket, shiny from wear and several sizes too big for him, and a chequered shirt which looked like it had been wrestled off a lumberjack. His hair was greased back and adorned with the occasional twig.

'Can I speak with you?' Amara said to Hobbs.

She ushered him to the edge of the campsite. He followed dutifully.

'You invited *Vincent* to join us?' she said. 'What do you think you're doing?'

Hobbs shrugged. 'Building bridges.'

'The guy has been nothing but rude to us, and you want to build bridges?'

'We need to resolve our differences. How else do you think it's going to happen?'

Amara threw her arms in the air. 'It doesn't work like that. He wants us to leave. That's it.'

'Just trust me.'

When they returned, Vincent had already made himself comfortable, perching himself on one of the tree stumps they used as stools. The nights were still warm, but he took the opportunity to warm his hands on the fire. He did it smugly, rubbing them together like he was coveting a pile of gold.

'What's for dinner?' he asked.

'Sausage casserole,' Hobbs said. 'It should be just about ready.'

He put on a pair of oven gloves, the cheap sort that don't really protect from heat. They were pastel-coloured, with flowers on, and looked like they were recycled from an old tea cosy.

'We're feeding him now, too?' Amara muttered.

Although Vincent must have heard her comment, he showed no sign that he didn't feel entirely at home. He struck up a conversation with Bong about the movies. His knowledge seemed remarkably up to date. Shortly after that, the conversation turned to politics, a positive mine-field at the best of times, even before taking into account Vincent's views. His main preoccupation was the number of Ukrainian refugees that had entered the country since the beginning of the war.

'If you ask me,' he declared, 'we should take care of our own people before letting others in. We have enough scroungers here already.' Vincent glanced pointedly at each campmate.

Hobbs handed him a bowl of casserole. It was the best thing they had eaten in weeks. Just buying the meat had blown their food allowance for the month. Vincent didn't even thank him.

'I mean,' he continued, waving his fork around to illus-trate his point, 'Geneva's been in a housing crisis for decades. All the expats turn up to work in organisations that don't pay taxes. They come in, take up the space, and don't give anything back.'

'Geneva seems to be doing pretty well for itself,' Trent said.

'Oh, you think so, do you? Try finding an apartment here. Can't do it for love nor money. And all the social hous-ing's taken by the bloody Ukrainians. I'll tell you what, it gives me sympathy for the Russians.'

Hobbs could feel Amara prickling next to him. He readied himself for confrontation. Fortunately, Bong diverted the conversation back to the movies.

'They make good baddies, the Russians,' he said. 'It's nice to see them making a comeback.'

Amara's nostrils flared. 'So, you're telling me that a good point about the invasion of a country, massive destruction and death of thousands of people is that Russians can be baddies again in your godawful films?'

Bong shrugged. 'Narratively speaking, yes.'

'And you think some of the things I say are controversial!'

Hobbs, forever the mediator, stepped in for the first of many times that night. 'It's good to have villains of all nationalities. The Nazis have been and gone, the Cold War's old news and even Middle Eastern terrorists are getting a bit tired.'

'Brits,' said Amara. Her gaze bored holes into Trent. 'They always make good villains.'

Trent coughed and looked away.

'Children, children,' Vincent said. 'Let's all agree we dislike each other. That's just fine. I hate everybody equally: the Ukrainians, the Russians, the Portuguese, Brazilians and everybody from bloody Whatsistan. They can all bugger off, as far as I'm concerned.'

'You've picked literally the worst city to be racist,' Amara said. 'There are more nationalities living here than anywhere else in the world.'

Vincent scoffed at that. '*Au contraire, mes amis*, it's the best place to be racist: plenty of targets.'

They continued their meal in silence.

A bit later, after Vincent had consumed his food and felt safe that he wouldn't miss out on a meal, he produced a list of demands. He had clearly spent a while working on them, scribbling them in pencil on the back of a Migros flyer. While the general theme was that they should get out of there, he pinpointed several specific gripes, such as Amara's "shrill voice" and Hobbs' excessive tidiness.

'As for you,' he said, addressing Bong. 'You need to get rid of that disgusting habit.'

'Which one are you talking about?' Bong said.

'I've seen you pissing up against the bridge like a dog.'

Hobbs turned to Bong. 'Is this true? There's a river ten metres away!'

Bong rolled his eyes. 'Remember that French expression we learned last week? *"J'ai la flemme."*'

'He means he's a lazy ass,' Vincent translated.

'Yes!' Hobbs said. 'Thank you!'

'Your friend's right, though,' Vincent told Bong. 'You're sleeping next to the greatest toilet in the world – the Rhône. And even better, foreigners swim in it downstream. Just think about them bathing in your piss. It's almost poetic.'

The evening went on too long. Vincent was all too ready to overstay his welcome. He left well after midnight. By then, everyone had got out their sleeping bags, but they were still shivering, staring into the fire's embers with sunken eyes. Only Vincent appeared to be still enjoying himself.

'*Au revoir, mes amis!*' he said, bowing with a flourish. 'Until next time!'

And he disappeared into the bushes.

As the campmates turned in for the night, Amara glared at Hobbs. 'Let's not do that again.'

Hobbs agreed.

Bong had decided to quit. It just wasn't the same interning with the International Refugee Agency without Hobbs. Outwardly, Bong may have given the impression of being so entranced by the horrific videos they watched that he barely noticed his companion's presence, but the truth was that he needed someone there with him. With Hobbs around, Bong could pull himself away; he could ground himself.

He made the decision whilst on a fake cigarette break. Those weren't the same, either, without Hobbs with him to share the sense of conspiracy. He strode past security, wielding his still-untouched box of cigarettes, but once he was safely out of sight, there was no one to giggle with. So, he just stood in the shadow of the concrete buildings, watching the trams pass.

It occurred to Bong that it should have been him, not Hobbs, who quit the IRA to look after Trent. When it came down to it, it was Bong's actions, not Hobbs', that brought Fredevich to the campsite, endangering them all. Hobbs had nothing to do with their failed heist. There had never been any question of the IRA offering a leave of absence for them to Trent recover from his beating: as far as they were concerned, interns were either working there or they were not. Bong should have taken responsibility. He should have left that internship and given up on all the opportunities it offered. But somehow, he couldn't make himself feel guilty about it. That was just the way things went. Besides, he was pretty sure that Hobbs had been looking for an excuse to leave. He'd hated that place.

Bong hung around for a length of time he judged it would take someone to finish smoking. As he turned the corner to head back to his little box room, he bumped into the most beautiful girl he had ever seen. She was dressed in a light summer dress, and her luscious curls tumbled over her shoulders. She was a splash of colour amongst the grey concrete, with pink lipstick, blue eyeshadow and red manicured nails. She was in her early twenties, still young enough to get away with clashing colours in the name of fashion.

To be more specific, Bong didn't bump into her; he stepped on her dog. It was a little Shih Tzu with bulging eyes and a nervous disposition that wasn't aided by having been trampled on. It yelped, and she picked it up, cooing at it like a baby. It tried to lick the snot out of her nostrils.

'*Désolé*,' Bong said.

The girl glared at him but didn't say a word. Women never talked to him. Standing on a girl's dog was just the latest in a long list of things Bong had done that had resulted in him being ignored by a woman. She pushed past him, whispering condolences to her little darling.

Bong watched her cross the road and enter the nearby park. He hesitated before following her. He wasn't a stalker, honestly. Bong had no more idea what to do with attractive women than admire them. He was just curious. And if they happened to bump into each other again, maybe he wouldn't step on her dog, and perhaps she'd go, 'Thank you for not stepping on my dog this time,' and they'd get talking.

As he entered the park, he spotted her in the shade of a sycamore. The Shih Tzu had deposited a little brown gift in the middle of the gravel path. She fished out a red plastic bag and bent down to scoop it up. This was quite a sight to behold, with her heels, high hemline, and low-cut dress that showed off more than she might have wanted as she crouched.

Without really thinking about it, he got out his phone.

This was every bit as depressing as Trent had expected.

They had a little table outside the Coop, emblazoned with the name Friends of the Disappeared and covered with leaflets. From there, they watched the shoppers go by. Trent tried to engage with them, to no avail. It was surprising how many people urgently needed to go shopping at H&M.

He tried all his techniques. He greeted them, smiling widely. He wasn't out there asking people for money; he was selling to them, and what he was selling was their souls. Charity was the path to a clear conscience. Only, no one there appeared to have a soul, or at least to care about it in the shopping blitz.

At one point, he even got so desperate as to follow Jenny's advice.

'If all else fails, ask them a question,' she'd told them at the briefing. 'People can't help themselves if someone asks them a question. It makes them believe we care what they think.'

'How would you feel if a family member just vanished?' he tried. Then, 'Who do you think should pay for the search if someone goes missing?'

In return, he heard all the excuses: "I've already given to another charity"; "My elderly parent's waiting for me, I have to get back before they die"; or simply "*Je n'ai pas le temps.*" The worst was those who ignored him. He had to jump out of the way a couple of times as they continued walking as though he wasn't there.

The young woman Trent was paired with had more success, thanks to her readiness to prostitute herself for charity.

'Thirty seconds with me, doesn't that tempt you?' she said to the men she approached. Nine out of ten agreed that, yes, it did.

Trent didn't even attempt to emulate her, knowing that if he'd tried that line on anyone, he would have been met with laughter or a police conviction.

He took a break, nibbling on a cheap supermarket sandwich while sitting on a bench beside the Rue du Rhône. He watched the rich people park their flash cars over the "no-parking" markings on the road. They didn't care. What was a little fine to them?

It was then that he had his idea.

He approached the next person who parked there and offered to keep hold of their keys. Their expression of incredulity softened when they saw he was wearing a suit. No one wearing a suit could be a con artist, could they? His association with a charity must also have helped. If someone was good enough to spend their Saturday fundraising, they must surely be trustworthy.

'I'll move it if I see a parking attendant,' he assured them.

Trent had to fight his jaw from dropping when they handed over the keys. It was staggering to see his plan pay off so easily. These people cared less about money than whether their pride and joy might get scratched or towed. Another concern was those horrible adhesives used to stick fines to the windscreen. It was next to impossible to get that stuff off.

Fifteen minutes later, when the car's owner returned to find their vehicle still there and fully intact, they greeted Trent with a wide grin and a handful of notes. They had cheated the system!

Trent reflected that there were two types of rich people: those who had made the money and those born into it. The first type was wily as hell; they knew all the tricks. They suspected everyone and saw hidden schemes in everything, mainly because they were the ones who devised such schemes on their way up. Trent understood this group well because he had once been one of them back in the day. There was nothing to be gained from approaching them.

Trent had been one of them. It was the second group he needed to target: those whose lives had been rosy and for whom it had not been necessary to develop a deep suspicion of humanity. Money was disposable to them. They were prepared to take stupid risks because the personal consequences were minimal. It was this group that parked in the no-parking spots.

Trent would not try to sell them their souls. Instead, he would sell them convenience. That worked better. And it was all for a good cause.

'I have a mission for you,' Trent said.

Serena smiled, and the world lit up. Trent felt certain it hadn't escaped her notice that it was he who struck up the conversation in that evening's French class rather than her.

'Tell me,' she said.

'Bong,' Trent said.

A flicker of confusion crossed Serena's face, but her smile didn't fade.

'He's one of my neighbours,' Trent explained. He chose that word carefully to avoid letting on that he was living out of a tent. 'And, well, it's an unusual name. Not the one he was born with, I think.'

'You don't say.'

'I need to know his real name.'

Trent didn't explain why. He suspected this woman wouldn't find it attractive that his campmates were pulling a teenage prank at his expense.

Serena slapped him on the arm. 'You've come to the right gal.'

They spent that lesson hatching a plan. Trent learned

considerably less French that hour than in preceding sessions, but that didn't matter. There was such a thing as priorities.

When they were finished, they roamed the building until they located Bong and Amara's class. Serena struck up a conversation with the tutor, an older gent who only had eyes for her. It was a masterful display on her part. She kept brushing back her hair as though she was shy while asking him all manner of questions about French grammar. How she knew so much about the language whilst still in a beginner class, that would have been an interesting question. Equally pertinent would have been why she was not asking her own teacher about this stuff. The guy didn't explore either of these avenues.

Trent snuck behind him and scanned the class register.

'Damn!' he hissed, but he managed to restrain himself from a louder outburst until he was outside.

Serena joined him a few minutes later, wielding a scrap of paper bearing the tutor's phone number, which she screwed up and threw away.

'What's the matter?' she said.

'He's in on it, too!' Trent sighed. 'All it said in the register was "Bong". How can they let people sign up for a course under a fake name?'

Serena nodded thoughtfully. 'Maybe it's his real name, then. Who knows what's fake these days? Trent Argent's not much better.'

'What do you mean?'

'It sounds like it's straight from a film noir!'

They ended up in a bar again that evening. It just came naturally: a casual offer of 'Want a drink?' from Serena and a response of 'Why not?' from Trent. Both knew what they were walking into, but they went through the motions of pretending they were just friends going out. It made Trent feel good, going about town with someone who looked as good as her. He was still feeling the high of his fundraising success. Maybe he did belong in the same world as Serena.

That evening's conversation was more involved than the last time. Serena continued probing about his love life, but he refused to budge. Quite apart from whether he was ready to talk about it, he didn't want to disappoint her, as he knew his tale was anticlimactic. He did, however, open up to her about his career before Geneva. It seemed only polite to give her something.

'I was successful,' he told her. 'I'm not saying that in an immodest way. Empirically, I was. We have a way of measuring such things in business, and it's called money.'

Serena ran a finger thoughtfully around the rim of her cocktail glass. He'd said the magic word, "money". That always made beautiful women stop and think. Trent had few cards to play in his favour, and it hardly required strategic mastery to opt for that one. If only he could still back it up.

'What sort of business were you in?' she said.

'Opportunities.'

'Is that some sort of banking thing?'

'No, it was about linking people with initiatives. Playing the moment. I worked with local councils tackling thorny community issues. Every problem has a solution; you just need someone to make the connection. That's what I did. In that line of business, if you play it right, you can help people and make a tonne of money out of it.'

'That's not how most people get rich.'

'I'm not most people.'

Serena laughed. 'Oh dear. It sounds like someone's

trying to salve their conscience. So, what brought you here, "*Pour sauver le monde*" and all that?'

Trent looked away. How could he explain his fall in a way that didn't make him appear as a soulless business tycoon who had been defeated? He still thought about the backwater village that had risen up against him. He remembered it every time he looked at the torn suit he had brought with him to Geneva. Had he tripped, or had they pushed him while he was making his exit? Should he talk about the gambling – his many failed attempts to prove he could stop losing? No, that was no better. What kind of sad, obsessive man fritters his fortune away like that? One that had lost a part of himself, a part that appeared insignificant to the naked eye but whose absence he felt keenly. He only hoped he could fill the hole by trying to make himself a better person.

Fortunately, Serena didn't let the silence last. 'I know what you are. You're a supervillain who grew a conscience, trying to make amends. Only, you weren't one of the fun supervillains with gadgets, lasers and minions. That would be far too interesting.'

'Thank you,' Trent said. It was one step up from "soulless business tycoon", he supposed.

Serena grinned playfully. 'In what reality was that a compliment?'

She ordered them another drink, and pretty soon, Trent felt the alcohol go to his head. He had not been drinking so much lately, not since the incident with Fredevich. He avoided alcohol when with his campmates because he knew he couldn't drink in moderation. Maybe he needed it less, too. There was plenty enough going on to keep him distracted.

'I was successful once, too,' Serena said when they had

been served. 'I was a top criminal lawyer back home, if you can believe it. Only, law doesn't travel well. American law counts for nothing here. Every country has to do it differently, and by the time I'd get on top of it, my husband would be moved on to his next assignment.'

'That sucks,' Trent said. He wasn't sure when he'd started talking like a teenager, but it seemed the right thing to say. Serena's accent was infectious.

'So now I have to be the pretty little wife,' she continued, stirring her cocktail. 'I've been doing it so long that I've almost forgotten what I am. What criminal lawyer looks like this?'

Trent took advantage of the opportunity to eye her up and down.

'One that wins all her cases, I imagine,' he said.

Serena pouted exaggeratedly. 'I suppose you think that's funny?'

'Well, I *am* a supervillain.'

They talked about anything and everything. Trent discovered he had a knack for talking with women – or he supposed he did, judging by Serena's reactions. He had never felt so entertaining. Her laugh had this playful lilt to it, and she would often throw back her head, tossing her golden hair behind her, fanning her breasts with a hand. They spent a long while mocking the bar's other clients, inventing backstories about them. The loud woman in the group at the table next to them was career-obsessed, sucking up to her boss to get her next promotion. The man alone at the bar with dark patches under his eyes was a new father who escaped from home to drink himself back to the life he used to have.

Serena whispered her theories to him conspiratorially, as though she were letting him into little secrets. Was this her way of flirting with him? More to the point, *was* she flirting? Why was she there, spending the evening with him? Trent would have been suspicious of anyone else, but with Serena, he was content to go with the flow.

They stayed late, until the staff had cleared the other tables and set about taking away their empties in a pointed fashion.

'I like hanging out with you,' said Serena as they prepared to leave. 'It's like I've finally found someone that speaks my language.'

Trent assumed she wasn't referring to the fact that they both spoke English. He fought down his initial rejection of the term "hanging out". That wasn't a thing Trent Argent did; it was too... inefficient. But intoxication had softened him, as had the fuzzy feeling he got from being the centre of this woman's attention.

'We should do this again sometime,' he agreed.

Serena grabbed his arm urgently as though she'd had an epiphany. 'A few of us are coming over to mine this Wednesday – a little afternoon *apéro* pool party. Fancy joining?

Even drunk, Trent's inhibitions around women wouldn't go away. When at his peak, he would have rejected her offer out of hand, aware that in the list of things that made great men fall, a woman was not far from the top. Still, her offer was tempting. He hadn't taken a proper shower in weeks, and there was only so much that could be concealed with a good dousing of aftershave. He'd considered paying the swimming pool tariff just to use the facilities. This was a cheaper option. He wondered if it would be acceptable to turn up with a sack full of dirty washing while he was at it.

He could recognise a trap, though. Traps were genderless, and they smelled to Trent like iron. His nose twitched as his instincts kicked in. He had avoided so many traps over the years that they took over automatically.

'I'm not sure that's a good idea,' he said, although a big part of him screamed that this was a very good idea.

Serena blinked. 'Why not?'

Trent gazed into her blue eyes. She appeared innocent and affronted, but this was a woman of glamour and conceit who concealed her true intentions just as readily as she applied her makeup. Yet still, he weakened.

'I'm busy this Friday. Another time?'

Serena smiled broadly. 'It's a date!'

'What's that smell?' Amara said from her tent.

'Bong!' Hobbs shouted when the odour reached him in his sleeping bag. 'We told you, you piss in the river. The river!'

Confused noises came from the third tent. 'It wasn't me!'

Dawn had barely broken, so they were all half asleep. Hobbs grimaced and crawled out into the open, where he was dismayed to discover that the smell was worse.

'Oh no,' cried Amara, 'he hasn't, has he?'

Vincent's urine had long dried by then, but the scent was pungent. As Hobbs inspected the site, he discovered that their neighbour from hell had relieved himself every-where. There were even stains up the side of their tents. Streams of moisture had flattened the campfire ashes.

'Who would have thought the old man had so much piss in him?' Bong intoned once he, Trent and Amara had emerged.

They all looked at him curiously.

'Shakespeare,' Bong explained.

'You know Shakespeare?' Amara said.

'Not personally. But it's bread and butter at theatre school.'

'You know Shakespeare, but you don't know what *flora* and *fauna* means?' Amara insisted.

Bong shrugged.

Amara turned back to the scene. 'He must have been saving it up. Filling bottles with it. How revolting!'

She stormed down to Vincent's lean-to to have it out with him. Nobody dared get in her way. It would have been a confrontation for the ages, but Vincent had made himself absent, leaving only the acrid markings of his territory behind him.

They set about cleaning up the place as best they could, taking their cooking pans down to the river to fill them with water, which they poured all around the campsite and up their tents. When they were done, it was difficult to tell whether they had truly rid themselves of the odour or if their noses had just adjusted to it. In any case, a half hour later, the place was a quagmire.

On his last trip back from the river, Hobbs could have sworn he heard laughter in the wind.

'We can't stay here,' Amara said.

Hobbs shook his head. 'We're not moving out. I refuse to give up on this.'

'Yes, fine, but I mean, look at it! I don't know about you, but I don't fancy standing around waiting for it to dry out.'

'It's like watching diluted urine dry,' Bong added helpfully.

'I have an idea,' Hobbs said.

Amara sighed. 'Your solution had better not be inviting Vincent to dinner again.'

'Come with me,' Hobbs said excitedly. 'There's somewhere I've been wanting to take you guys for a while.'

The Salève was the nearest mountain to Geneva. Its face was sheer. The crumbling rock appeared to be held together in places by hardy trees and bushes. It looked like God had made a miscalculation when laying out the land, realising that he had built it too high, then cutting it away abruptly in the hope that nobody would notice. The various rock strata were visible. It was a geologist's dream.

The quarry chipping away at its side diminished its grandeur, making it appear like a glorified construction site. If God believed that humankind might be intimidated by this "mountain", then He had underestimated its desire to extract wealth from dirt or put a telegraph tower and ice cream stand at the top.

To the locals, the Salève was known principally for obstructing their view of Mont Blanc. But it was Geneva's mountain, and woe betide anyone who might disrespect it.

From its foot, Hobbs couldn't help but be impressed. It was tall enough to block out the sun. The morning's humidity lingered longer there. Trent appeared in awe of it, too, although he informed them that this was principally because he had spent the past few years in South England, where they call a mound of dirt a hill and a hill a mountain.

They were at the lower station for the cable car, whose lines were suspended across the autoroute and up, over the quarry, to the top at about 1400 metres in altitude.

Bong paled as they entered the cabin.

'I didn't realise you were afraid of heights,' Hobbs said.

Bong nodded slowly. 'It's not natural.'

'Listen,' Amara said softly. 'This thing has been running for over a century. Why would it collapse now?'

'Law of averages,' Bong replied. 'If nothing's gone wrong in a hundred years, it's bound to happen now.'

'That's not how statistics work.'

As the doors closed, Bong put his head between his knees, inhaling deeply. The mechanism started, and they accelerated on their upward journey. Bong's panic was intoxicating. Hobbs wouldn't usually have considered what might happen if the cables snapped, but it was now all he could think about. He turned away from the view and avoided looking at the void of air beneath them. He watched the rock face come closer as they got higher.

'We're halfway,' Trent said as they passed the other cabin on its way down. His voice was light and full of relief.

Bong's heavy breathing filled the cabin. The other travellers gave him a plethora of dirty looks. They were kitted out with mountain bikes or paragliders and had done this a thousand times before, rarely with such drama.

Hobbs closed his eyes and breathed deeply, too. He had lived through moments like that before, those which he knew would end but which somehow lasted an eternity.

They all looked a bit green when they reached the top. They pushed themselves out of the cabin, holding tightly to the rails.

'If you don't mind, I'll walk down,' Bong said.

Nobody minded.

A gust of wind greeted them as they left the terminal (a concrete monstrosity that had evidently not been built with any intention to beautify the area). It whistled in their ears, carrying just a hint of the snow that still covered the peaks of Mont Blanc. It was not unpleasant, not in the height of summer. And the air up there felt clean, not like down in the valley where Geneva fermented.

This was just what they needed.

'Breathe it in, just breathe it,' Hobbs instructed. 'This is what air's supposed to smell like!'

Unfortunately, just upwind of them, someone had decided to light a cigarette. Apparently, that was the best accompaniment to the view.

They moved to the far end of the viewing platform, where they sat on a wall and spent a few more minutes finding their feet. Hobbs wished he could say that Geneva looked beautiful from there, but it appeared like the detritus washed to the mouth of a river. Framed by mountains on two sides and the lake on the other, it was dwarfed by nature. Their lives were down there, amongst those grey-brown buildings and construction cranes. Hobbs thought about the hours they had spent labouring away down there. It all seemed so pointless, so insignificant. He had wanted to go up the Salève to put things in perspective; he didn't like what he saw.

He must have been looking downhearted because Trent laid a hand on his shoulder.

'This was a good idea.'

Hobbs looked into the eyes of the older man. On balance, he was glad he had taken a gamble on him, inviting him into the fold. Yes, there might have been teething pains while they shuffled to make space for him in the group dynamic, but ultimately, his presence was positive. Hobbs was painfully aware of the expression, "You can choose your friends but not your family" – he had muttered it to himself many times over the years. This peculiar group felt like his family now, and he'd been fortunate enough to have a say on who joined it.

Just then, a group of hikers coming up the mountain path glared at them for taking the easy way up. At that moment, one of the kids in their backpack seat realised that they had dropped their toy somewhere on the way up and decided to share their misery with everyone assembled. Shortly after that, someone decided to make a contentious work call a few metres away.

It was time to move on.

They trudged up a rocky footpath for fifteen minutes until they reached the viewpoint at the very top of the Salève. From there, they could no longer see Geneva, but they did have a breathtaking view from the other side of the mountain, at the Alps and the Mont Blanc. Again, Hobbs was awestruck by the enormity of nature. Those mountains had been born millions of years before him, and they would outlast him, unchanged. The only impact that humanity had made on them was to reduce their snow covering by pumping pollutants into the air. Hardly a legacy to be proud of.

Hobbs stretched his arms out to the sky. 'It puts everything into perspective, doesn't it? This is it! This is what we're living for! Not all that shit down in Geneva. Here. We're here! Fuck me, we're alive!'

Amara glared at him.

'What's the matter?' Hobbs said.

'Nothing. I just don't need to roar expletives to enjoy the view.'

Hobbs shrugged. For a moment, just a moment, he didn't care about what other people thought. 'To each their own.'

Amara was shivering as she walked over to Trent.

'He brought us here for *this*?' she said.

Trent smiled at her. The Salève, it seemed, was not for everyone, but he, at least, was happy to be there. Weeks into his stay in Geneva, this was the first time he had left the city. The mountains seemed so close – like you could walk to them. Trent would never have attempted that, of course, and wouldn't even have dreamt of scaling them on foot – he knew his limitations – but the bus ride had been doable even for him.

Amara sat on the grass, waiting for Hobbs to finish his spiritual moment. Trent hesitated to join her. She was exuding an aura on which you could hang a "Do not disturb" sign – and she was never the warmest to him at the best of times. Still, his time with Serena was rubbing off, not just in his increased resilience for Americanisms such as "awesome" but in a growing belief that conversation could be an end in itself, so he decided to give it a go.

'Hobbs reminds me of someone I used to know,' he mused, sitting with her. 'A good soul.'

He was thinking about Eric, a straightforward man he had recruited temporarily to his cause back in England. Eric's prime motivation had been to do good for the community to repay it for accepting him. How naïve that had seemed to Trent back then. It had made Eric so easy to manipulate. Now, it seemed praiseworthy. He wondered what had happened to Eric in the five years since he had turned on Trent.

He thought, too, about a journalist he used to know, one whose name he could not bear to utter. She was rarely far from his mind. Was that just because there were echoes of her in Amara – in their profession and their cynicism? No, it was more than that. The journalist's story was wrapped up in Trent's own. In a peculiar way, she was part of him.

This was what Trent's life was like: a repeat of the same events and the same people. Perhaps that gave him a second chance to do right by people. Failing that, it helped at least to make death bearable, knowing that to carry on would be to replay the same script, only with different actors.

'He deserves better than us,' Amara said. 'Which reminds me, I've been wanting to ask you something.'

'Shoot,' Trent said – another of Serena's expressions.

'The other week, when Fredevich showed up looking for his phone, you had it. You'd snuck away with it in your pocket. Why was that?'

Trent caught his breath. He had hoped that episode was past them, minus a few lingering bruises. He had taken one for the team; that was the accepted story. No one had asked probing questions. Until then.

'I saw them coming,' he said. 'It was obvious that's what they were after, so I took it. I was hoping to lure them away. It didn't quite work out how I planned.'

Amara's dark eyebrows knitted. 'And you didn't think to warn us?'

'There wasn't time.'

Amara looked away. Trent felt sure he had failed to convince her of anything, but he kept quiet. It would only have raised suspicion if he'd tried to augment his story further.

'You're a strange one,' Amara said eventually. 'You turn up drunk with this ridiculous story about wanting to turn your life around. About having been some "big deal". And we just accept it.'

'What else do you need?'

'Tell us about that suit of yours. The one you keep in that vacuum pack.'

'How do you know about that?'

'I saw it when we were moving your tent.' Amara grinned mischievously. 'Is it your dead father's?'

Trent picked a wildflower and considered how to respond. Amara didn't really want to know about him. She was trying to goad him into giving away something incriminating.

'My father's alive and well, thank you,' he said.

'I never hear you phone anyone.'

'My mother requires a bimonthly activity report, which I send by email.'

'I'd like to meet her.'

'No, you wouldn't.'

At that point, Bong squealed with delight a few metres away. He was brandishing his phone (because everyone's primary impulse is to check their phone when they're up a mountain).

'A thousand followers!' he shouted, punching his fist in the air.

Trent and Amara regarded him questioningly. He shuffled across the grass towards them.

'Look at this!'

Bong had opened his TikTok account. Since leaving his internship, his mobile phone had barely left his grasp. He had been tapping away at it relentlessly for days, pausing only to wipe the sweat from his brow. Trent had judged this to be in response to his campmates' consternation about him quitting to pursue a new venture into social media. Hobbs had been particularly scathing about Bong's choice, doubtless because he regretted leaving the same internship a few weeks earlier.

'It's reckless!' he'd said. 'What a wasted opportunity! Yes, it might not pay, but it's the foundation of a career. It'll haunt you for years, walking away.'

Everyone had understood Hobbs' response to be a case study in projection. Bong had objected to being mothered, but he still wanted to prove Hobbs wrong. And by the sound of it, he might have succeeded.

'It's my channel, #Glamurouspeoplepickingupshit,' Bong explained.

'What?' Amara said.

Trent shielded the screen to keep out the sun but still couldn't make anything out.

'I've been taking videos of people who have a dog as an accessory,' Bong said. 'You know, those little yappy things all the it girls have?'

Amara scoffed. 'Baby substitutes.'

'Exactly. They think they look so good in their top-brand clothes, carrying those little rats around dressed up like dolls. Well, those dogs shit like the rest of them, and they've got to clean it up. That's when I start filming.'

'You've been taking videos of girls picking up dog poo?' Amara said. 'How have you not been arrested?'

'Everyone loves it,' Bong insisted. 'A thousand followers! That many people can't be wrong!'

Amara glanced at Trent and then back to Bong. 'Is this why you haven't been applying for jobs?'

'Absolutely!' Bong sprung to his feet. 'This is just the beginning. The beginning of something great!'

CHAPTER 6
INTO TEMPTATION

T hey were setting Trent up for failure by sending him to fundraise door-to-door in Cologny. With his clipboard, he could get spotted as a fundraiser two miles off (the length of some of the driveways). Iron gates, security cameras and intercoms protected these properties. It was what was called, in common parlance, a hint.

The Cologny residences were impressive, to say the least. Many were built on the slope down to the lake, affording them unfettered views of the best part of Geneva – the wet bit, which hadn't been built on. Their grounds were extensive and carefully maintained. Trent suspected that half of the community (those not there to benefit from lower taxes) were employed to tend them. The architecture was an exercise in showing off – all glass and widescreen televisions where there should have been walls.

Bong would have loved it there. More than once, Trent saw a glamorous person picking up shit.

Trent hid his clipboard behind his back as he approached the next gate. In retrospect, this probably just made him look like a bad hitman. He wondered briefly if anybody apart from charity fundraisers bought clipboards these days. Did they alone keep the clipboard industry afloat?

Still, if his recent success at street fundraising was anything to go by, this was a job at which he excelled. His supervisor, Jenny, had sworn (in a good way) when he'd handed over the cash. If he was so good in the Rue du Rhône, just think what he could achieve in Cologny!

He was outside the final residence on the street. It was a particularly nice one – at least, it looked it from the little Trent could see over the tall bushes. It had extensive grounds, and he could make out a balcony on the first floor.

He pressed the intercom and waited, steeling himself for another rejection. After this, he would be done for the day, ready to go back and listen to Jenny swear (not in a good way). He prepared his spiel. 'I'm sorry to bother you. I wonder if I could take a few minutes of your time to tell you about one of Switzerland's biggest unrecognised problems...'

The light on the camera turned on. He drew in a breath. Then:

'You came!' It was a female voice. 'What perfect timing!'

The gate whirred open.

Trent hesitated before entering. This was mainly due to shock, but he was also dealing with the various warning alerts that had gone off in his brain. He had been invited into a secure compound by a person or persons unknown. He had no idea what he was walking into, and once that gate closed behind him, he would be trapped. Who knew what kind of slave labour these Cologny residents used to sustain them in the manner to which they had become accustomed? And where had their fortune come from?

Maybe they were traffickers, preying on poor people like him to harvest their organs.

He shrugged off the last thought. Who in the world would want any part of his body?

Trent entered.

A path of carefully maintained paving slabs led across a pristine lawn to a swimming pool. The deckchairs were empty, but several empty cocktail glasses sat on the poolside table. Trent approached carefully. His eyes flicked to the building's large windows, searching for movement, but he couldn't see anything through the dark glass. The patio doors were wide open, so he headed towards them, assuming that whoever had let him in had done so from a panel indoors.

It was then that she emerged. The first thing Trent noticed was the flesh – there was so much of it. Her legs, chest and stomach were bare. She wore a skimpy, dark blue bikini. Her hair was tied up, and her makeup was immaculate.

Serena.

'Trent!' she called. 'So good of you to come!'

She strutted towards him in her strappy heels. If Trent had been cognizant of such things, he would have questioned the combination of high heels and bikini, but he wasn't really thinking at that point. He was just staring.

He still had the presence of mind to hide his clipboard.

'You missed most of the fun,' Serena said. 'My guests left ten minutes ago. It's just you and me now, but that's fine. Let's get you a drink!'

Before he could respond, she grabbed him by the arm and pulled him into the building.

The living room was a cold, modern design, all clean edges and glass. An oversized leather sofa, which looked like it had never been sat on, gazed onto a television that covered an entire wall. A spiral staircase, painted black, led upstairs. The room also housed a large marble bar. Bottles of various spirits lined glass shelves behind it, and a man-sized wine refrigerator buzzed determinedly.

'You live here?' That was all Trent could manage.

'We're just renting,' Serena replied.

Trent didn't even want to consider how much the rent must have been on that place. Serena didn't work, but her husband must have been making a pretty penny.

Serena seemed to follow his thoughts because she said. 'Hunter's out at work. Won't be back until late. It's just you and me for now. Cocktail?'

She didn't wait for his response or ask him what he wanted before she started pouring. She had all the instruments that people have to show off when making cocktails, all in stainless steel. Trent perched on a stool and watched her.

When she was done, she thrust a glass into his hand. He took a sip. His eyes watered as the back of his throat burned.

'What is this?'

'Various things. Mainly absinthe.' Serena giggled conspiratorially. 'I've always gone by the adage, "If it's illegal somewhere, it's probably worth trying."'

'Didn't you say you were a lawyer?'

'Not here.'

Serena grabbed Trent again by the arm and led him back out to the patio. He left his clipboard behind on the bar. She didn't seem to notice.

'Did you bring your trunks?' she asked. When Trent shook his head, she added, 'Well, you can take your shirt off anyway. Get some sun on you. It's good for vitamin D, you know.'

Trent was aware of this, although he was unconvinced that Serena's sole concern was his vitamin level. Still, he obeyed. It was against his better judgement, but he was beginning to realise that he had left it on the other side of that automatic gate.

At the sight of Trent's bare chest, pale and bony, Serena wrinkled her nose.

'It doesn't look like that sees much sun. Probably best to be careful. Better put your shirt back on before you get burnt.'

'I'll be okay for a few minutes.'

'Put it back on.'

And so, Trent re-dressed. He didn't blame her. He knew he wasn't a pretty sight. He couldn't remember the last time he had exercised, and his bruises from his beating at the hands of Fredevich's cronies hadn't yet faded entirely. One might say that he had the physique of someone wasting away, but there had never been much there in the first place.

'Are you going in?' he asked, gesturing towards the pool.

Serena snorted. 'If you've spent as long as me on your hair and make-up, you wouldn't even think about it. Besides, I hate the thing. It makes me feel like a goldfish, swimming back and forth all day.'

'Is that what you do with your day?'

'That and drinking.' Serena raised her glass. 'There's nothing much else to do in this country except sit around and get implants. And I'm running out of body parts. Breasts, lips, I've even had my butt done. Who in their right mind intentionally makes their butt bigger?'

She gestured to her bum as she said that. Trent tried not to look, and succeeded instead in staring at her breasts.

'I've had those done, too,' Serena said, 'although I bet you couldn't tell. They do it well over here.' She leaned forward. 'Come on, feel them.'

Trent gulped back his astonishment. Then, he remembered she had a head-start on him with the alcohol consumption, so he raised the glass to his lips and took a long drink. He wanted to cough, but that was not the done thing.

'I'm sure your husband is very appreciative,' he said, hoping that his mention would jolt them both to their senses.

'I don't do it for him,' she spat. 'I do it for me. Hunter doesn't even notice, anyway – he's so wrapped up with his job. But that's okay. He does his thing, and I do mine. Occasionally, I do something to help him remember I'm here.'

Trent hesitated. Was she referring to the modifications she had made to herself, or something else? Was Trent just a tool here, something she used to get back at her husband?

'God, you men are all the same!' Serena continued before he had time to ponder that thought further. 'Emasculated, masculated, you think you're the only reason women want to be attractive. The world doesn't revolve around you, you know? Not anymore.'

That wasn't the only thing that had changed over the decades. A few years back, Trent would have had no qualms about getting it on with another man's wife, not that he'd ever had the opportunity. And if he had, he'd never have used the term "getting it on" – he wasn't stuck in the 70s. Either way, things were different now. Trent had a conscience. At least, he was trying to nurture one.

He tried to step back from the situation. He reasoned

that it wasn't vanity that made Serena draw attention to her body. She had cultivated her looks, crafted them. She could judge her physique as one might an external object. She knew she was attractive, and it wasn't arrogance that told her this; it was an objective fact for which she had paid a lot of money.

Trent tried to make himself feel repulsed. She was just so... obvious, a walking, talking example of what society had determined that men should desire. But society had programmed him well. Object though he might about it, he couldn't pretend he didn't desire her.

'Speaking of Swiss precision,' Serena said after it became clear that Trent was rooted to the spot, 'there's something I want to show you.'

She stood and grabbed him by the hand. For a moment, Trent objected to being led around like a child, but then he realised he was enjoying it.

She took him back inside and up the spiral staircase to the main bedroom. It was expansive, taking up the best part of the upper floor. Again, it was sparsely decorated. A king-sized bed dominated the space. Its sheets were tucked in neatly. Not, he suspected, by her.

Serena disappeared into a walk-in wardrobe. When she emerged, she was carrying a red leather briefcase, which she set on the bed before unlocking the clasps. Inside was an extensive array of Swiss watches, gold and silver, all ticking expensively.

Trent whistled.

'It's my husband's collection,' she said.

Trent looked without daring to pick any of them up. Trent had never met Hunter, but he felt his presence strongly, and while Serena might act breezily about it, opening that briefcase was a finger gesture to her husband

and his abandonment of her. This was his private collection, and it might as well have been pictures of him in his underwear. Even if nothing else happened in that bedroom, she could draw satisfaction from its exposure.

Trent looked from the watches up to her. Then he saw it. A smile from five years earlier. It was on Serena, but it was not her face. He had seen it many times in the intervening years, but he rarely remembered it because it appeared on the edge of sleep or when he was intoxicated enough to see things that weren't there.

It was only there for a second, but that was enough.

'Excuse me for a minute,' he said. 'Where's your bathroom?'

Serena pouted, but then she said, 'You can clean up in there.'

The bathroom was tiled like a mosaic. It must have been completely impractical and as slippery as hell, but Trent suspected that the designer's primary concern hadn't been practicality. It looked expensive. It must have taken weeks for an artisan to grout those two-centimetre squared tiles into place, one by one, line by line, so that visitors could remark that it must have taken a lot of time and been expensive.

Trent splashed water on his face and regarded himself in the mirror. The same Trent was peering back at him with its old-before-his-time look. The wrinkles around his eyes were more pronounced than they had been a few years earlier, but it was still him. Only this wasn't his life. Trent Argent didn't get seduced by women. He didn't allow himself to be used in a power game with her husband. And he certainly didn't let desire push aside good sense.

He stared at himself for a few minutes until his breathing steadied. Then, he took a deep breath and headed back to the bedroom. He couldn't un-choose the path he had taken, so he might as well enjoy all it had to offer.

Serena was sitting on the edge of the bed.

'Ready?' she said.

There was nothing now to hide between them, no point in pleasantries. He felt a wave of anticipation rush through him.

'Ready,' Trent said.

She grabbed him by the collar and pulled him into the bed, displaying more strength than her slight frame suggested – not that Trent was the heaviest of men. The briefcase of watches tumbled to the floor, spilling its contents. Neither of them gave it a thought.

Then, she was on top of him, and her lips were on his, engulfing him. Her breath was heavy with absinthe, and her tongue was in his mouth. Lights flashed before his eyes as he struggled for breath.

She pulled back to regard him, this man that she had conquered. Her hands lowered, and she began to unzip his trousers.

'You can keep your shirt on,' she said.

He didn't mind.

Hobbs hadn't been listening for footsteps. He was gazing towards the river, specifically at Vincent's makeshift shelter. They hadn't seen him in days; it was only a matter of time before he inflicted some other mischief on them. Hobbs planned to be ready. He had no intention of letting their campsite become the location of a dirty protest again.

So, their visitor was almost on top of them before Hobbs noticed.

It was a tall man in his forties. He was dressed in expensive-looking clothes and carried himself with an air of authority.

'Trent Argent?' he said in a deep voice with a heavy American accent.

Had Hobbs been braver, he might have claimed ignorance. No, it wasn't a matter of bravery: this man had about him an aura that demanded compliance. There was no question that Hobbs would mess him around. It was the natural order of things.

'Um... Trent?' Hobbs called.

Trent emerged bleary-eyed from his tent. It had been a while since Hobbs had seen him hungover. Trent's short streak of sobriety had already reached an end. If that wasn't obvious that morning, it had certainly been the night before, when he had returned late, making an almighty racket while trying to sneak into his tent discreetly. The noisiest thing on a campsite was somebody trying to be quiet.

At the sight of Trent, the man's thin lips curled into a sneer.

'My name's Hunter,' he said. 'I believe you've been sleeping with my wife.'

Hobbs observed the scene. The tall man, proud and noble, and the wreck that was Trent, who was still on his hands and knees at the entrance to his tent. For a moment, he wasn't sure whose side he was on. The whole narrative dictated that it shouldn't be Trent's.

'You don't need to say anything,' Hunter said. 'Serena's told me everything. I think she enjoyed it, actually.'

Trent blinked.

'I'm not a thug,' Hunter continued. 'I'm not going to threaten you. But I will say that I have some influence in this city. Your life is about to get a whole lot more interesting. I just wanted to size you up first. Frankly, I can't see the attraction. Then again, it's always been less about them than me.'

And with that, Hunter turned on his heel and left. It would have been more impressive had he not been standing in a puddle of mud. He slipped a little as he set off, but he recovered quickly and strode away.

Trent still hadn't said a word.

It was Bong who spoke first. He had been plucking away at his guitar at the far end of the clearing, practising a rendition of Crowded House's *Into Temptation*. From there, he had heard everything.

'It would be fantastic, he said, 'if everyone could stop inviting people here who want to get us.'

From the bushes, Vincent had listened in, too.

He had spent much of the previous few days there, hidden from sight, eavesdropping on his unwanted neighbours' mindless chatter. He wouldn't say it passed for prime entertainment, but in situations such as his, there was little competition. He did it hoping to find a string to yank on – an idea for another prank. Urinating over their stuff, that had been just the beginning. Now, that was entertainment!

This new development troubled him, though: the sharply dressed man. It seemed that people could just drop in now to threaten his neighbours. It was getting too busy there. If there was one thing Vincent had learnt from being homeless, it was to stick to the quiet places. People were trouble – especially those with money.

Was it worth the risk staying there? Much as he might enjoy messing with his neighbours, he had grown tired of their chatter. No amount of sniggering and passing loud judgment (in the depths of his brain) could get past the fact that they were young and clueless. They knew nothing of the real world. They hadn't lived through personal tragedy, hadn't grappled with despair, or stared teary-eyed into the face of the world's general indifference. Maybe they thought they'd had it bad, but they hadn't, not really. They had no idea how bad things could get, walking around in those little bubbles of theirs.

No, no, enough was enough. It had been fun messing with them for a while, but that game had run its course. It was time to leave.

Vincent scrambled down the hill to his lean-to. He took a moment to look at it, as though saying goodbye to an old friend: the stained mattress and the screen of leaves and branches, which had sheltered him from many prying eyes. It wasn't much of a home, but it had served him well.

Still, there were other bridges in Geneva. He packed up his few possessions and gave a final salute to his home and a finger gesture to its invaders. Then, without a word, he left.

Thus, for Trent and his friends, the Vincent problem was solved.

Not that Trent was in any way short of things to worry about.

Serena didn't sit next to him in the next French lesson. She didn't come to his class at all. Trent tried not to think too much about it, but the intricacies of the French language didn't hold his attention for long. He kept glancing at her empty desk, thinking about what had happened a few days earlier. He was an obsessive, he knew that, but it was new for him to obsess about sex: the physicality of it, the feel of Serena's skin. He fixated on it like a teenager.

He thought, too, about what Amara and Bong had told him about Serena a few nights earlier. She had a reputation. There was a reason why the other members of the French class weren't captivated by her in the same way as him. It was the same reason packs of animals move together while predators stalk them through the undergrowth.

As he passed one of the other classrooms on his way out, he glanced in and saw Serena. She was chatting intensely with a young-looking guy in spectacles, laying a hand on his arm.

Trent's legs failed him. He had expected this, but that hadn't prepared him for witnessing it with his own eyes. He grabbed the doorframe for support but couldn't stop looking at them. After a few moments, Serena looked up. She smiled and waved before returning to her conversation.

It was then that Trent knew for sure now that she hadn't seen anything in him. Their connection went no deeper than convenience. He'd come along when she had exhausted the existing supply of men. Now that he'd been conquered and fresh prey was available, she had moved on.

He would have felt used had he not gone into it with his eyes wide open.

Trent Argent had never been a sexual predator – far from it – but he *had* played with people's affections to get what he wanted. His first girlfriend, at the tender age of twenty-two, hadn't been as wily as him. She had trusted him completely. It was this that had enabled him to take advantage of her.

Caroline wasn't the woman who haunted his dreams; that was Zoe, and she merited her own story. He hadn't thought about his first girlfriend for years, and that probably said as much as was necessary about how he felt for her.

He met Caroline during drinks with colleagues, a friend of a friend of a friend. Trent had still been in his first sales job, but by then, he'd been planning to start his own business. She hadn't been his target from the start. No, something else had drawn them together. Trent still couldn't imagine what she saw in him. He hadn't felt the same, but he'd been swept along by the novelty of a woman showing interest in him.

They dated a few times, first for coffee, then drinks, then dinner, and gradually, her story unfolded. She'd inherited her father's business empire, which was sustained by a panel of advisors after his death. This was fortunate because she was sweet and naïve, without a commercial bone in her body. The protective arm her father had wrapped around her during her early life made her vulnerable to people like him.

All the same, he didn't ask Caroline for money. He wouldn't be "that guy". He just spent time with her. He would even go so far as to say he enjoyed it. She knew what he wanted in life – that he needed money – so it was simply a matter of waiting.

They were out walking on a quiet path alongside a meadow, talking about their weeks, when she suddenly announced, 'I'd like to invest in you.'

Trent looked away, aware that his face would betray

him. He hadn't yet learned how to control his micro-expressions.

'What do you mean?' he said.

'I think you have a great idea. I believe in you. I've got the money. I want you to use it.'

After going through the motions of objecting that they shouldn't mix business with pleasure, he accepted – on highly favourable terms for her, he might add.

After that, he tried to continue the relationship, but his heart wasn't in it. He'd got what he wanted, and no matter how much he tried to convince himself otherwise, his passion lay elsewhere. Their relationship became one of business. He paid her back when things took off, no issues there, but the unwritten contract they'd entered – the promise of a continued romantic relationship – fell by the wayside.

It was Caroline who finally broke it off. She told him she loved him and that he'd broken her heart. Trent felt sorry for her – he really did – but his overwhelming emotion was excitement. His new venture was taking off.

That had been the end of Trent's love life until he met Zoe. It was only now, years later, that he understood how love can make you wilfully ignore what's right in front of you. He and Caroline couldn't be together; their paths were so different. Her eventual realisation must have been agonising.

He wondered what had become of her. Had she gone on to live the life she'd desired with him but just with someone else? For a fleeting moment, he wondered if, by some strange coincidence, she had ended up with Dean, his first betrayal. He shook off the thought. Just the idea of it felt like the world laughing at his life choices. Or had he turned her off men entirely? Was she still a spinster, the head of a multi-million-pound empire sustained by a cutthroat approach to life she'd learnt the hard way?

Either way, Trent felt sure he was the only one who still felt the loss of the story they had never spun. She had most likely forgotten all about him, but he remembered her then – and, finally, he felt.

∾

Jenny looked stern behind her plastic desk. 'I'm going to have to ask you for your I.D. Badge and clipboard.'

Without a word, Trent dumped both on the scuffed surface.

'You know,' Jenny continued, 'we're all behind you spreading the word. But spreading the *seed*, that's not what you're paid for.'

Trent turned away. There was little point in further discussion with someone who had clearly invested time rehearsing that line. He walked through the reception, descended the building's old winding staircase, and buzzed himself out of the main doors. He breathed in the fresh (although not by Salève standards) air.

Serena's husband was a man of his word. He had lodged a complaint with Friends of the Disappeared the following morning, and the rest – the chain of events resulting in Trent being unceremoniously stripped of his clipboard – had been inevitable.

'Geneva's a small town,' his employment advisor had told him once. 'Everybody knows everybody.'

At the time, Trent had taken Edouard's comment to reference the value of networking. Now, he saw the other side of the message. It had been a warning: "Don't piss anyone off."

He had well and truly failed at that.

So, Trent was unemployed again. He wasn't heartbroken about it, having had his fill of fundraising. It did, however, make his fiscal and administrative situation more complicated. The clock was still ticking on his permit. If he didn't have a job before it expired, he would be returning to the UK in failure.

He could only hope that Hunter's complaint would be the extent of his revenge. But deep down, he knew it was just the beginning.

STEP 3 – BE PART OF SOMETHING GREATER

CHAPTER 7

THE SETUP

06:00 – COLOGNY, GENEVA

awn crept across the ceiling of the master bedroom. It blossomed quickly, projected from the contraption on the bedside cabinet, which also piped out a recorded morning chorus of birds long since dead.

Hunter Pickering opened his eyes and gazed across the pillow at his wife. Serena was still sleeping deeply, with no reason to get up at that hour. She looked so pure lying there, almost angelic. Hunter was well aware that she was anything but innocent, but it pleased him to think of her that way. He remembered how she'd been years earlier, before they had decided to prioritise his career over hers. So hopeful, so determined. He had little desire to consider too deeply what she had become.

If he'd known their choice would ultimately lead her to infidelity, would he have advocated for a different path? He contemplated this for a moment, but not for long. Their decision had brought him power and respect; it had taken them from the USA to Geneva and the lifestyle they now enjoyed. To get anywhere in life, one needs to make sacrifices.

Outside, the real dawn had already been and gone. Hunter threw on his dressing gown and slipped between the blackout curtains out onto the balcony. He didn't need his sandals: the sun had warmed the flagstones. He looked out onto the Lac Leman, across the millionaires' yachts to the UN buildings atop the hill on the far bank, where he spent most of his days.

Today would be special: a culmination of months of planning. It would go differently than anyone had envisaged.

Today was a good day for revenge.

07:19 – COMMUNITY ORGANISATIONS CONFERENCE CENTRE (COCC), GENEVA

The security staff arrived, as usual, just over two hours before the start of the event. There was little for them to do in terms of setup – the janitors had done the heavy work the previous evening, setting out the tables and chairs in the welcome area and various breakout rooms. Delivering large international conferences was a day-to-day task for everyone who worked there. The different variants of floor plans and configurations had been calculated years earlier, so it had simply been a case of deploying whichever option had been selected for the day's event.

Security arrived at that hour because it was not uncommon for conference leads to suffer from nerves. They would turn up ridiculously early and flap around arranging banners and displays, biting their nails whenever they paused for thought. Somebody had to let them in.

The security staff regarded the conference organisers with pity. They had witnessed successful conferences and complete failures, on topics as diverse as disaster preparedness and currency management systems. One major commonality was that they always ended. Good or bad, interesting or impenetrable, it would all be over by evening, and a different conference would take place a day or two later. There was nothing to get worked up about.

These were the same people who had spent the early part of their careers at concert performances by musical legends, not to enjoy the act, but to stand with their backs turned to the stage, watching the crowd and trying to look tough. They were a breed in themselves. Some would say these people were superhuman; others that they had no souls; still others would question why they should be interested in your shitty music.

Still, they were essential to the smooth running of events. They didn't just let people in; their careful diligence ensured that the thousands of people who descended on the conference centre would leave that evening in one piece.

That day, they would be put to the test.

07:57 – COMMUNITY ORGANISATIONS CONFERENCE CENTRE (COCC), GENEVA

'Fancy meeting you here!' Hobbs said.

Hobbs held the door open for Trent, grinning broadly. Trent humoured him by not rolling his eyes, but that was the best he could manage. They had walked to the conference centre together.

They would both play roles that day. Hobbs' smile had earned him a place with the volunteers at the welcome desks. There were three volunteer teams supporting the event – welcome area, reporters, and general support – and Trent would be coordinating the latter, making sure that presentations were ready in the meeting rooms and that no one sneaked into a session they hadn't registered for. He had been afforded that honour after distinguishing himself by wearing a suit to his recruitment interview. They'd talked to him like he was some sort of hotshot. It occurred to him that there was a massive disconnect between the stringent security arrangements imposed on conference attendees and the cursory screening the volunteers underwent. Their primary qualifications were being able to speak English and being willing to work for free.

Bong would join them a bit later. He had been disqualified from his initial role at the welcome desks after advertising his intention to greet all attendees with the phrase 'Welcome to my COCC!' He had been relegated to the reporting team, which was based in a back room somewhere.

Evidently, whoever named the building *Centre de Conference pour les Organisations Communautaire* had only a rudimentary understanding of English and/or acronyms.

Once they had got through security (bodies scanned; bags searched for whatever weaponry someone might wish they had to hand after several hours at a conference), Hobbs bid Trent farewell with a salute and made his way to the welcome desks. There, he would greet conference attendees, hand them a name badge, and listen to them complain about the delays at security. He'd also have tote bags to give out containing leaflets and a refillable flask, the one concession to the good old days of freebies. They had stopped distributing the usual knick-knacks (key rings, USB sticks and other junk destined to gather dust on desks around the world) as a concession to protecting the environment. The flask was more environmentally friendly – or so it was claimed – although most attendees already had an extensive collection of free flasks from other events gathering dust at home.

Another proof of the organisers' environmental credentials was that they had refused to send the flasks back when someone noticed that a typo got through quality control. The "Water and Sanitation Summit" had been inadvertently rebranded "*Waster* and Sanitation Summit". On spotting this error, they decided to double down on it, ensuring that the conference's new name was displayed consistently across the programmes, banners and the bright yellow T-shirts the volunteers wore. It was the kind of who-blinks-first strategy typically employed by confidence tricksters.

Trent headed to the "control room" on the conference centre's lower floor. Its name suggested something grander than it actually was, conjuring images of monitors screening the CCTV or complicated machinery that belonged in a recording studio. It was a small, plain room with a square table and a few tatty-looking plastic chairs. There were no monitors, and the lighting barely worked, flickering for a few seconds every minute. The volunteers had been instructed to report there at the beginning and end of their shifts.

Trent had been provided with a walkie-talkie, but he was unsure how much use it would be, as they had been instructed to keep them on mute so as not to disturb the workshops. Still, he clipped it to his belt. It was his badge of office, granting him the same authority that a high-vis jacket might at an outdoor event. It wasn't an office he had ever aspired to, but he had to make do.

He sat down at the table and pulled out the register of

the volunteers interviewed and trained in the preceding weeks. It was a fair bet that half of them wouldn't turn up, but they had prepared for that, having recruited more than needed. This was the only way to ensure the event's smooth running.

08:19

'Thank you, Trent, for confirming I am here,' Amara said.

She had little patience for bureaucracy, particularly when it placed any semblance of power into the hands of people like Trent Argent. She would have thought twice about getting him involved if she'd known it would lead to this.

Amara's organisation, Reporters Everywhere, had agreed to cooperate with Geneva Conference Volunteers to support the event. They were anticipating that the conference centre, which could hold thousands, would be filled to capacity with people coming together to discuss the meaty subject of water and sanitation (a big draw, if ever there was one). Accordingly, a plea had gone out through both organisations to get friends and family involved. With Hobbs, Bong and Trent all out of work, they had been perfect candidates to be "volun-told".

Amara had hoped this would gain her points within her organisation, although this now seemed unlikely. For logistical reasons, resources were being pooled under the direction of Geneva Conference Volunteers, a sensible choice given the size of the conference, and a strategy that many of the humanitarian organisations represented that day resisted when working together in the field.

She turned away from Trent and headed to the room next door, where the reporting volunteers were setting up.

It felt good to turn her back on Trent. There was something about him that put her on edge. She couldn't quite place her finger on it, but she was confident that the truth would surface sooner or later.

Bong was waiting for her when she arrived. When her organisation had found out about his social media success filming rich people picking up dog poo, they'd decided this made him a prime contender to join her team. It made sense, she supposed, or as much sense as did any of them being there in the first place. It would be their job to take notes of the various sessions and post updates on social media to maintain excitement about what was happening – because it was a great idea to encourage those who had flown thousands of miles to get there to pass the time on their phones.

'Ready?' she said to Bong.

'I was born ready,' Bong replied.

Much as Amara found this a ridiculous expression, it didn't seem beyond the realm of possibility that Bong had been born with a mobile phone in his hand. It was the way things were going of late: babies in pushchairs transfixed by whatever programme their parents were streaming on their phone to stop them from crying.

Bong proceeded to demonstrate the posts he had already scheduled for the morning. Each hour, he planned to post an update on which sessions were underway. His intended audience was those who preferred to get their information from a mobile device rather than a programme.

'That's amazing value-add, there,' Amara said.

'Thank you,' Bong said, missing the sarcasm.

Amara wondered whether the conference's rebranded title, which Bong wore proudly on his T-shirt, might be accurate in his case. She bit her tongue, got out her laptop and logged in with the other wasters.

08:30

The first attendees arrived at the centre. These were mainly people who had been up at 3 a.m. due to jetlag. After working their way through security, they were fatigued enough to take a second breakfast of croissants and patisseries in the networking area.

08:45

Trent's walkie-talkie scratched to life. It wasn't supposed to do that.

He raised it to his ear and tried to make out the words. It sounded like the message was being played from a 1970s tape recorder. He'd imagined the technology would have moved on since then, but evidently not.

'*Central to Trent, over.*'

Trent didn't respond immediately. He had thought *he* was Central. After all, he was in the control room.

'*Central to Trent, over,*' the message repeated. 'Please respond.'

Trent moved the walkie-talkie to his mouth as though it were a poisoned chalice, what with all the germs breathed over it during its many years of service. He doubted it had been disinfected once in all that time.

'Trent here, over,' he said.

'*Please report to the administration office.*'

And that was it. Trent looked around to see how the other volunteers in the inappropriately named control room had reacted. No one had paid the slightest attention.

He grabbed Cynthia, a young woman who'd displayed some bitterness when he had been designated coordinator instead of her. She seemed completely uninterested in him being summoned but was more than willing to take on the lofty responsibility of registering the rest of the volunteers.

Now, to find the administration office.

Trent had received a tour of the facilities the previous day to help him direct participants if asked. The administration office hadn't been a particular highlight of the visit. Trent remembered that it was also tucked away on the minus one level, but that still left a large area to scour. Any signage that might have helped him was concealed behind the stands and banners of various community organisations, so it took him a fair amount of time to find it.

He knocked lightly and pushed open the door to reveal a medium-sized room containing a few desks and workstations. It was all very plain, much like the volunteers' control room, but some people had personalised their workstations with trinkets and family photos. A figure Trent hadn't expected to see was sitting on one of the desks. Tall, handsome and supremely confident, a man Trent had last seen not threatening him in a highly threatening manner.

'Glad you could join us eventually, Trent,' Hunter Pickering said. There was a coldness to his tone, but his face betrayed nothing.

Oh, shit, Trent thought. He was feeling eloquent that morning.

Trent had known that Serena's husband was a bigwig in Geneva – she had told him as much – but he hadn't dreamed that Hunter might be involved in this event. But he was wearing a name badge with the sponsor's logo, had access to the administration office and even had a walkie-talkie, so there could be little doubt about his authority.

Trent's mind raced. This was it. This was how Hunter would take revenge for him having slept with his wife.

'We have a situation,' Hunter said.

Agreed.

'My organisation has received information about a threat to this event,' Hunter continued. 'Apparently, someone harbours a grudge against one of the participants and wants to share it with us all. We've received a bomb threat. We're on the lookout for suspicious packages. Sports bags, parcels, anything left unattended.'

Trent's brain reconnected but struggled to keep up with what was happening. He had expected Hunter to send him home, at best, but his rival was instead letting him into a confidence.

'Are you going to cancel?' he said.

'Do you have any idea how much these events cost? People have travelled here from all around the world. No, we're pressing ahead, keeping a close eye on things.'

'You've informed security?'

'Well, of course I've told security! I need more than that. I need you to be my eyes and ears.'

Trent wasn't convinced he was the perfect choice for that role because he could barely believe what he was hearing. This was quite obviously a trap. What was he supposed to do? It was hardly as if he could refuse to look out for a bomb, but he half suspected if he found one, Hunter might have rigged it to blow up in his face. Or else this was a wild goose chase. Either way, he was a helpless pawn in this.

At Trent's hesitation, Hunter fingered a piece of paper on his desk. 'Strange, it does say on your CV that you're a "Motivated self-starter, able to operate at the highest level of *integrity* and *discretion*."' He practically spat out the last words.

'That's me,' Trent said helplessly, although he hadn't felt like a poster boy for either virtue when sleeping with this man's wife.

'Well, that's just what I need.'

Hunter stood. He was taller than Trent remembered and more muscular – generally better-looking than Trent, who was feeling very small at that point.

'They gave you emergency training, I assume?' Hunter said.

Trent nodded. He remembered a jumble of coded messages intended to alert those supporting the event of a situation without alarming the participants. They'd told the volunteers about Dr Brown (the codeword for a threat of violence), Mr Sands (fire), and various other people that Trent hoped didn't have real-life equivalents in attendance because that would be a recipe for panic and confusion.

'Good,' Hunter said. 'Hopefully, it won't come to that. I need you to circulate and keep an eye on things discreetly. Security is already stretched hard. They'll do a sweep of the venue, but we need someone on the lookout continuously. Are you up to it?'

Trent nodded again. You don't mess around when someone mentions the word "bomb". (At least, Trent didn't. Hunter was an unknown quantity in that respect). It didn't seem to be an option to say "no".

'I can tell the other team leads, I assume?' Trent said.

Hunter shook his head. 'I know what volunteers are like. First, it will be whispers, then someone will get excited, and it'll stop being whispers. Then, the participants will start getting wind of it, and we'll have a full-blown panic on our hands. No, keep this to yourself.'

Trent's mouth opened and closed wordlessly. There had

to be a way of getting out of this, but he was too rusty to work out what it was.

'Good,' Hunter said at Trent's silence. He strode to the door and opened it, gesturing for Trent to leave.

'I'm relying on you,' he said as he ejected Trent into the basement corridor.

CHAPTER 8
THE HUNT

09:18 – COMMUNITY ORGANISATIONS
CONFERENCE CENTRE (COCC), GENEVA

The security lines grew. Many participants had turned up early to avoid the queues, which were the stuff of legend, to the extent that the opening address was known in some circles as the graveyard shift. It was common for only half the attendees to have made it into the venue by that point.

The security crew worked diligently but without any sense of urgency. If ever a risk vector (the dehumanising name with which they referred to participants) exhibited any frustration, they took longer frisking them. In theory, this was because twitchiness was a sign of malevolent intentions; the truth was that they were no more willing to have someone ask them to hurry up than a farmer would be for a sheep to tell him his job.

By the time participants arrived at Hobbs' welcome desk, many were ready to explode. They didn't understand that as a volunteer, he wasn't paid to take their abuse. He didn't play that card, anyway, for fear that it would have made them look at him as a lesser person.

So, Hobbs withstood the outbursts. He allowed people to rant at him, speak over him, snatch their name badge off him, and call him "boy" (a word which, when he reflected on this later, he realised could have been much worse). A few people demanded how to register a complaint, but they didn't listen when he walked them through the process because it delayed them further. Still, he kept his smile. The only indication of his stress was that his voice rose an octave.

Registration was in full swing when Trent pulled him to one side.

'This is hardly the time,' Hobbs said.

'It's serious,' Trent said.

They found a little alcove behind the welcome area. A few of the volunteers had left their bags there. Trent eyed them suspiciously.

'We may have a Mr Jets in the building,' Trent said.

Hobbs scratched his head. 'I don't remember seeing him on the register.'

Trent pulled Hobbs closer. There was a directness to him that Hobbs hadn't seen before. 'A bomb.'

Hobbs' eyes widened. 'Really? How do you know?'

'Hunter Pickering told me.'

Hobbs took a moment to digest this. 'The husband of the woman you slept with?'

'Yes. He's a VIP here.'

'How does *he* know?'

'That's not important. The main thing is we need to keep control of the situation.'

Judging from the wild look in Trent's eyes, it didn't appear to Hobbs that he was in control of anything. He felt the same. He hadn't signed up for this. He was there to say "Good morning" to people and give them a welcome pack. He didn't recall seeing bomb disposal as part of the role description.

Still, he couldn't walk away from this. The tricky thing about important roles was that they involved responsibility. If Hobbs wanted to better himself and make an impact on the world, he needed to be ready to step up. That might sound like his father talking or perhaps one of the teachers at the military school, but no, it was Hobbs himself. He had come to Geneva looking for opportunities to make a difference. One had fallen right into his lap. He couldn't turn away.

'What do you need me to do?'

'I need your eyes and your ears,' Trent said in a hushed tone. 'You see everyone as they come in. If any of them look suspicious, let me know.'

Hobbs ran a finger down his temple. 'Define "suspicious".'

Trent sighed. 'I don't know, what about that guy?' He indicated a tan-skinned man wearing a white robe and a headscarf, checking in at the desk behind them.

'What's suspicious about him?' Hobbs demanded. 'Apart from that he's Arabic?'

Trent reddened, but he stood his ground. 'Look, Hobbs, you'll know what you're looking for when you see it. Hopefully, there's nothing, but if you see something that looks out of place, call me.'

He waved around his walkie-talkie, which it appeared they were now permitted to use.

'I don't do racial profiling,' Hobbs insisted. 'You're going to have to give me something more to go on than that.'

'I don't have anything more. Look, just keep an eye out;

that's all I'm asking. This is your chance to be the hero. If you see anything, let me know right away. And please, whatever you do, keep this to yourself. We don't want to start a panic.'

As Hobbs returned to the welcome desk, he took a moment to question whether his annoyance with Trent was entirely reasonable. They were both under pressure, and maybe he shouldn't have pressed Trent for answers he didn't have, but racial profiling was just unacceptable. There was more to it than that, though. He was beginning to resent Trent. The man always fell on his feet. Hobbs was still out of work and desperate, whereas Trent, who by his own admission was sleeping around and pissing people off, had been selected as one of the team leads.

Why was it that success only ever came to those who didn't deserve it?

Still, despite all that, Hobbs did what he was told. He kept an eye out. Whether this was the result of his innate instinct to obey or his desire to save the day, he didn't know.

09:30

The welcome and keynote speech began. They had decided to go ahead on time, even though half of the conference participants were still queueing for security, because it was a crammed agenda. Besides, this was Switzerland, and everything there must run on time, dammit!

The event was opened by a representative of one of its sponsors, an organisation whose initials were so well known that Amara had no idea what they stood for. Amara looked on from the row at the back of the room assigned to the reporting volunteers. Setting aside the many empty seats, the scene was all very impressive. On either side of the stage hung enormous banners with the conference title, "Waster and Sanitation Summit". As a backdrop, the image of an African woman carrying a bucket of water on her head reassured people that they had turned up at the right place and the topic of water would be very much on the agenda. Flags of the countries represented that day were draped from the front of the stage. The attendees were just as colourful, from all around the world, some dressed in suits, some casually, and others in their national garb. It felt like a wedding whose dress code had been communicated poorly.

Hunter Pickering. Amara noted down the name of the person opening the event. It seemed familiar somehow, but she couldn't quite place it.

'Welcome,' Hunter said. 'Welcome, everyone, and thanks for joining what promises to be a groundbreaking event. As my organisation is a sponsor, I get the honour of welcoming you to this Waster and...' He paused, having noticed something for the first time. '*Water* and Sanitation Summit.'

Hunter kept his other remarks short, probably keen to get off stage and discover who was responsible for the blunder. He finished by inviting the keynote speaker, a Dr Kensington, to the stage. Amara quickly gave up copying down the various letters that followed Dr Kensington's name. She prepared to focus on what he was saying, readying her fingers on her laptop, which was balanced on a tray table folded out from the side of her chair.

She had been assigned to take notes of the session, alongside several other interns, hammering away on keyboards next to her. The hope was that by combining their reports, the people in charge might be able to piece together a vaguely intelligible record of what had transpired.

Dr Kensington smiled broadly as he took to the stage. He was wearing jeans, a white shirt, and an unbuttoned suit jacket. His beard was neatly trimmed. He had the air of someone who spent his life feeling very content with himself. A few people applauded, and he lapped it up as though at a presidential rally.

'Well, well, well,' he said. 'Thank you so much for travelling all this way. We have a packed auditorium today.'

Delusional, much? Amara thought, glancing at the empty seats.

Dr Kensington's face turned grave as he turned to the subject of his address: 'Today, I'm going to talk to you about a subject very close to my heart. The saying goes that some people think best on the toilet. But what if they don't have a toilet?'

A few of the participants nodded at this incisive comment, which had put a whole new spin on the subject. Amara rolled her eyes.

'Just think about all that wasted brainpower,' Dr Kensington continued, turning to the next slide, which contained a bewildering array of bar and pie charts. 'If we could harness it, think of the good it could do to humanity!'

Amara glanced towards the interpreters' booth to the right of the stage. It was these people that she admired the most. Already, they were hard at work, translating this drivel into a multitude of languages, speaking into microphones that broadcast to participants tuned in on their headsets. Amara wasn't sure what she was most impressed by: the intensity with which they worked, listening and talking simultaneously, the relentlessness of it all. Or was it that they managed to retain focus for hours on end at incomprehensible speeches such as this?

Amara chastised herself. She had been to so many of these things that she'd grown jaded. Her father's voice sounded in her ears: *Cynicism is the highway to a closed mind. If you close your mind, my dear, you close out the glory of the world.* Now, there was a man who somehow managed to find joy in the world, even though he worked the same dull factory job year after year. She missed him and wished she could afford to go back and visit.

So, in honour of her father, Amara typed.

09:38

Since when did Trent Argent start following instructions?

The little voice in Trent's head had started piping up a lot lately. Worse still, it tended to refer to him in the third person, which he assumed was psychologically worrying. But he set this aside. He had more pressing issues to deal with.

I always followed instructions, he replied to himself. *Or at least gave the appearance of doing so. One had to maintain the illusion. It was the grand plan that mattered.*

What's the grand plan now, Trent?

Trent considered responding, but he knew without a shadow of a doubt that the little voice would find it hilarious if he replied, *I'm just trying to save lives.* Anyway, it wasn't as though he was obeying mindlessly. He had already gone against Hunter's wishes by confiding in Hobbs, and he'd speak with Amara after the keynote address. That way, he'd have friends on the lookout in two key locations: the welcome desks and the auditorium. And if they did spot something, Trent certainly wouldn't be contacting Hunter. Yes, it might be against procedure for him to call the bomb squad without consulting anyone, but it would be perfectly defensible.

Trent continued his tour of the facilities.

The COCC comprised three levels. The basement, where the volunteers had set up, housed several small meeting rooms for breakout sessions, plus the administration offices. The ground floor contained the security checkpoint, an expansive welcome area, and a few other meeting rooms. The large conference rooms were on the upper level, which also hosted a cafeteria and the entrance to the upper rows of the auditorium – an impressive space spanning two floors of rack seating, gazing down out on a stage. It was all lit with warm, calming lighting and carpeted in a pastel grey/green, just dense enough to absorb the racket of hundreds of people chattering without impeding wheel-chair access.

All told, Trent had a lot of ground to cover.

His next destination was the toilets. He had been putting this off until after the event began because it was many participants' first stop after the welcome desks. The constant stream of people hadn't lessened, but Trent figured he couldn't delay it further.

It was a standard public toilet, with a grey linoleum floor speckled with bits of glitter. A fanfare of hand dryers heralded his arrival, as did an automatic air freshener, which pumped out spray as soon as he entered. Those things went off consistently whenever he entered a room. Trent tried not to take it personally. After all, he had been sleeping rough under a bridge for weeks.

Trent wished it had disbursed more deodorant. This place was revolting. Were people in such a hurry to make it to the keynote address that they felt it acceptable to trash the facilities? Toilet paper was strewn on the floor, and the wall beside the urinals was splashed as though someone had been startled midstream. Judging by the smell, several participants had yet to be formally introduced to a toilet's flushing mechanism.

The irony of the facilities being in this state at a sanitation conference was not lost on Trent, but he didn't pause to ponder this further. He was already growing dizzy from holding his breath.

He checked the corners and the surfaces for suspicious packages. Then he pushed open the cubicle doors to check inside. A few were occupied (fortunately, whoever was in there had managed to operate the lock, so there were no nasty surprises), so Trent took a quick glance beneath each door. He waved around his walkie-talkie beforehand as though that permitted him to do so.

Then, he got out of there.

Outside, catching his breath, Trent considered whether he should check the women's toilets. He was sure he had the remit for it, but there seemed something innately wrong about the idea. So, he never found out if they were in a better state. Or if they contained a bomb.

10:15

The crowds at security had settled down. The latecomers arrived and breezed through, much to the chagrin of people getting coffee just inside, who had been standing there the best part of an hour.

10:21

Amara glanced at the clock. Despite the prompt start, they were already running late. The keynote address was supposed to have finished five minutes earlier, but Dr Kensington was still in full swing.

At 10:10, after 35 minutes on stage, Dr Kensington had announced, 'And now I've reached the end of my opening remarks, let's consider my process in more detail...' This had been met by a murmur of discontent amongst attendees (those still awake), but he had pressed on regardless.

Five minutes later, the volunteer beside Amara had slid her a bit of paper, which she identified as a hastily assembled "jargon bingo" card. She had set it to one side, thinking it disrespectful (her father's voice again), but she picked it up again when Dr Kensington turned to reveal his learnings about working in a fourth village without fresh water. The most remarkable thing about this village was its resemblance to the preceding three.

She grabbed a pen and readied the card.

'Solutions-focused.' Check.

'Results-oriented.' Check.

'An innovative, agile, trust-based approach to community involvement.' Check. Check. Check. BINGO! She almost jumped up, brandishing her card.

Then, Amara noticed Trent. He was standing by the stage, scanning the audience with squinted eyes. Was he looking for her? She considered waving to him but thought better of it. There was little enough excitement in that auditorium that the spectacle of one person beckoning another would attract hundreds of stimulus-craving eyes.

She watched him continue his search. If he spotted her, he gave no indication. He seemed more interested in a sports bag left in one of the aisles. He mounted the steps and regarded it closely before being shooed away by its owner.

Some people lose their nerve in battle. They were a long way from open conflict in that conference centre (although that depended in part on how much longer Dr Kensington continued speaking), but Amara was aware that the pressures of running a large event impacted people in different ways. This was all too much for Trent. She looked forward to that evening with a mischievous joy, and the garbled account he'd give of what the hell he had been doing.

She was so caught up with trying to work out what Trent was up to that she didn't notice Bong join her, not until he started tapping loudly at his mobile phone.

'What are you doing?' she whispered.

'It's my new channel,' Bong said. '#outoforderornot.'

Amara had never felt the slightest bit of interest in Bong's social media exploits, but after 50 minutes of Dr Kensington, it seemed the most fascinating thing on the planet. She leaned across to get a good view of Bong's phone but could only see a series of text messages.

'The trick is to get two phones,' Bong explained. 'That way, you control both sides of the conversation. Then, you just make something up.'

'You make up a text exchange?'

Bong nodded. 'People lap it up. They fall over each other to have their say. They love a scandal.'

'What sort of things do you write about?'

'All sorts. Could be an inconsiderate neighbour or a boss asking for something unreasonable. It mustn't be too obvious, but someone's got to be out of order. Then I just post it, pretending someone's been in touch wanting a second opinion. Look. This is the most popular one so far.'

Amara took Bong's phone and scrolled down the messages supposedly screen-shotted from some husband's phone. The exchange between the imaginary husband and his imaginary female work colleague skirted the wrong side of appropriate, as the subject migrated from business to more personal matters. He gave several awkward compliments and seemed fixated on his colleague's weekend availability. Her responses were cold, but she didn't discourage him, either.

There were 273 comments below from people who believed that the exchange was scandalous and that the fictional wife should either 1) divorce her husband immediately, 2) encourage him to go to marriage counselling, 3) cut off his balls, or some combination of the above.

'Impressive,' Amara said, handing back the phone. And it was impressive. Bong had displayed a level of nuance she thought beyond him. Certainly, his previous channel, #glamourouspeoplepickingupshit, hadn't suggested such a profound understanding of the human condition.

'Don't people realise it's fake?' she asked.

Bong shook his head. 'They're too busy being outraged.'

10:53

The auditorium doors swung open, and the participants flooded out. They weren't due a break, but the conference organisers had taken pity on them and released them for fifteen minutes while they tried to reassemble an agenda from the torn-up pieces their keynote speaker had left them.

A few participants remained in the rack seating, slouched in their seats, dizzy and seasick. Such a response was customarily reserved for the afternoon sessions. In that respect, Dr Kensington had been efficient, progressing them early to levels of human misery usually reserved only for the later parts of a conference.

In the interpreters' booth, they removed their headsets and sighed with relief. They had lived through similar sessions before, but it had still been a shock to the system so early on. The team leader rallied them with a few words:

'We're made of sterner stuff. Take a break, recharge your batteries, then let's take it to 'em. Let's get back out there and INTERPRET!'

Her words were greeted by a collective 'Hurrah!' It was not for nought that they had won Amara's admiration.

The welcome desk was quiet. Hobbs was nowhere to be seen.

10:54

Hobbs rounded the corner of a ground-floor corridor. The buzz of the crowd softened behind him. He edged forward gingerly, listening carefully for noises up ahead.

Someone whispered.

This part of the building wasn't being used for the conference. It contained meeting rooms that were too small for that day's numbers. There were six doors ahead, three on each side of the corridor.

Hobbs wasn't sure where the whisper had come from, so he would have to try each in turn.

A few minutes earlier, from his post at the welcome desk, he had observed a pair exchange a glance. There was nothing suspect about that in itself, but they had ignored him when he'd called after them, directing them to the auditorium.

Would he be able to remember their faces if the police

asked him later? He thought hard. The man had been wearing a pressed suit and a hideous tie. Not a crime in itself, either, although some would argue it should be. He had black hair and well-kept eyebrows.

Well, that should narrow it down in a line-up, Hobbs!

The woman wore a business suit. Dark hair pinned up behind her head. Maybe in her thirties... he had never been much good at guessing people's age.

The first door was locked. He moved on to the second and turned the handle carefully. It didn't budge, either.

Then, he heard the rattle of keys.

A door opened ahead. It was around the corner in the corridor, so he couldn't see it, but he heard the bottom of a door stroke the thin carpet.

He didn't try the next few handles but tiptoed to the corner and peered around. By this time, the door had closed. There were another couple of entrances to meeting rooms before the corridor terminated with a fire exit.

Hobbs drew in a breath. Should he fetch help? In the training, they had impressed upon all the volunteers that they shouldn't try to be heroes if it came to an emergency. But Hobbs couldn't resist the idea of being a hero. What better way to stand out from the crowd?

So, he approached the next door, pressing his ear to it, poised to react to any sound.

A woman giggled.

This gave Hobbs pause for thought. Admittedly, he was a novice in the world of counterterrorism, but he deemed it unlikely that someone would titter like that whilst setting a bomb. Then again, nerves affect people in different ways.

He had come this far. No going back now.

Hobbs reached for the door handle. Should he turn it quickly and startle them? That way, he would benefit from the element of surprise. Or should he open the door quietly and peek in, giving him time to assess the situation before deciding what to do?

This all became academic when the door opened in front of him. The man was there. His eyebrows were just as neat as Hobbs remembered, and they were pressed into a frown. He had removed his jacket, and his tie appeared to have been loosened.

'What are you doing, sneaking around here?' the man demanded.

Hobbs peered past and into the room. The woman was perched on a table. She, too, had removed her jacket, and the top button of her blouse was undone.

'Um...' Hobbs said. 'I thought you were lost.'

'I *work* here,' the man said, as though that should have been self-evident. That explained, at least, how he had unlocked one of these meeting rooms.

'Understood,' Hobbs said, and he backed away.

The man shut the door quickly after that. The lock clicked shut. Hobbs stood there for a moment, not knowing quite what to do. Then, the woman giggled again.

I told you, Trent, Hobbs thought to himself. *I told you!*

CHAPTER 9

WE GOTTA GET OUT OF THIS PLACE

T rent had officially had enough.

He had been wandering around the COCC for two hours looking for a bomb, which he now believed did not exist. The closest he had found was a plastic bag filled with other plastic backs (itself an anomaly in these days of bag-rationing, but hardly explosive). By most empirical standards, the non-existence of a bomb was a good thing, but Trent was furious. He was angry with Hunter for setting him up to run around like a frantic dog and livid with himself for playing along with it. What was he supposed to do, abandon his duties and spend the whole day on the lookout?

Enough was enough.

He had returned to the administration office to tell Hunter this, only to find the room empty. He'd tried contacting him on the walkie-talkie, but the only response had been another volunteer telling him angrily to shut up. So, now Trent was searching for Hunter rather than a suspect package (although if he saw one, he wouldn't ignore it; he wasn't sure enough of himself for that).

Trent considered himself a rational man, but something had happened to him when Hunter had mentioned the word "bomb". It was one of those innate, primal instincts that he had worked so hard over the years to suppress. There was a place for instinct in business, of course, but not when it stopped you thinking properly. A rational Trent wouldn't have abandoned his post, passing his coordination duties on so readily to the power-hungry Cynthia. He would have insisted on involving the other coordinators rather than confiding only in Hobbs. He would have considered walking away and calling Hunter's bluff. He would have questioned things more.

Trent slumped on one of the sofas in the coffee area. The conference participants were being called back into the auditorium, so there were a lot of people milling about. He hadn't managed to find Amara to tell her what was going on, and he was no longer sure he wanted to. He considered sending her a message and was pleased to discover that some degree of rationality had returned to his reasoning when he questioned doing even that. What would his message read, exactly? "Look out for a bomb. And don't tell anyone!" That was hardly likely to result in a calm, measured response.

From where Trent was sitting, he could see the upper floor of the conference centre across a large atrium through which the escalators ascended. Plenty of people were up there, too, and he could hear the clang of metal trays as the cafeteria staff prepared for the lunch break. He recalled the looks they'd given him as he'd searched for an offending package beneath the dining tables. When he had waved his walkie-talkie at them in explanation, they had regarded him uncomprehendingly, but they hadn't stopped him.

Trent was well aware that a lunch can make or break a conference. Check the feedback forms of any meeting, and the food is by far the thing that's commented on most, especially if it is bad. Napolean said, 'An army marches on its stomach'; any long-haul airline will tell you that people settle down when they're fed, and any conference organiser will say, 'Make sure you get the bloody food right!'

While Trent was gazing up, he spotted Hunter leaning against a barrier. Hunter was looking right at him, but he betrayed no sign of recognition.

Trent jumped to his feet. Now was his opportunity to confront this man. He had no idea what was to be gained by doing this, but rage engulfed him now. He pushed through the crowd to the escalator and took the steps two at a time, his heartbeat pounding in his ears. When he reached the top, he located the spot where Hunter had been. There was no one there.

Trent looked around wildly. The participants were almost done filing into the auditorium, but he couldn't see Hunter among them. The catering staff continued their business, and a few attendees were still at the tables finishing their snacks and coffee. There was no one else around.

Trent gripped the barrier to steady himself as he caught his breath. What now? He was severely tempted to walk away, to just leave, but then Hunter would have won. Trent would get known as someone who'd abandoned his duties in the middle of a crisis; there would be no coming back from that.

He needed to tell someone. The director of Conference Centre Volunteers had been present during their onboarding, but he hadn't seen her since. She was undoubtedly busy hobnobbing with various dignitaries, but she had to be told what was happening. Trent had to cover his back.

The moment he resolved to do this, the alarm went off.

It was ear-piercing, conversation-stopping, thought erasing. Every nerve in Trent's body leapt to life. For a moment, everyone froze. One participant screamed. Was this really happening?

Then, people in fluorescent jackets appeared. To be more precise, the catering staff and people flanking the auditorium doors donned the fluorescent jackets they'd had secreted somewhere. It was like a bad flash mob.

'Please proceed calmly to the nearest fire exit,' they announced, gesturing towards the escalators.

If you want us to be calm, turn down that bloody noise! Trent thought. He felt a little bitter that any authority granted by his walkie-talkie had been so easily trumped.

After the third repeat of the instruction, people started to move. Their reluctance stemmed, perhaps, from shell-shock but more likely from irritation that their conference had been interrupted by a bloody fire drill. Those still in the cafeteria grabbed handbags and binders of important notes that could not be allowed to perish in whatever calamity was befalling them. A few savvy people took their coffees with them. Those less smart among them stuffed what remained of their Danish pastries into their mouths in one go and struggled to breathe as they made their way out.

Trent went with them. It occurred to him that he had failed, that whatever threat had been made against the conference was coming to pass despite his best efforts. He didn't dwell on that long – the noise did not allow it. He did what he was told. In some areas, Trent considered himself the master of his domain. Emergency protocols were not one of them.

A crowd gathered at the top of the escalators. They had been turned off because why make this easy?

At this point, someone grabbed Trent by the shoulder.

'Trent, help me! You can't let me die!' It was Cynthia, the young woman he had deputised to take over his duties. 'I have a daughter!'

Cynthia's eyes blinked at different times to each other, and a shudder kept running through her body. It was like a computer virus had hacked her brain and was trying to control her body. It was contagious, too. The people around her reeled with every one of her convulsions.

Trent didn't have time to question why her having a daughter made her any more worthy of rescue than other people. He recognised that if he didn't deal with her quickly, they'd have a full-blown panic on their hands.

'Come with me,' he said.

He led her to a little staircase the volunteers used to get between the levels. It was technically a fire exit, but nobody had noticed it. He took Cynthia down one level into the entrance hall. The main doors had been flung open. Bright light flooded in from outdoors. People were running towards it.

'Go,' he said, pointing Cynthia towards the exit. It felt a bit like he was releasing an endangered species back out into the wild.

'Thank you, thank you!' Cynthia kissed his hand, and then she was off, fleeing to freedom. That was the last he saw of her.

Trent took a moment to collect himself. The alarm was

still going, so it wasn't easy to string together a coherent thought, but it occurred to him that someone ought to check on the other volunteers. Cynthia clearly hadn't done so. Someone had to take responsibility for ensuring they got out safely, regardless of whether or not they had a daughter.

'Save the children, save the children!'

The plea came from Trent's right, a quieter part of the conference centre, where community organisations had been allowed to erect their stands. Trent's initial reaction was that this didn't seem the most appropriate moment for self-promotion. Then, he saw a group of young people standing beside a billboard for the Geneva Youth Council. One was in an electric wheelchair, which appeared to have decided it would be a fantastic time to break down. A couple of the kids were trying to push it, but the mechanism had jammed.

The person shouting was wearing a fluorescent jacket. They clearly understood that their role was to bark at people rather than help them get out.

Don't be a hero, Trent. That's what they'd said at the training, although they hadn't mentioned his name specifically. And if anyone wasn't a hero, it was Trent. Still, were it to get known that he had rescued a bunch of children from a burning building, it couldn't be bad for his CV, could it? "Other relevant experience: Hero."

Trent approached the group, trying to act calm. The children's faces exhibited a range of emotions, from excitement to fear and all-conquering panic.

'Hi,' he said. 'I'm Trent'

Trent had less idea about dealing with young people than how to defuse a bomb, but this wasn't time for thinking. He grabbed the wheelchair's handles and tilted it onto its back wheels.

'Sorry about this,' he said to its occupant, but it seemed to work. With two of the older kids, he succeeded in pushing the wheelchair towards the exit, where they were greeted by a couple of fluorescent-jacketed women who took over.

Trent turned to look back into the conference centre. Fewer people were running around now. Those left appeared to be the smart-arses that didn't take this sort of thing seriously. Still, he hadn't recognised any faces. Where were the volunteers?

He was about to head back to the staircase when someone grabbed him by the hand.

'Save the planet!'

Trent didn't have time to object before he was dragged back towards the community organisation stands. His captor was an old man with wild hair and a firm grip. They passed the youth council's display and approached one made by hand, all foil and tissue paper.

'You've got to be joking!' Trent said.

There before him was a human-sized model of the planet Earth.

'Help me move it, please!' the old man pleaded.

'Leave it behind!' Trent said.

'I can't! I spent months working on it!'

It took Trent only a moment to realise that this idiot was going nowhere without his craft project. The quickest way to get him out was with the globe. He reached out and gently nudged it. He was surprised to discover that it was fairly light. He suspected it was made from papier-mâché, painted blue, green, brown, and white to represent the various continents.

Together, they pushed the globe from its pedestal and rolled it to the exit. There was a metaphor in there somewhere, but Trent hadn't the slightest inclination to try and find it. He smiled, embarrassed, at the fluorescent jacketers as he handed over his charge.

Again, he turned and headed back to the staircase.

'Save the whales!' came a voice to his left.

Trent kept on walking.

He descended the little staircase to the basement.

It was calm down there. The alarm was just a whine in the background. That explained why he hadn't seen any volunteers upstairs: no one had heard it. He hastened to the control room, where he found about fifteen team members sitting calmly, typing up their notes. Bong was among them, tapping away on his phone.

'What are you doing?' Trent said.

Bong looked up at him, amused.

'Well, it's called a mobile,' he said. 'It connects to this thing called the internet.'

'We've got to get out of here.'

'Why?'

At that moment, someone pushed past Trent. Hands clapped loudly.

'People, people, it's time to move out!' It was a man's voice. 'There's a fire in the building.'

The volunteers jumped to their feet.

'Leave your laptops,' the man instructed. 'You can come back for them later.'

The man turned to Trent, and he saw who it was. Authoritative and confident, the perfect person to evacuate people calmly from a building. Hunter Pickering.

Hunter glanced at Trent, and just for a moment, Trent

glimpsed his true intentions. The edges of Hunter's lips curled into a smile.

11:26 – EMERGENCY ASSEMBLY POINT, CONFERENCE CENTRE FOR COMMUNITY ORGANISATIONS (COCC), GENEVA

It took Amara's eyes a few minutes to adjust to the daylight. She had been inside for the best part of the morning, bathed in strip lighting.

She made her way to a low wall on the opposite side of the street, pushing her way through the crowd. The conference attendees had gathered into groups; some continued heated conversations started inside, and others speculated about what was happening.

She sat on the wall and gave herself a moment to calm down. She'd got caught in the crowd fighting their way out of the auditorium. The fire marshals had instructed them to remain calm, and most people had achieved this outwardly, but in reality, it had been a case of everyone for themselves. No matter how far humanity had come or how much they tried to project themselves as civilised, in the end, it all just came down to self-preservation.

She hated people sometimes.

She took a moment to reflect on the irony of this, given her chosen profession, for what was journalism about if not people? Had she known this when deciding on a career? Or had her motivation been simply to break into a new life, which wasn't driven entirely by revenue and productivity? Perhaps she was deceiving herself to think those factors didn't drive everything in this world, but she had to believe it. The alternative was too depressing.

A few minutes later, the fire trucks arrived. *Les sapeurs-*

pompiers, she remembered from her French lessons. She had never had massive respect for firemen, painting them as thrill-seekers who liked to show off their fancy equipment, but she now wondered if she needed to re-evaluate that assessment. There they were, running towards a danger from which hundreds of people had fled.

And what was that danger? They still didn't know. Some conjectured it was a fire detector malfunction, others a slice of bread stuck in a toaster. She couldn't help but imagine it was something more sinister. What was wrong with her brain?

She only hoped her friends had made it out okay, too. She would go looking for them as soon as she felt steadier on her feet. Whilst she was at pains not to let them know it, she cared for them and would hold herself personally responsible if anything happened. After all, she was the one who had got them involved in this event.

Some diplomats had left their cars in the no-parking spots between the building and the fire hydrants. The *sapeurs-pompiers* took great delight in smashing their side windows to run the hoses through. Amara wasn't sure this was entirely necessary, but there was a point to be made.

She sat there and watched them work.

13:03 – ADMINISTRATION OFFICE, COMMUNITY ORGANISATIONS CONFERENCE CENTRE (COCC), GENEVA

There were three of them there this time – Trent's jury.

He didn't recognise the man behind the desk, but his badge indicated he was the facilities manager. He was a rotund man with a wine-coloured face. He caressed the arms of this chair as he regarded Trent.

The second jury member was the director of Geneva Conference Volunteers. She was a gaunt-looking woman with wispy grey hair and a severe expression. She seemed none too pleased to be there and stood beside the door as though in a hurry to get out.

Their chairman was Hunter Pickering. He was perched on the edge of a desk, just like the last time.

They'd been back in the building for almost an hour when Trent had been summoned. The conference was set to restart after lunch, and people were still making their way through security. Everyone had to be scanned again before being allowed back in. Were it not for the prospect of a free meal at the other end of the queue, most would probably have returned to their homes or hotels already.

The word was that a fire in a wastepaper bin had triggered the alarm. Now, what anyone was doing introducing a naked flame to a wastepaper bin was anyone's guess, and Trent had doubted it at first. But down there in that office, Hunter confirmed the rumour.

'There's no accounting for stupidity,' he concluded after reporting the development.

The man behind the desk gave out a forced-sounding laugh. 'You've got that right!'

Hunter turned to Trent, 'Speaking of stupidity, I wanted to have a little word. Thomas and I have been going over what happened, and we reckon we had a near-miss. The alarms on this floor failed to go off.'

'That's right,' Trent said. 'When I got down here, I could barely hear them.'

'Yes, yes,' Hunter said. 'We've discussed that, and Thomas has agreed to organise a full audit before we hold any other events here. Isn't that right, Thomas?'

'Absolutely,' the facilities manager said. 'We can't be too safe with these things.'

It's a bit late for that, Trent thought.

'That's not exactly what I want to discuss,' Hunter said. 'I'm more interested in your role in all this.'

'My role?'

'The volunteer team was the last to be evacuated. They could have been left in a burning building for all we knew.'

Trent's forehead furrowed. 'That's why I went down to check on them.'

'Oh, *that's* why you went down?' Hunter feigned surprise and glanced at the others to confirm that they had reacted similarly. 'Ten minutes after the alarm started. Top of your priority list, was it?'

Trent shifted from one foot to the other. 'I was in the cafeteria when the alarm went off.'

'Ah, so you admit it! You were responsible for the volunteers, and you were upstairs eating.'

So, that was where Hunter was going! It seemed an incredible leap, but he seemed intent on pinning the blame on Trent. Trent had to tread carefully now. No matter how spurious Hunter's claims might be, he had a way of expressing them which seemed unimpeachable, like common sense.

'I had someone deputise for me,' Trent said. 'And I wasn't eating – I was doing what you asked. Running around, being "your eyes".'

Hunter spluttered out a laugh. 'What *are* you talking about?'

'The bomb threat! You asked me to circulate, looking for anything suspicious. That's why I was up there. Exactly where you wanted me!'

Behind Hunter, Thomas's red face turned even redder than its usual base colour. 'What bomb threat?'

'Indeed,' Hunter said. 'I think our friend here is suggesting I'd fake a bomb scare just to watch him scramble around like a headless chicken. And that I'd wait until he was furthest from his post before lighting a fire at my own conference just to make him look bad? Does that sound about right, Trent?'

Trent hesitated. This was, in fact, precisely what he thought, but it was out of the question to suggest it after Hunter had made it sound so ridiculous. He reflected that sometimes, the best way to disguise the truth is to wave it in people's faces.

At this point, Thomas tried to play the peacemaker, although Trent doubted his heart was in it. 'Listen, guys, I know what it's like when these things happen. Everyone wants to point fingers. The truth is, we don't know for sure how the fire started, but the important thing is that everyone got out safely.'

Trent glanced at the other person in the room, the director of Geneva Conference Volunteers. He would have expected her to come to his aid, not Thomas. She had slunk into the corner, trying to tuck herself away.

'You have no authority over me, Hunter,' Trent said. 'If you have an issue with my behaviour, you should take it up with Geneva Conference Volunteers.'

'And that's exactly why Edith is here,' Hunter said. 'What do you think, Edith? I'd call it a dereliction of duty, wouldn't you?'

'You're talking about me as though I'm a paid employee,' Trent objected. 'I'm a volunteer!'

Again, Hunter feigned surprise. 'Surely, you're not suggesting that you're less responsible for your actions because we don't pay you? I'm not sure most people working in this sector would agree with you on that point.'

Trent looked to Edith for support. She was watching the two of them go at each other as though she were a spectator at a tennis match. No matter. Trent had a strong suspicion that she wouldn't be much use to him anyway. There was too much at stake for her. On one side, she had a representative of one of Geneva's biggest international organisations, upon whose endorsement she relied for her own organisation's existence; on the other, she had someone she had been working with for barely a few weeks, and who could easily be replaced by the next loser who walked in off the street.

He did not have to wait long before she confirmed this suspicion.

'I quite agree with Hunter,' she said. 'Whether or not someone gets paid for a job is no indicator of its importance.'

'Thank you!' Hunter said, vindicated. 'And I'm sorry, Edith. I know this is your domain...'

'Oh no, no!' Edith waved a hand at him as though petting a child. 'It's wonderful when an event's sponsors get involved. It helps make it a real team effort.'

Trent didn't feel like one of the team. He was doomed. He would continue to fight for form's sake, but the battle was already lost.

Hunter returned his attention to Trent. 'It's very clear that as team coordinator, you were responsible for making sure your volunteers got out.'

'And that's exactly what I did,' Trent objected.

'Ten minutes late.'

Hunter was prowling around the room now. Thomas and Edith withdrew visibly, giving him space to rant.

'I dread to think what might have happened. This is Geneva, for Christ's sake – one of the safest places in the world. We build these state-of-the-art facilities and write safety procedures, but in the end, it always comes down to people. If there's one weak link in the chain, we all fail.'

'Let's just cut through the crap, Hunter,' Trent said. 'This is a setup. You're just trying to get back at me for-'

Hunter's eyes flashed. 'For what, Trent?'

His stare bore into Trent, who fell silent.

'I won't work with you again,' Hunter said. 'A bad reference from one of us, and you won't be working for anyone. Geneva's a close network. Rumours travel quickly. So, do yourself a favour and get out of here before you make things even worse for yourself.'

Trent considered arguing further, but it wasn't worth it. These two were so deferential to Hunter that nothing was likely to budge them. So what if he exposed Hunter's true motives? It was hardly as though Trent would be any better off were it to get known he'd slept with another's wife. People's view of relationships may have developed significantly in prior decades, but infidelity was infidelity. It didn't make anyone feel clean.

Without uttering another word, Trent walked out of the office. Beyond that, his next steps remained unclear. His immediate priority was getting out of the building. Then, out of the city, and maybe out of the country. When it came down to it, a big part of him just wanted off the planet.

Unfortunately, his trial was not over. Hunter caught up with him before he reached the exit and walked with him the rest of the way. Now that they had acted out the scene in front of the others, they could talk properly.

'Well done, Trent, you played your part well. I particularly enjoyed watching you scurrying around the building, looking for a bomb.'

'Thank you,' Trent said weakly.

He was surprised to find that he bore Hunter little ill will. Truth be told, he was impressed. Hunter had manoeuvred him into a lose-lose situation. On top form, Trent would have found him a worthy adversary; in his current state, he was just outclassed. More than anything, he felt curiosity. How had Hunter managed to thread together such a trap? And why such an elaborate one at that?

Hunter's next comment went some way towards explaining it: 'I want you to know that I'm the reason you got that coordinator position in the first place. A recommendation from me goes a long way. It wasn't your experience. It wasn't your qualifications. It was me. Build them up, then knock them down; that's how I do it.'

Okay, I get it, Trent thought. *Geneva's your stomping ground. Mess with you and I'm in trouble.*

But one thing still didn't add up. He figured he might as well ask about it. There was nothing more to be lost.

'Why would you sabotage your own conference? Surely there are better ways to get back at me without jeopardising something you've paid a lot of money for?'

Hunter smiled. 'You overestimate the value of these conferences. They're all just talk; we never get anything meaningful decided. We organise these things to build a community, that's all. What better way to bind together a community than a shared traumatic event?'

Trent knew then for certain that he would have to leave Geneva. He had been bested by a man willing to go to further extremes for revenge than he could have dreamed. There was no way this could end well for him.

17:26 – QUAI DU SEUJET, GENEVA

Trent was drunk.

He hated that word. It sounded so unrefined. Several cans in, Trent wasn't sure he could write the word "refined", never mind act it. To top it all off, he was still wearing his yellow "Waster" T-shirt.

He pushed himself off the bench and stumbled to the nearest bin, depositing his can into it. The Geneva police were less tolerant of littering than intoxicated behaviour, and getting fined would be the perfect end to a perfect day.

You should have seen it coming, Trent. You've got rusty.

The voice in his head spoke louder whenever he was inebriated. He had forgotten about this when he had started drinking. Now, it was too late to do anything about it.

So, I should have known Hunter would start a fire at a large international conference just so I would look bad? Trent almost said this out loud because the very idea that he might have predicted it sounded even more ridiculous than Hunter's scheme itself.

You knew he was after you. You should have left at the first sign of trouble.

Trent couldn't find much fault with that point. Every time he had run into difficulty, it had been because he'd stuck around too long. Persistence was for the foolhardy.

He played you, the voice pointed out helpfully. *He knew he could take advantage of you being desperate.*

Sometimes, Trent hated the world he lived in. When he'd been at the top of his game, it had seemed like a fascinating puzzle to hack. What were people's levers? How could he manipulate them? When a plan came together, it felt like a thing of beauty. For the past few years, though, he had always felt one step behind, like the outcome had already been decided upon, and he was inevitably the loser.

So, it had come to this. He'd gone to Geneva, believing naïvely that people there were trying to make the world a better place, but beneath it all, everything boiled down to money, power, and who was fucking who. He had hoped for more.

Trent wasn't one for revenge. It served no business purpose, as far as he could see. More often than not, it damaged the perpetrator as much as the target, just as it had done for Hunter, no matter how he might deny it. Okay, maybe Trent came out the worse out of that one.

But once, just once, Trent had succumbed.

It happened during his fall from grace. He'd been living out of bed and breakfast in the middle of nowhere, keeping costs down, making the little money he had left stretch as far as possible. He'd spent his days in a café trying to cook up opportunities to dig himself out of his hole, and his evenings in the pub trying to forget about it all. These should have been clues that it was not an ideal time to approach him for money, but his former colleague, Mince (an assumed name), must have been just as desperate. He had tracked Trent down and laid his cards on the table: unless Trent coughed up, he would expose his network of dubious schemes and bogus companies.

Trent had refused. Even though he'd mislaid the business acumen that had supported him earlier in life, he'd still been aware that it would be a grave mistake to succumb to blackmail. And it wasn't like he had the money to meet Mince's demands anyway.

Mince had been livid. A hot-blooded fake American, he was used to getting his way. He had followed through on his threats, exposing Trent in the only way he knew how:

with a letter to a national newspaper, setting out what he knew about Trent's business network in detail. The newspaper, ravenous for content but lacking the resources for more than a cursory investigation, had published an article on its website. Hardly anyone read it, but the damage was done. Trent had already been forced to dismantle most of his empire, and this was the killing blow for the rest. What appears on the internet stays on the internet forever. There went his hopes for a comeback.

More significantly, a sacred trust had been broken: of two men going into illicit business together. All trusts of that kind are sealed with pacts of mutual destruction. Trent never went into business with people he couldn't control. In this case, his power had been built on the fact that Mince lived a while as Grinderman (also not his real name), a mercenary with a reputation for atrocities committed during a civil war in his home country. "Expose me, and I'll expose you", that had been their agreement.

Trent had spent a day considering how to respond. He had staggered around the village with an ever-diminishing bottle of malt whiskey in hand. He had already been exposed; there was little to be gained from revealing Mince's past. But as the level of whiskey had dropped, such qualms had drowned. At the end of the day, he sent a typographical-error-ridden anonymous message to the police. A week later, Mince was arrested.

Trent hadn't followed Mince's trial; he'd been too wrapped up in his own misery for that. He hadn't needed a blow-by-blow account to feel satisfied that Mince had got what he'd had coming to him for a long time.

Trent thought of Mince as he drank, his loud voice and fake smile. He thought about the damage that human beings do to each other when lines of self-interest cross. He was no better than Hunter.

Whatever the truth, one thing was indisputable: the kindling flame of Trent's career in Geneva had been well and truly trampled out. He would have to find greener pastures elsewhere.

Trent grunted. Even the metaphors were out to get him.

When there was nothing left to drink, Trent began the long trudge along the riverbank back to the campsite.

STEP 4 – FACE YOUR PAST

CHAPTER 10

BEFORE TAKEOFF

'Are you Trent Argent?'

Trent turned to the woman who had addressed him. She looked harmless; at least, she wasn't visibly holding any weapons (which was probably sensible at Geneva airport's check-in desks), so Trent allowed himself to respond, 'Yes.'

The woman didn't seem satisfied with this. She wrinkled her nose and insisted.

'*The* Trent Argent?'

Trent smiled to himself. You know you have arrived when people start referring to you using the definite article. Still, something was unsettling about this woman's manner. There was a hint of wildness in her eyes, a jitteriness to her movements. She looked familiar, too. Her dark hair was carefully styled to contour her face, and a streak of black eyeliner enlivened her eyes. Her lips were thin. She was biting the bottom one.

'Um, I think so,' Trent said.

The world jolted to one side. Trent's head reeled. His vision rocked.

The stinging sensation on his cheek only arrived a few seconds later when his body caught up to what was happening. He pressed a hand to his face and looked back at the woman, wounded. A self-satisfied smile had spread across her face, lighting it up. This made Trent finally recognise her, even before she said, 'That's for Nancy.'

And she turned on her heel and walked away. Trent gazed after her, but his body was still in shock. He noticed a few bystanders grinning.

'Zoe?' he called.

She didn't turn back. He followed her as soon as his legs started working again but stopped himself from running. He didn't think chasing someone in an airport was a good idea, not with armed security officers around.

The woman disappeared into a crowd. Trent cursed himself.

Had it truly been Zoe? He thought about her every day but had somehow failed to recognise her. Yes, she styled herself differently now. Gone was the mass of frizzy hair. Her youthful enthusiasm had twisted into bitterness. This woman looked much older than the one he remembered.

Had the past five years been as hard on her as they had on him? Well, it didn't matter now. She had gone.

Trent glanced up at the timetable and noted that his flight was delayed. Typical! Geneva's airport had a reputation for efficiency, in the finest Swiss tradition, but there was no accounting for the budget airlines. Flights were organised with such little turnaround time that a delay in Brussels or Luton could have a knock-on effect and send the whole timetable crashing.

It did mean that he had a bit of time to track down this woman. But where would he start? He didn't remember her having a suitcase, so she probably didn't need to check anything in, but how sure was he about that? And anyway, what would he do if he found her? Offer his cheek for another slap?

He decided not to hang around and headed for security. That was the next hurdle, the pressure point, and it was vital that he didn't miss his flight. Once he was through, he could rest a bit more easily. And perhaps mount a search of the waiting area.

The security gates were the next floor up. He hopped on an escalator and got his boarding pass ready to scan. After the ticket check, he was sent to queue for a security gate.

That's where he saw Zoe again. As luck would have it, they were in the same line.

A young family was struggling to fold up a pushchair ahead of them. Others were getting out their fluids and putting them into the transparent bags for the scanners (it was a mystery to all why they hadn't done this at home). Still less excusable were the passengers standing there without a care in the world. They would get flustered at the gate and waste ten minutes fishing in various pockets for the liquids and various prohibited items they had forgotten to pack in the hold luggage. There were maybe ten people ahead of them, so it was likely to be a bit of a wait.

But that didn't matter.

'Hello, Zoe,' Trent said.

Zoe looked at him and then turned away. 'Hello, Trent.'

So, there it was, the two of them standing together as though the past five years hadn't happened – and in particular, the most recent five minutes. What were they to do? Ask, 'How've you been?' as though this was perfectly normal. So, they stood and said nothing.

That's for Nancy, Zoe had said. Nancy Spiller. Trent pictured the young woman from the remote village of

Ramstead, who was so friendly, welcoming, and naive. Nancy had been one of Trent's victims. At least, he felt confident that that was how Zoe would paint it. "Victim" was such an ambiguous but emotionally charged word. It was hardly as if he had abused her or murdered her or some such horrific act. He had just tried to help her.

Trent had been afforded a fantastic opportunity to snap up several properties in Ramstead at a bargain rate. He had provided her with cheap lodgings in one of them, knowing that Ramstead was on its way up due to the money the council was putting into it, money that had seen him hired to help out there in the first place. It should have been a win-win situation, but the villagers had got wise to his machinations far sooner than in any of the places Trent had profited off before that. He had been forced to sell up, leaving Nancy and her baby on the street.

Every business has its victims; that's what the old Trent would have said. Most of the time, they're less visible: child labour or people slaving away the other side of the world. People cared less about that. It was just the way things worked.

Trent didn't say any of that, even if a part of him still believed it. He was aware that one of his cheeks was probably burning red, and it would have been easy enough for Zoe to make him symmetrical.

'I'm sorry about Nancy,' he said.

Zoe must have heard him, but she didn't respond immediately. Instead, after a few moments, she said, 'This line's going nowhere.'

'What?' Trent said.

'They changed shifts. There's no one manning this gate anymore.'

Trent leaned to one side of the line to see past the other

passengers. Zoe was right. The staff had presumably clocked out at the end of their shifts, abandoning the security gate. Trent supposed that the people directing the queues should have moved them to another line, but they appeared to have overlooked this detail. The nearest staff member, at the ticket gates, was busy showing someone how to pull up their boarding pass on their phone, and Trent couldn't see anyone else around.

'Hopefully, someone will be along soon,' he said.

Zoe glared at him as though he had just mansplained something to her. She looked around for someone, anyone, whose attention she could grab.

Trent kept quiet at first, but the more he thought about it, the more he realised this was it. This was his only opportunity to make up with this woman who had haunted his waking thoughts for five years. She was a captive audience. Yes, he might risk another slap if he pushed it too far, but he had to try.

Letting go of Zoe was the only selfless thing he had ever done, and he had regretted it ever since. With her at his side, printing stories in this local rag, he could have turned the tide when the villagers turned against him. But he had already sent her off to pursue her career. It had seemed like a kindness at a time, encouraging her to set aside their burgeoning relationship, but his doubts had emerged soon after.

'I'm really sorry about Nancy,' he said. 'When things changed in Ramstead, I had to sell up. I've always regretted it. I didn't live up to my promise to her.'

'I heard you the first time, Trent.'

'Okay. I'm sorry. But please, just tell me, did things work out for her?'

Zoe sighed and looked to the heavens.

'They rehoused her in Tralford,' she said, eventually. 'She'd hardly ever stepped outside of Ramstead, and there she was in a big town.'

'That must have been tough for her,' Trent said, trying carefully to coax out more.

'In the end, it was probably for the best. There was no life for her and the baby in Ramstead. In Tralford, at least, she got help. It was kind of the jolt she needed to make something of her life. She's started training as a teacher.'

That was something, at least. A few months after Trent had retreated from Ramstead, he had tried to check up on people there. It was the first time he'd done this with somewhere he'd worked – it didn't pay to look back – but Ramstead was different. It had been impossible for him to get any real information. He hadn't dared venture back in person, and her father, in his nursing home, seemed to have forgotten he had children.

'And Terrence?' Trent said, remembering the baby's name. 'How's he doing?'

Zoe turned to him now. 'Terrence the Terror, I used to call him. God, he made his mum's life hell. The things kids put their parents through! If an adult were to do half those things, we'd call it gaslighting or some other form of psychological violence. The police would be around there in a heartbeat, then the lawyers, then the tabloids. They'd be branded a monster, and their name would be in every headline in the land. But no, it's okay for a child to do that twisted shit, and the parent has to put up with it. Be grateful about it, even, because you're expected to love your child, no matter what.'

'Come on, he's just a kid. It can't be that bad!'

'Thank you for proving my point.' Zoe paused a second to let that sink in. 'Funny enough, he's turned into a well-balanced boy. He's just about to start his second year at school. Ah, EXCUSEZ-MOI, EXCUSEZ-MOI!'

Those last words weren't intended for Trent, but one of the airport staff walking by. There was still no movement at the gate, and the passengers were growing twitchy. The staff member, who looked like she had somewhere else to be urgently, regarded Zoe with her mouth agape as though she'd just witnessed an animal talking.

'This queue is going nowhere,' Zoe said.

'Just please be patient, madame.'

'I have a plane to catch.'

'So does everyone. We do advise all passengers to arrive two-and-a-half hours before their scheduled flight time.'

And off the woman went, leaving them in the queue to nowhere. Zoe huffed and puffed. Trent wasn't sure how much of that was due to her being stuck and how much was because she was stuck with him.

'When's your flight?' he asked.

'It's been delayed. But they don't know that.'

As Zoe's agitation grew, so too did Trent's. He wasn't usually an anxious person, but he couldn't afford to miss his flight. He had taken a risk booking it for the same day as his interview, but it had been the best way to avoid a hotel bill. Flying in and out on the same day would be exhausting, but his funds were running short.

This job was Trent's final chance. His name was mud in Geneva, and the ninety days on his permit were up. When an opportunity in Paris had come up, he'd leapt at the chance. The Zoom interview went well. They had seemed impressed by his experience helping UK communities. When they'd asked to meet him in person, he hadn't questioned it, even when he'd seen the price of the flights. Still, they were cheaper than train tickets. If one thing alone could explain the state of the Earth's atmosphere, that was it.

All eggs in one basket. If this interview didn't work out, Trent would be on a bus back to the UK to claim unemployment benefits.

For the sake of his sanity, he tried to keep Zoe talking:

'How's your father?'

Probably not the best choice of subject. Zoe's father had been an abusive man. Trent had only known him as an old man being cared for by Nancy, but she'd never been coy about what happened when they were younger. His being taken into a care home was probably the best thing that could have happened to Nancy, even though she wouldn't accept that at the time.

'He didn't last a year in that place,' Zoe said.

'Oh, I'm sorry.'

Zoe brushed this aside. 'Some people aren't built to live in residential care. He was always too independent. He never liked anyone helping him.'

'Except Nancy.'

'That was different. She was his daughter; he saw that as her duty. But letting strangers help him, no, that was weakness.'

'So, he didn't accept help?'

Zoe shook her head. 'It was the opposite, actually. The moment he accepted he needed help, that's when he gave up. It was like a piece of him had been taken away. After that, there was always something missing from his eyes, and he just faded...'

Zoe looked at her feet, and for a moment, the security queue was the last thing on their minds.

'It's a terrible thing to lose a parent,' she said. 'Even one that made your life a misery. It's the history you lose, the memories, the connection to the past. You realise that all those things from childhood, those stories he used to tell, you're the bearer of them now. You're the only one around to make them important.'

Just then, a fuss started further up in the queue. People started shouting in French. Now, that caused a reaction from the airport staff. If anyone knew how to complain effectively, it was French speakers. A few minutes later, a crew arrived at their gate and set themselves up slowly, studiously avoiding eye contact with passengers and ignoring the grumbling. A few minutes after that – following the predictable delays with people forgetting they were wearing belts or watches – they were through.

Trent and Zoe didn't speak as they unpacked their liquids into the tray and passed through the scanners. The great responsibility of sorting their belongings into various categories weighed heavy, so it deserved all their concentration. As Trent did this, he reconciled himself to the idea that the moment had passed. He wouldn't see Zoe again after this. The little contact they'd had would have to be enough. It had answered some questions, at least, and quelled some regrets. He doubted it would stop him thinking about her, but it would have to do.

To his surprise, Zoe was waiting for him at the other side of the scanners.

'Where are you flying to?' she asked.

'Paris.'

'Me, too.'

'10:20?'

'Yes.'

An expression of foreboding crossed Zoe's face. 'Show me your ticket.'

They put their phones side by side, and the strange

reality became clear. Seats 19A and 19B. They would be sitting together.

'What are the fucking chances?' Zoe said.

Concerned that she might find him somehow to blame, Trent quickly said, 'Must be fate.'

'Me and fate have always had issues with each other.' Zoe put her phone back in her bag. 'Well, I suppose if we're going to be sitting with each other for the next few hours, we'd better get reacquainted. Come with me. Let's catch up properly.'

Switzerland was one of the few countries Trent had visited that still had a smoking area inside the terminal. It was a vacuum-sealed bubble, such that you might see in films about people trying to contain a contagion. Several fans sucked up the offending air, but the odour remained, the ghost of a smell.

There were about a dozen people in there, all supposedly enjoying their habit whilst looking unremittingly depressed.

'When did you start smoking?' Trent asked as Zoe lit up.

'You're judging me,' Zoe said, sitting on one of the wipe-clean plastic seats. 'I can't believe that, of all people, Trent Argent is judging me!'

Trent uttered a few words of denial, but he quickly gave up. He was an excellent liar, but knowing when you were stretching credibility was key to the art of lying. He had always detested smoking: the smell of it, the mess. He'd thought twice about following her in there, not wanting to stink of smoke for his interview.

He couldn't understand why someone would get into it

in the first place. Of all the habits to take up, why that? Even football wasn't that bad (and he was quite aware that many people would disagree with the characterisation of football as a bad habit). He asked Zoe this in a roundabout way.

'I'm not going to try to explain it to you,' Zoe said. 'You won't know 'til you've tried it. You understand things more when you experience them. I remember my sister always looked down on young mums. She could be so judgemental. She said they were irresponsible. Then, that councillor got her pregnant, and her outlook changed.'

Trent could understand that from his own experience. He used to look down at people for many things he'd gone on to stoop to. He would never have imagined himself as an alcoholic with a gambling addiction, but that's what he had become. The first time he'd dabbled with online poker, it had been like a seed that had lain dormant in him since birth had finally been watered. It had sprouted, and its tendrils had spread quickly, entwining every cell of his body.

'You didn't answer my question,' he said.

She smiled enigmatically at that. 'Okay, try this, then. There's an old saying: when in France, smoke.'

Trent was pretty sure that wasn't how the saying went, but even so, there was a more fundamental flaw to her argument. 'We're in Switzerland.'

'You were never one to let the facts get in the way of anything. Actually, I live in Paris.'

So, she's on her way back home. 'Ah, really? So, this is a visit?'

'I've been covering the peace talks.'

With the UN having a headquarters in Geneva, it was common for the city to host talks between two warring countries. Trent had no idea which two countries had been engaged in the latest mediation, but he assumed it was important.

'Wow,' he said. 'How'd they go?'

'These things get worked out by bureaucrats sitting in dark rooms together. We only see a small part of it, the bit they want to be public. But they had a positive resolution, if that's what you're asking. How about you? What are you doing here?'

Big question. Trent decided it was best to answer her in bite-sized segments. 'I was working at a conference last week. The Water and Sanitation Summit.'

'I heard about that. There was an incident there, wasn't there?'

'A fire.'

'Where Trent Argent goes, disaster follows!'

Trent realised that they were heading back towards the subject of how he messed up things for other people. It was best to divert from that one. 'So, covering the peace talks, hey? You've moved up in the world.'

Zoe shrugged. 'I've done okay for myself. Had my fair share of knockbacks, but I've kept going. There's not really much else to do.'

'Other than curl up and give in.'

'That's not me. You know, there was one thing I remember hearing again and again when I was growing up: "Ramstead sticks together. We help each other." Such a lie! The only thing I learned from Ramstead is that you have to stick up for yourself and yourself alone. Turns out, if you learn to do that, you'll go far in this world.'

Trent scratched his nose. 'I'm beginning to think there's another way.'

Zoe laughed. 'That's rich, coming from you! You're the one who told me to leave my family and focus on my career.

You sent me away, and you didn't even come to say goodbye.'

'Another one of my regrets,' Trent said.

'Well, aren't you full of them?'

'Excuse me, can you keep it down?' It was a man with a large cigar, who clearly believed that tobacco should be enjoyed as in the old *Hamlet* adverts. He lounged in his seat like Winston Churchill.

They both looked at him for a moment. Then, they started giggling.

'We get all sorts in these places,' Zoe whispered. 'It's just like in supermarkets. All human life is there.'

'Nicotine's a real unifying force,' Trent said.

They spent the rest of their time in the smoking booth people-watching. With Zoe's encouragement, they took turns whispering stories to each other about why the other occupants had taken up smoking. The fifty-something over there did it as a child to be cool; the young woman at parties, socialising with her friends; others as an excuse to go outside and get away from their children. Their conspiratorial chat reminded Trent of that time with Serena. Only, this felt more genuine, like two old friends catching up.

Is that what they were, old friends? Certainly, if you looked at their story, they were not. Back in the UK, they had used each other: Zoe for stories to feed her editor, and Trent to influence what went in the press. But there had been something more. They had been on a date of sorts. And their influence on each other's lives was more significant than either cared to admit.

They stopped when another man came up to them.

'Have you visited St Paul's Cathedral?'

'Pardon?' Zoe said.

'It has a gallery of whispers. You can hear everything

201

there, from the other side of the gallery. This room's a bit like that.'

They should have been embarrassed, but instead, they collapsed into fits of giggles again.

'Come on, Zoe said, stubbing out her cigarette. 'I'm finished.'

They heard the chanting long before they saw the group. It sounded like somebody was off to watch football. Trent couldn't distinguish the words, but people only made that kind of din during football matches. The sport involved switching off the brain, which made them receptive to nonsensical singing.

A male voice directed proceedings, shouting out a line, which the others repeated at the top of their voices. There was so much testosterone around that Trent could almost smell it.

The crowd parted as the mob entered the departure area. Trent realised he'd been wrong. There were seven or eight men aged from their twenties up to their sixties, and none were wearing football strips. They were all walking with the distinctive sway of the inebriated. Most were dressed casually, in jeans and short-sleeved shirts, but they had various... adornments. One stood out in particular. He was wearing a tiara and a sparkly bra over his T-shirt. He tottered around in heels.

A stag party. That would probably have been Trent's second guess.

'Let's just hope the gods of fate haven't put them on my flight, too,' Zoe muttered.

Trent blinked when they got closer. He recognised the

stag: his square body and inconsistently-shaved beard. The clothes were familiar, too. When you camp with someone for weeks, you get to know their wardrobe.

'Bong?' he said.

He cursed himself as soon as he spoke. The first rule of interacting with mobs is not to interact with them. He hoped Hobbs hadn't heard him over the singing, but of course, he had.

'Ah, Trent, Trent!' Bong wheeled around to address the rest of the group. 'This is my good, good friend, Trent!'

'Hello, Trent,' they all shouted.

Trent glanced apologetically at Zoe. He excused himself from her for a moment and ushered Bong to one side. This solicited various wolf whistles from members of his group. Then, the singing recommenced.

'What's going on?' Trent said. 'You never told me you were getting married.'

In point of fact, Trent had never seen Bong with a woman. The very idea of him courting someone seemed unlikely. Pursuing, maybe.

Bong lowered his voice. 'It's a cover.' He didn't sound as drunk as he had first appeared.

'A cover for what?'

'We're on a business trip. Environmental conference.'

A few things clicked into place then. Not many, but a few. A week earlier, Bong had announced to the campmates that he'd been headhunted to join the social media team of a large foundation. His activities on TikTok had caused quite a stir. This organisation wanted to be "where it's at", and apparently, faking adulterous relationships and making videos of people picking up excrement was that precise location. Bong had accepted the job on condition that he could continue his extra-curricular activities.

According to him, that was where the real money lay, not working 9-5 in an office.

But Bong wasn't in an office. He was in an airport, dressed like a drag queen who'd given up halfway through getting ready.

'We have to go incognito,' Bong said. 'We've been getting some bad press recently. Some right-wing blogger made this.'

He got out his phone. Trent leaned in to watch the video. He had been doing this so often of late, with all the rubbish that Bong insisted on showing them, that he felt a crook in his neck.

A plain-looking man adjusted his cufflinks.

"Declan Runrig, President, Ellipsis Foundation", the caption declared.

'Our climate change-busting team has been travelling the world, saving the environment,' Declan said proudly.

And then the music cut in – the theme tune to Team America, World Police. *In the montage that followed, various faces (presumably of the Ellipsis Foundation's climate team) were superimposed over footage of the Team America dummies jetting to various locations around the world. There they were beside the Egyptian pyramids, then Mount Rushmore, and then the Sydney Opera House; each scene was interspersed with them flying in their (presumably highly polluting) jet aeroplane.*

'Travelling the world, saving the environment.' It was Declan's voice again, but this time, it sounded like it had been hacked. It became some sort of electro-rap.

'T-t-travelling the world, s-s-saving the environment.'

It continued. Pictures of various world landmarks flitted across the screen at an increasing rate as the sound and images crescendoed into a climax. There was the Eiffel Tower, the Great Wall of China, and the Taj Mahal.

'T-t-travelling the world, s-s-saving the environment.'

And there were the Niagara Falls, the Colosseum, the-

'I'll stop it there,' Bong said, and he pocketed his phone.

Trent fought back a smile. 'That's pretty witty for a right-wing blogger.'

'I know, right? They're usually more shouty.'

Trent nodded. 'So, that's your solution? Pretend you're on a stag do?'

'Not all of us,' Bong said. 'The big boss was very concerned about the carbon impact, so he's getting there by solar-powered yacht. Left three weeks ago. We would have gone with him, but he didn't want to leave the office unstaffed that long.'

Trent realised that Bong was not alone in distinguishing between caring about the environmental impact of international travel and being concerned with how it would appear. The planet was doomed.

Then again, there was a certain unfairness in how the court of public opinion perceived such matters. Climate change deniers were prepared to utilise every tool at their disposal to win the battle. If climate activists were to have any hope of countering this, they needed to network, mobilise, coordinate, and sometimes, perhaps, catch a flight. There were limits, of course, but refraining from travel entirely was to tie their hands behind their backs. For a right-wing blogger to criticise them for travelling was rather like someone trying to secure a strategic advantage for their side. Or a superpower invading a small country, targeting its infrastructure, and then lamenting the injustice of that country not holding wartime elections.

At that point, a sturdy man with a low-cut T-shirt and nipple tassels, whom Trent would later learn was the country director for Sweden, called to Bong.

'Oye, oye!' replied Bong. Then, he addressed Zoe for the first time. 'Pleased to meet you, woman.'

'Likewise,' Zoe said.

And off Bong went.

'You have interesting friends,' Zoe said neutrally.

'Thank you,' Trent replied.

'They're calling us to the gate,' Zoe said.

'Already?' Trent said. 'I thought the plane was running thirty minutes late.' He checked the flight tracker on his phone. 'It still says it's over Belgium.'

'Let's not question it. Come on!'

As they made their way to the moving walkway, Trent hoped she was right. If their plane left when it was supposed to, it wouldn't be a bad thing at All. He had allowed plenty of time between the flight and his interview that afternoon, highly aware of the perils of travelling, but he could see that buffer being eaten away, little by little.

They stepped onto the walkway. Trent had never been sure of the etiquette on those things. Should you stand still and let them carry you, or walk and take advantage of the boost? He decided to stop and chat with Zoe, much to the dismay of other passengers, who pushed past, knocking him pointedly with their bags.

'You look good, by the way,' he said. 'If I'm allowed to say that.'

Zoe rolled her eyes. 'It's a bit creepy, but I suppose I'll allow it. You're not looking too bad yourself.'

'Really?'

Zoe's cheeks inflated until she couldn't hold it in any longer. She burst out laughing. 'No. You look terrible! What the hell happened to you?'

'I've been living under a bridge the past few weeks.'

Zoe raised her eyebrows. 'As you do.'

Trent wondered what else he should tell her. Just sprinkle a few facts about himself – that would be enigmatic. Then again, those facts involved him getting roughed up by a crime lord's henchman, having sex with a married woman and getting fired, so maybe it was better to start from the top.

'I've been looking for work here. Keeping costs down. The price of hotels is scandalous.'

'Ever heard of Airbnb?'

'Staying in someone else's home?' Trent shuddered. 'No, it's not for me.'

He stumbled as he reached the end, facing backwards.

'So,' Zoe said, stepping gracefully off, 'the great Trent Argent ends up sleeping under a bridge. How the mighty have fallen!'

Her eyes grew distant as she savoured the moment.

'It was a prolonged fall from grace,' Trent admitted.

Zoe smiled wickedly. 'I want to hear all about it!'

Trent would have to tell it later because they had to separate to go through passport control, and on the other side, their flight was calling "Final Boarding".

'What the hell?' Zoe said. 'They only called us to the gate five minutes ago!'

'We'd better hurry,' Trent said.

He hated being at the beck and call of others, but this

was no time to argue about it. He could not miss that plane. They were in the new part of the airport, where they boarded the budget airlines the furthest they could from the "proper" ones. He and Zoe had a long walk ahead of them. A few people had overtaken them already, trailing suitcases whose wheels were ablaze as they raced for their plane.

Trent took the next few metres at a stride before realising that Zoe was no longer with him.

'There's only so fast I can walk in these heels,' she said when she caught up.

Trent tried to walk slower, but it was so difficult. His whole body was straining like a dog on a leash. He tried to keep his cool, but Zoe must have noticed.

'Go on, go ahead,' she said. 'Abandon me. You're an expert at that.'

'That's low.'

When they finally arrived at the gate – the furthest away, of course – Trent was about ready to burst. It was then that he noticed there was no queue for boarding. Worse still, there was no one at the gate. The estimated time of departure on the board was now an hour later than planned. The other passengers were milling around, looking several shades of confused and angry. They had gone from the false hope of leaving early to the reality of being late.

'There we go, they've done it again!' Zoe sighed.

'What's going on?' Trent said. He was beginning to accept that he was less experienced in international travel than her.

'It's an old trick. Call everyone to the gate early so they can be herded onboard as soon as the plane arrives.'

'Well, that's just lovely!'

'Welcome to modern travelling!'

Zoe plopped herself down on the nearby seats. Trent paced around for a few minutes, trying to calm himself. It now seemed a real possibility he would be late for his interview. An hour's delay would still just about be okay, but who said that would be the end of it?

'What's the problem?' Zoe said after watching him march back and forth for a while.

'I have an interview in a few hours,' Trent said.

'Close to the airport?'

'Other side of Paris.'

Zoe jutted out her chin. 'You *are* aware there's a public transport strike today? Half the trains are cancelled.'

Trent raised his face to the heavens in a silent scream.

'Just call them,' Zoe said, sounding quite content that she wasn't in his shoes. 'Tell them you're delayed. See if you can reschedule.'

'Okay, okay.'

Trent detested being in that sort of state, especially in front of someone else. It made him feel weak. He hated following Zoe's advice even more, but he did so. He got out his phone and called the number they'd given him. No answer. They were probably in other interviews.

'Leave a message,' Zoe suggested.

This was one piece of advice too far for Trent. 'Who listens to their messages these days?'

He resolved to try again as they were boarding. He forced himself to stop pacing, concerned that he might use up his daily energy quota on that useless act, and went to sit next to Zoe.

'What's this job, then?' Zoe said, probably as much to distract him as anything.

'Six-month contract, with the possibility of a permanent role,' Trent said. 'Happiness Officer.'

Zoe doubled over with laughter. It seemed greatly exaggerated, but the more Trent thought about it, the more he could see the amusing part.

'Trent Argent, Happiness Officer,' Zoe chuckled. 'You've got to be joking!'

'Alright, alright. I'm a different person now, Zoe.'

'How so?'

'I came to Geneva to help people.'

'You went to Ramstead to help people, supposedly. "Community Troubleshooter", wasn't it?'

'I *did* help people.'

'And got rich off it!'

'A fortunate side-effect, that's all. But that doesn't matter. I've changed. You might not believe it, but I have.'

God, he sounded like a cheating husband now. Just when Trent thought he'd hit rock bottom, there was always another layer to descend.

'It's easy for men to say they've changed when it serves them,' Zoe said. 'For all I know, this Geneva thing could be part of one of your schemes. I'm sure there's plenty of money to be made in humanitarian work. Maybe you own the company that manufactures the refugee shelters, or something.'

Trent's eyes widened with innocence. 'This is how you try to calm me down?'

'They do say the best form of defence is offence.'

'That makes no sense!'

'Distracted you from the flight, though, didn't it?'

They were quiet for the rest of the wait. Zoe got out her laptop and started typing. Trent pretended he had something to do on his phone, but he was really just stewing away.

Eventually, a voice came over the speakers to announce boarding. By this point, the other passengers had already started queueing, prompted by the arrival of airline staff a few minutes earlier. Zoe didn't budge. Their plane still hadn't arrived, and they needed to disembark those passengers and clean it before anyone could board.

'They're just jostling over space in the overhead lockers,' she said.

Trent had a small backpack and Zoe a laptop bag, both of which could fit under their seats, so there was little point in them entering the arena of battle. Still, it took some effort for Trent to stop joining the queue. He didn't know whether this was due to his eagerness to get on board and get the flight over and done with or the innate desire of all English people to join queues.

He tried phoning his prospective employer again. Still no answer.

'Leave a bloody message!' Zoe said.

Trent didn't.

They boarded eventually and made their way to their seats. Zoe was at the window, and Trent found himself sandwiched between her and a man with hairy arms, who immediately staked a claim to their shared armrest. Trent decided he had bigger fish to fry, but privately, he was seething.

He wrote a short email explaining the situation to his prospective employer. It wasn't a voice message because he didn't feel he could back down on that now. He only hoped they would check their emails between interviews.

They didn't talk much as the boarding completed and the plane made its way towards the far end of the runway.

The constant stream of announcements – safety, a non-apology for being late due to baggage handling at the previous airport ('It's always someone else's fault,' Zoe remarked), and their in-flight service – made it difficult to concentrate on anything else. Messages were piped out to the passengers at deafening volumes as though they were barking to inmates in a military camp.

Then, the plane just sat there.

'Does it normally take this long?' Trent said

The speakers came to life again. 'This is your captain speaking. Air traffic control has just informed us that there's a restriction on flights coming into or out of Geneva Airport. There's a fire in one of the neighbouring buildings, and we need to wait until it's been brought under control.'

Zoe repeated her earlier statement: 'Where Trent Argent goes, disaster follows.'

Trent buried his face in his hands. Was Hunter responsible for this fire, too? Was he still hounding him, even as he tried to leave the country? Whatever the truth, it was now certain that Trent would miss his interview. He tried calling them again, but he and Zoe had the misfortune of being seated close to the front. One of the flight attendants instructed him to put his phone in flight mode. She kept an eagle eye on him after that.

He just had to hope the email would be enough.

CHAPTER 11

AN EVENING IN PARIS

The engines powered up. They were finally moving. The plane reached the end of the runway and turned to point down it.

Zoe grabbed Trent's knee.

'You don't mind if I, do you?' she said. Her voice sounded frail.

'Um, sure, okay,' Trent said.

'I'm terrified of flying. No matter how many times I do it, there's something about putting my life in other people's hands that scares the shit out of me.'

The engine noise intensified. Zoe's grip tightened. He could feel her fingernails digging into his flesh.

'We do that every day, you know?' Trent said. 'Every time we leave the house or get into a car, we put our lives in other people's hands. Someone could crash into us, whatever we do. It's true in everything we do in life.'

He tried to sound matter-of-fact about it, hoping that adopting a reasonable tone would help calm her and reduce the pain he was feeling around his knee.

'So, your solution is to make me terrified of *everything*?

Thank you *very* much. Well, call me oversensitive, but I find having thousands of feet of empty air beneath me really heightens my sense of vulnerability.'

The engine roared, and the plane accelerated, pushing them back in their seats. Trent looked out of the little window and tried to think about anything other than whether Zoe's nails were about to draw blood. The grass beside the runway became a blur. Then, the view tilted, and they were in the air quite effortlessly, as though it was perfectly normal. Which, of course, it was. Thousands of flights took off every day and had done so for decades. But there remained something special about how humankind had transcended the rules of nature, sending metal tubes full of bodies and luggage into the sky. It never ceased to astound Trent.

The plane rose higher still, and the ground fell away to reveal the whole of Geneva. It was as though a veil had been lifted. This was how it really looked, away from their petty concerns. Trent thought back to his visit to the Salève. He'd had a similar feeling then. And there it was, beyond a few fields and settlements. It looked tiny now – definitely more of a hill than a mountain.

A few minutes later, the plane levelled, and Zoe removed her hand.

'Thank you,' she said.

'Any time,' Trent said. He didn't mean it. 'Do you normally grab a man's leg when you take off?'

'There's not normally enough meat on a woman's.'

The announcements resumed, this time for the airline's bistro service. At the mention that they weren't carrying hot food, the many passengers planning on ordering a cheese toastie came together in a collective groan. The alcoholics cheered at twice the volume on hearing that the drinks service would be provided as usual.

'Distract me from my misery,' Zoe said. 'I want to hear about yours. Tell me, Trent, how *did* you end up sleeping under a bridge in Geneva and working for a sanitation summit? The last time I heard of you, you were selling off your stake in my childhood village and evicting my sister and nephew.'

'Quite a change,' Trent said.

'Quite a change.'

Trent thought for a second. Over the past few weeks, he had told various versions of this story to his campmates, Serena, and even himself. Which version should he tell Zoe?

The truth, Trent. Tell her the truth.

'Ramstead was the first place I really lost,' he said. 'Don't get me wrong; in business, you accept that you can't win every time. The trick is to make sure you win more often than you lose – or if you win, you win big to cancel out the failures. But it was more than that in Ramstead. I feel like I connected with people there. And when they turned on me, that made me question a lot of things.'

'As it should,' Zoe said.

'This problem was, it was just the start of my misfortunes. One night, I don't know, I was looking for a little distraction. I had been drinking. I didn't used to drink, but I'd started a few weeks before. I told myself that was Just a little distraction, too – a way to soften things. Nothing at all to worry about – until it was. Anyway, that night, I tried my hand at online poker. Just a little game to prove I still had it. Only I didn't. So, another game, then another...'

Zoe laughed incredulously. 'You're not about to tell me you lost your fortune to online poker?'

'The losses in Ramstead had already hit my finances pretty bad. The poker just finished me off.'

'But still... that must take persistence.'

'That's one of my defining traits, unfortunately.'

Just thinking about it made him feel idiotic. It was stupid gambling, stupid, grubby online gambling. It takes forever to lose a fortune like that. It's not like visiting a casino, going all-in and losing your car, house, wife and children in one blow. No, with online gambling, you lose little by little. He'd watched himself fritter his money away. He'd had plenty of opportunity to stop it, but he hadn't. It was this that dispirited him most.

Not that it had ever been about the money for Trent. Money was just a way of keeping score. The truth was that Trent was an addict. It had taken him years to recognise that part of himself. It wasn't Ramstead that had brought him to ruin; it was his inability to let things go and accept defeat.

'And then you had a revelation...' Zoe prompted.

'I got to the bottom, and it didn't seem worth the effort to crawl back up, not if it meant going back to the life I'd led before.'

Zoe shook her head incredulously. 'You amaze me. You speak like you've grown a conscience, that you want to atone for what you've done. But let's examine this more closely. You got where you were because you got played by a bunch of villagers and couldn't handle it. You're just trying to prove them wrong by pretending you've turned over a new leaf. There's nothing noble about that.'

Her bitterness was still there, but it was less sharp now. It remained well-rehearsed, but it lacked something in the performance.

'Listen,' Trent said, 'I understand why you think that, but believe me, I've changed.' There he went again. 'Don't pretend you haven't, too.'

'I've adapted to survive. That's very different. Don't get me wrong, I'm glad if you've turned over a leaf and want to fix the world, but don't forget it was people like you that got us in this state in the first place. Do you know what, it's not you I'm disappointed in; it's me. I knew what you were. People like me get into journalism to expose people like you.'

'We made good news together, though, didn't we?' Trent said in a conciliatory tone.

'We made *your* news.' Zoe paused briefly before laying a hand on his leg, which was still tender from take-off. 'Look, let's not talk about this anymore, not while we're stuck together like this. Anyway, these things happened years ago. There's no point in carrying them with us any more than we need to. These things define us. They make us stronger. We have to accept that and move on.'

Trent nodded and smiled weakly. It was the closest he came to forgiveness. It would have to do.

An hour into the flight, the captain came over the speakers to instruct the cabin crew to prepare the cabin for landing. He then mentioned casually that they were expecting turbulence as they approached Paris.

'Oh, God!' Zoe said.

The flight attendants completed a final tour of the cabin, collecting rubbish and checking that everyone was belted in with their tray tables stowed. Trent didn't read too much into their economy of words as they called out, 'Rubbish?' He had already noted that they cut out every extraneous word during the drink service. 'Would you like any sugar with that?' had been clipped down to 'Sugar with that?' and 'That'll be twelve euros twenty' became 'Twelve euros twenty.' He understood it, of course. Interacting with people could be exhausting, especially if it was routine. Best to cut off the fatty gristle.

He looked across at Zoe. They hadn't talked much during the past half hour. She'd got out her laptop and pretended to work; he'd pretended to be preparing for his interview. He wondered if she had been thinking about him as much as he of her. He'd spent his time contemplating who she once was and who she had become, and trying to shake off the pervading sense of unreality.

Zoe had paled visibly since the announcement. Trent rubbed his tender knee and prepared for another assault.

The plane dropped ten metres. People screamed. Something banged.

Zoe grabbed his knee, digging her nails into his flesh. He gritted his teeth.

The engine noise changed frequency, as though slowing and speeding up. They dropped again. The lighting flickered. In the row behind them, someone vomited. The smell wafted its way quickly to Trent's nostrils, and he felt like he might do the same.

A terrible thought occurred to Trent then. He realised that if he were to die on that flight, he would have nothing to show for his life – just a collection of dirty clothes in a tent and a vacuum-sealed suit with a scuff on the knee. What kind of an existence was that? Sure, his parents would mourn him when they heard the news, but then they would carry on, their daily lives unchanged.

What about his campmates, Hobbs, Bong and Amara? It was a sobering thought that these people he'd only met by chance a few weeks earlier figured so high in his list of potential mourners. It made sense, though: they were the future. They *had* a future. If they remembered him, that would be something.

And what about Zoe? Would she care if he died? Actually, the question was redundant because she would most likely be dead, too. He was getting delirious now.

The plane descended through the clouds, and there was Paris below them. Wind buffeted them from side to side, but it was less violent than it had been higher up.

With a buzz, the undercarriage opened. Zoe's grip tightened again. Trent would have grabbed the armrest for support but for the hairy man's arm, so he held onto his other knee instead. He wondered if he would still be able to walk after this.

The ground neared. They were coming in fast, too fast, by Trent's judgement. Fortunately, Trent was not a trained air pilot, so his judgment was wrong. The plane touched down with a bang; then it reared up momentarily before being guided back down as though the pilot was trying to tame an over-excited pet.

Then, the brakes kicked in, and the plane screeched slower. When it was moving no faster than a bus, Trent realised he had been holding his breath. He let it go.

'Oh, my dear God!' Zoe sighed.

A few passengers clapped, some in a sarcastic way, but most were just glad to be alive. Trent didn't have the energy to move his hands.

He closed his eyes. They had made it.

~

'This is your captain speaking. I'm afraid there will be a slight delay in disembarking. Due to strike action, the Charles de Gaulle airport is operating with limited ground staff. We're in a queue waiting for them to attach the air bridge.'

'Oh, for heaven's sake,' Zoe said. 'How hard can it be? Just push the bloody lever!'

Trent wasn't listening. He had taken his phone off flight mode and checked his emails.

'They got it,' he told Zoe. 'The interview's been rescheduled for tomorrow.'

'That's great,' Zoe said, 'because we're going to be spending the night in this plane!'

'I was supposed to be flying back tonight,' Trent said.

He hadn't meant it as a hint; it was a statement of fact. Now that he knew he would live beyond the next few minutes, his brain was processing the next steps.

'Well, I wouldn't recommend trying to sleep under a bridge in Paris. I don't think the tramps here are as hospitable as in Geneva.'

'Oh, you'd be surprised,' Trent said.

'You can crash at mine if you like.'

Zoe's words hung there for a few moments. Trent knew he should snap up the offer, but something made him hesitate.

'It's a couple of stops on the RER,' Zoe added. 'I have a spare sofa and a shower. You can make yourself look presentable for tomorrow.'

The old Trent would have considered all the arguments for and against. He would have thought about the relative merits of a comfortable bed versus the cost of a hotel. He'd have considered the journey time at peak hours the following morning and questioned how much sleep he would get on a sofa. The new Trent didn't think about any of that stuff. He just said, 'Okay. Thanks.'

Zoe nodded as though a significant decision had been made.

Twenty minutes later, they were released from the plane. The same bustle commenced as when boarding, with everyone leaping to their feet to get a few places further up in the escape queue. Trent and Zoe took it easy. Although they were both desperate to get off that plane, they lacked the energy for a fight.

When they finally stepped onto the air bridge, Zoe announced, 'Well, that was the journey from hell. The worst flight I've ever been on, stuck with one of my exes. If you think I'm going any further without a cigarette, you've got another thing coming.'

So, Trent followed her to the smoking zone outside. When they got past the terminal doors, they joined a diverse group of addicts, topping up their nicotine levels before or after a flight. Trent's first taste of Paris air was tainted with cigarette smoke. Looking back, it was pretty representative. But something else was on his mind right then.

'You think of me as one of your exes?' he said.

It wasn't as if their relationship had gone anywhere. One date, which had ended with them discussing work, and that was it, apart from a bit of flirting. Yes, maybe their bond had gone beyond that, but that didn't make him an ex. If he wasn't an ex, then he was undoubtedly a groupie. He felt that way whenever he had a conversation with someone smoking. It was like they had pulled him there with the sheer weight of their personality, like a planet keeping moons in orbit through its gravitational force.

Zoe had a faraway look as she blew out a stream of

smoke. She stood silent for a few seconds, perhaps lost in contemplation or maybe just enjoying the chemical hit.

'My other exes and I actually kissed,' she said, eventually. 'It's kind of part of the definition. But yes, we had something. It could have been more, maybe.'

'Life got in the way,' Trent said.

'It has a way of doing that.'

Trent felt a lump in his throat. Zoe's words were a validation. Several times over the years, he had questioned whether he had made the whole thing up, that their relationship had been anything more than business. It was scary how, under analysis, anything could be up for grabs. Things that seemed so clear at the time could melt away beneath the microscope.

He looked up at the sky. It was late afternoon by then, around about the time Trent would have been finishing his interview had the day gone as planned. The cloud was low and constant, bathing everything orange. He felt lighter than he had done in years. The obsession he'd been harbouring had been based on something. That made it more acceptable.

'You know that whatever we had then was transactional, right?' Zoe added, as though reading aloud the small print at the bottom of a contract. 'We were using each other.'

'I know,' Trent said. 'And I regret it. I think about it every day, what we could have had together.'

Zoe scoffed at that. 'What is it with men and their "What ifs"? A girl smiles at you, and you fantasise about her for the next twenty years!'

'Sometimes the unknown is better than the reality.'

'You're going to tell me now that you haven't had other relationships?'

Trent smiled thinly. 'I never found much space for them.'

Zoe looked away. 'It was the life you chose, Trent Argent. And if you expect me to feel sorry for you about it, you're in for a long wait.'

Trent couldn't argue with that. He could, perhaps, have nitpicked about whether he chose that life or if others imposed it on him: his parents, his upbringing, or society's need to put everyone into boxes defined by their jobs. He thought it unlikely that this would have much sway on Zoe. They had already come so far over the course of a short flight.

'What about you?' he said. 'You've had other relationships?'

'Of course!' Zoe laughed. 'All dysfunctional in their own special way.'

She stubbed out her cigarette. She had smoked it intensely, like someone gulping down water after days of traversing the desert.

'Come on, let's go,' she said.

Although they had to wait a while for the next train, Trent's first trip on the Paris underground went smoothly. This was somewhat surprising after the briefing Zoe gave him:

'Make sure your bags are zipped up. Consider anything in an unzipped pocket as stolen. Don't check your phone when the doors are open. Someone can swipe it and be off before you know it. And whatever you do, never make eye contact with anyone.'

Quite like London, then.

A torrent of air greeted them as they emerged onto the streets of Paris. Zoe lit up again, repeating, 'When in Paris...'

A few steps later, Trent stood in some dog muck.

Zoe smiled as he tried to scrape it off on the curb. 'Yes, Paris does have a dogpat problem.'

They cackled like two drunk people sharing a private joke. Back in Ramstead, loads of people would have been in on it. "Dogpat" was the term used there to avoid offending delicate sensibilities.

'It seems so small now, Ramstead,' Zoe said. 'It used to be my life. Just think, I spent my childhood in a little dot on the map that no one's heard of.'

'It always did seem small,' Trent said. 'But maybe even more so now. I wonder how big it would be compared with Paris.'

'The size of a park, probably. Or my street. Speaking of, it's just down there. Come on.'

The Paris boulevards were wide, but the buildings were tall. Apartment building after apartment building was stitched together almost seamlessly, all different styles, new and old. If Trent had more time, he would have spent a few moments taking them in. He hadn't been to Paris before, had never had reason to do so. Now that he was there, he felt bombarded by the history of a city that felt both worn-out and vibrant.

'You know, I've been thinking about what you told me earlier,' Zoe said as they walked. 'Your gambling addiction and your revelation. Have you ever considered that you might have had a breakdown? It made you a different person.'

Trent was taken aback by the straightforward way she suggested this. 'I didn't come here for psychoanalysis.'

'Well, I didn't check in this morning intending to meet you. Hear me out. Having a breakdown isn't like losing the plot and running around naked, gibbering. It's more subtle.

It's having realisations that shake you to the core. They make you unable to continue operating in the way you once did. Does that feel more like it?'

'I didn't have a breakdown,' Trent said. He was too strong for that.

'It can happen to anyone,' Zoe persisted. 'Especially those of us who've gone through our lives convinced we've got it all worked out. Trent Argent has always been the best. He's always been one step ahead of everyone else. He's never let anyone get to him. What happens when that proves untrue? You start questioning it, and the whole house of cards comes tumbling down.'

Trent almost stepped on another dog turd. He swerved just in time to avoid it.

'I don't like "breakdown",' he said. 'I prefer "midlife crisis".'

'Midlife crisis sounds so mundane! It screams of adultery or buying flash cars.'

'I used to have a flash car. The leather seats were too slippery, and the annual service cost a fortune.'

'Well, there you go, then!' Zoe stopped outside a blue door with an elaborate metal grill over the window. 'This is it. Are you ready?'

Zoe's apartment was on the fourth floor. The elevator was occupied by someone trying to fit a wardrobe into it, so they climbed the well-worn stone stairs spiralling upwards around the lift shaft. Their motion activated the lighting as they ascended, and natural light came in from the small windows that looked out on the building's courtyard.

Trent wasn't convinced he had scraped all the dog muck off his shoes, so he left them beside the welcome mat on the doorstep. Not that Zoe's place was the cleanest he'd ever seen. A thin layer of dust covered the floor. It was heavier towards the corners, where activity had kicked it aside. Other than that, the first thing he noticed was how frugal it appeared. The famous sofa, which would be his comfort for the night, sat opposite the front door. It was tiny, with wooden arms, and looked like it would give him backache if he sat on it for more than twenty minutes. Beside it was a desk and an office chair covered with coats. There wasn't space for much other furniture. This room contained a small kitchen, too, with a buzzing fridge-freezer, microwave, and a two-ring stove. There was one window and one other door, which Trent presumed led to the bedroom.

The place screamed student accommodation. But it was probably all she could afford in the centre of Paris.

'Let me get us something to eat,' Zoe said, taking off her bag and throwing it onto the desk. 'There's fresh water in the tap if you want some.'

Trent realised that he had barely eaten all day. An over-priced packet of crisps on the plane, that was it. It was well past the hour that British people consider to be dinner time and into the period when the French would typically sit down for an *apéritive*.

Five minutes later, Zoe had finished rustling up two plates of cheese on toast. Trent smiled to himself. You can take the girl out of England, but you can't take the England out of the girl. He rinsed a couple of glasses and filled them with water.

That was their dinner.

When they finished, Zoe chucked the plates in the sink

and announced that she wanted an early night. Trent felt the same way. It had been a physically and emotionally intense day, and the more rest he could get before his interview the next morning, the better.

He looked at the sofa and considered his strategies. How could he manoeuvre himself into a position vaguely comfortable for sleeping? Should he fold himself up between its arms and risk cutting off the blood circulation to his legs, or try to position his backpack so he could use it as a footrest? Neither option seemed particularly appealing.

Zoe disappeared into her bedroom but returned a few minutes later.

'Are you seriously going to try sleeping on that?' she said.

Trent blinked. 'I thought that was the idea.'

'For a man who built his career off manipulating others, you can be surprisingly thick sometimes.'

And she returned to the bedroom, leaving the door ajar.

Trent regarded the sofa for a few moments. He remembered his visit to Serena's place, when he had stared at himself in the bathroom mirror and thought of Zoe. There he was in Zoe's apartment, and it was almost unimaginable. What a day it had been! It had started with her slapping him, and now he was in her front room with an open invitation to venture further.

He didn't wait long.

Zoe's bedroom was just as small as the rest of the apartment. Her wardrobe comprised a couple of metal frames, and a double bed took up most of the space.

'It's one of the few luxuries I afford myself,' Zoe said. She was sitting on its edge. 'If you don't get a good night's sleep, what do you have?'

Trent was inclined to agree with her. After all, he had

spent several weeks sleeping on the ground and didn't feel better for it. He sat next to her. Perhaps it would have been polite to comment on how comfortable the bed felt, but they were well beyond that.

Then, the undressing began. Zoe made the first move, unbuttoning his shirt. He looked down at his exposed torso, just as unimpressive as ever.

'You know when I said you look terrible?' Zoe said. 'It's not entirely true. You look like the world's roughed you up a bit, but it suits you. It's more genuine. I like it.'

Then, it was his turn. He slipped her jacket off her shoulders and reached down to lift her top. She raised her arms to help him, and it soon fell to the floor.

Although the Zoe that Trent had met that day was older in spirit than he remembered, she had the body of a young woman. Her skin looked soft, and her breasts were pert, nestled in her brassiere. Something surprised him, though.

'That's a few tattoos you've got there,' he said.

Zoe glanced down at herself. Her chest and arms bore several delicately drawn images of birds, butterflies and leaves. 'You didn't expect it?'

'You keep them well hidden.'

'I've got to think of my career. Besides, they're not for show; they're for me. They're my way of putting things behind me.'

Trent's brow furrowed. Marking your skin permanently, how could that do anything other than ensure you carry your scars wherever you go?

'It's a bit like the new year,' Zoe explained. 'People hang onto it as a way of starting with a fresh slate after an awful year. I don't wait for 31st December – I force the issue. I get my tattoo to tell myself something's over. The pain's a release. I'm moving on.'

Trent still didn't understand, but he decided not to question further. The fact was that this woman he had been thinking about for five years was opening up to him. He touched the tattoo on her arm. Somehow, this made their first contact less intense than it might have been. It wasn't about the physicality; he was examining a piece of art.

The image was of a bird escaping a cage, drawn in fine lines. The little thing seemed to have a broken leg, but its wings were spread majestically as it launched itself from the open door of its prison.

'What did the world do to you?' he said.

'That's the one I got to say goodbye to Ramstead.'

Trent examined it silently.

'And this one,' Zoe said, pointing to a flower blooming in her wrist, 'this was when I left Tralford. I felt like I had my whole life ahead of me then. That it was finally taking off.'

Trent moved his fingers to touch that one, too. Then – he didn't know what overcame him – he kissed it tenderly.

'And I got the one on my back to say goodbye to Covid,' Zoe said.

Trent leaned over to look at it. In between her shoulder blades, in glorious yellow, the sun was emerging from a cloud. Trent wanted to tell her he knew exactly where she was coming from. Their release from Covid restrictions had been like hope had been granted for a new life. For him, it had not lasted long.

He kissed her on the shoulder.

'This one's for an awful boss I had. I got it when he was sacked.' Zoe pointed to a tattoo on one side of her chest. 'And this one's a health condition I won't bore you with.'

Trent didn't look closely at these images before he kissed them.

'And this one...' Zoe pointed to a tattoo above her left breast. It was a wildflower tangled in a vine. 'This one was to say goodbye to you.'

Their faces were close as Trent regarded that one. Their quivering breaths mingled. The flower – a dandelion, perhaps – was in full bloom, and a strand of ivy was twisted around it. There were no colours, but the textures had been brought out carefully. There were a thousand things that tattoo could mean. All that mattered was what it meant to her.

Trent looked up into her eyes, which were softer than before. There was a light in them that had been missing.

Zoe held his gaze. 'I'm not getting another.'

'You won't need to.'

They didn't talk after that; they just experienced each other. Trent's brain – which had been driving him for decades, analysing, plotting, charting out his every move and weighing up the consequences – fell silent, stifled by those parts of him that had lay submerged for so long.

Their first kiss was a revelation, the tenderness of her lips, the way their mouths closed around each other. There was a faint taste of her smoking habit, but he didn't let it put him off.

They raced to remove the rest of their clothes, kissing as they did so. It made the job ten times harder, but they were drawn to each other by an invisible force. After all those years apart, they could no longer bear the distance.

They fell back on the bed. Trent's body moved by itself. He found this unsettling at first, but the spell did not break. Their bodies moved together, directed wholly by nature, without thought, without doubt. For a few moments, they became one.

As they lay together in the aftermath, with bedsheets tangled and flesh glistening, Trent kept his skin pressed against hers. He would not let her go. Not this time.

'So,' Zoe said, 'is the reality better than the unknown?'

Trent rolled over and kissed the side of her neck. 'I'll never have to wonder.'

～

The following morning, Trent felt like every muscle in his body had relaxed. He hadn't realised that they had all been tugging away, 24 hours a day, for every day of his life until then, never giving up, never relenting. Most of the effort had been futile. He only recognised this as they rested that morning.

Another realisation struck him, too. His time with Serena had made him question why he had never entertained relationships with women. He had been considering this on and off before then, too, ever since the well-oiled machine of his life had broken down. He used to tell himself that he never had time for a relationship, but he realised that this was only partially true. The truth was, he had never met someone he'd considered his equal. Was that arrogance or something deeper-rooted? He thought back to his childhood and how his mother had drilled into him, from early infancy, that he was different and would change the world. An unrealistic aspiration, perhaps, but one that had come to ingrain every fibre of his being. It had been a lonely life. Even after he rejected her grand plans for him and decided to forge his own path, he had still been looking for a perfect woman.

His revelation in Zoe's bedroom was that he'd been

looking for the wrong thing. There was no such thing as the perfect woman. And even if there were, that wasn't what he needed. He was a flawed, selfish, shallow man; the perfect woman for him must have her flaws, too. As he looked around that mess of an apartment – the clothes strewn over chairs, the ashtray on the windowsill – he realised he had found her. He'd used her, and she'd used him, but that just confirmed it. Zoe was the perfect woman for him.

Zoe was taking a shower through all this. She emerged, wearing just her underwear. No shyness, no self-conscious-ness. There was nothing between them anymore.

'Can we see each other again?' Trent said. The words slipped from his lips like a hidden thought.

Zoe studied him for a few seconds. He couldn't read what was going on behind her eyes. Then, she looked away. 'I don't think so. I like the new you, I really do, but I've got to protect myself.'

A part of Trent felt like he should object. If he truly wanted Zoe, the least he could do was put up a fight. He should be arguing against this! But he kept silent. This was how it needed to play out; he had known this all along.

She picked up her jeans, slipped them on, and went about her morning routine. He was just a spectator.

'There's probably something in the fridge that's in date,' she said. 'If you pull the front door closed on your way out, it'll lock. Good luck with the interview.'

She picked up her make-up bag and returned to the bathroom. A few minutes later, with her day self ready, she grabbed her keys and handbag and put on her coat. Trent said nothing. He didn't move. He just lay propped up in bed, watching, taking it all in. He didn't dare to think, either, lest his thoughts crowd out the experience and he miss something.

'I'm glad we did that,' Zoe said before she left. 'I was always curious about what it might have been like.'

Only once the door had closed did he allow himself to lie flat. He gazed up at the ceiling.

You've seen it now, he thought to himself. *Touched it, tasted it, lived it. Let's see if that lasts you another five years.*

STEP 5 – FOLLOW YOUR PATH

CHAPTER 12
A NEW BEGINNING

'So, this is it,' Hobbs said.

'I think so,' Trent said. He scanned the area his tent had occupied the past few months to check he hadn't missed anything.

'If we find anything, I'll let you know.'

Hobbs said this because it seemed the right thing to say, but he knew it was unlikely. Each of them had so few possessions that it was nigh-on impossible to leave something behind.

There was another freed-up spot on the campsite. Bong had moved on the week before, renting an apartment in town. He had found success sooner than the others, and his new job was going well. Life in social media moves faster than real life.

Hobbs seemed to be spending all his time lately saying goodbye to friends. He didn't like it. Okay, so Bong was just downtown, but none of them had heard from him since. Trent would have even more of an excuse to fall off the radar in Paris.

Hobbs' new family was dissolving. He supposed that was the way with families as they moved out into the world, but with ties of blood, those bonds endure. Hobbs was beginning to doubt his campmates would bother keeping in touch.

Hobbs moved in and hugged Trent. He was careful about it. Trent had recovered from his injuries at the hand of Fredevich's thugs, but he still had a perpetual air of fragility about him. Hobbs worried that if he squeezed Trent too hard, he might break him.

Trent returned a look that read, "You didn't tell me you were a hugger."

'I wish you the best,' he said.

'You, too.'

Then, it was Amara's turn to bid Trent farewell. Following Hobbs' example, they hugged, too, but it was stilted. Neither of them felt entirely comfortable.

'Was I wrong about you?' Amara said.

'That depends,' Trent said. 'What did you think about me?'

'Oh, it's too late for that now.'

'Then I guess we'll never know.'

Amara brushed a strand of her sleek black hair from her face. 'Good luck with everything.'

'You, too.'

And that was it. Trent slung his bag and rolled-up tent onto his back and scrambled up the slope to the metal stairs that lead to the Pont Butin. Hobbs and Amara watched him from a now very sparse-looking campsite.

Hobbs wondered how long it would be before Amara left, too. She appeared to be well-established in her reporting internship role; it was only a matter of time before they offered her something.

He sat down on a tree stump and tended to the stove. The water had already started boiling. Since Bong left, they had been going through fewer matches getting it lit, and Hobbs now had a teabag just to himself, not shared between three. Amara always took coffee.

'And then there were two,' he said.

Trent paused at the top of the steps and looked through the branches to the campsite.

He had never thought it possible, but he would miss living there. Not the hard floor and lack of facilities; not that. And not the birds, either. Trent had never been a huge fan of nature but hadn't actively disliked it before moving to Geneva. He existed, and nature existed, generally in different worlds; they could get on like that. It was a different story when birdsong woke him at the crack of dawn. Some people found it pretty – relaxing even – but Trent knew that beneath the surface, it was just birds bigging themselves up and looking for sex. Was that their contribution to the world, in all honesty?

He would miss the dawns he was obliged to experience, though. After a time, he had come to appreciate the freshness of the air, the stillness, the lack of traffic crossing the bridge above. This was how humankind was supposed to live, experiencing the day from dawn to dusk, not tucked away in artificially darkened rooms with artificially comfortable beds.

He was looking forward to having a proper bed, though.

His phone pinged. He fished it out of his pocket quickly. Every day since he'd left Zoe's apartment, he had checked his phone feverishly, hoping beyond hope that she'd had a change of heart and wanted to see him again.

It was a message from his mobile provider informing him about their roaming fees.

Trent trudged towards the bus stop. He hadn't acquired any new possessions in Geneva, but his backpack felt heavier than before.

He tried to cheer himself up by thinking back to his interview with the John R. Percival Foundation. It had taken place the morning after his voyage with Zoe and had gone staggeringly well. Whether due to fatigue, heartache, or the fact that he had been doing far too many interviews lately, Trent had approached it differently. He hadn't tried. He had just gone through the motions. This must have been interpreted by the interview panel as quiet confidence.

By this point, Trent had been well-versed in being interviewed. He knew how to respond to all the standard questions: priority management, getting up to speed quickly, and managing difficult situations. He'd answered them efficiently, waiting for the big questions that would follow, those whose aim was to get beneath his skin and pick him apart. Trent had been philosophical about it. There was no accounting for what they would make of his personality. It was the one thing he had learned not to take personally.

Those questions never came. Instead:

'You advertise yourself as a community troubleshooter. That's exactly what we need. We have trouble in our little community. Will you shoot it for us?'

Trent had maintained a poker face. The title of his last job in the UK was something people tended to latch onto, and he had grown to accept it. He couldn't blame them for raising it: it was, empirically, the most interesting thing about him. Behind his neutral exterior, he'd battled the urge to tell them those days were behind him.

'Absolutely,' he'd said.

∾

Two days later, Trent was sitting in the office of Charles Bingham, president of the John R. Percival Foundation. It was a plushly-furnished affair, but the awful art on the wall caught Trent's eyes the most. He wasn't sure if he preferred the idea of them having been painted by Charles or a professional artist. If it was Charles, this man must have been deluded to want to advertise such output. It was all weird angles and bungled perspectives. Then again, if he'd paid good money for them, it was just as damning an indictment on his judgement as it was on the world of art.

Trent already had reason to question this man's judgement. After all, he had hired him after the most spurious of interviews, after all.

'Thank you for making yourself available so quickly,' Charles said.

He was a sharply dressed man with a fine head of grey hair that would be the envy of anyone in their sixties. However, his suit interested Trent the most: its crisp-cut edges, gold buttons and seamless seams. Back in the day, he would have asked for the tailor's name.

'It was my pleasure,' Trent said. It sounded better than, "Thank you, I desperately needed the money."

'Tell me, what do you know about the John R. Percival Foundation?'

Trent had done his research, of course. 'Staff of forty-five, making grants to nonprofits around the globe working in the fields of climate change, women's rights and disarmament. It manages the estate of the American businessman John R. Percival and distributes around two hundred million dollars a year. It's regarded as one of the top foundations operating out of Paris, where he retired with his French wife.'

'So far, so Wikipedia. Tell me, were you able to discover anything more insightful about us?'

There, Trent struggled. The little information he had found was based on various philanthropy resources – a few lines and some statistics, nothing more. The foundation didn't even have a website.

After watching him flounder, Charles said, 'Don't worry, Mr Argent, your ignorance is a comfort to me. That's how we intend it. This foundation operates below the radar. We're not interested in having a high public profile with all the scrutiny involved. Perhaps the most significant thing you need to know about us is that we adhere closely to our founder's values.'

'John Percival,' Trent said. It was a mistake.

'John Percival was a scoundrel and a thief,' Charles puffed. 'We don't talk about him here. But his son, John R. Percival, was one of the foremost businessmen of the nineteenth century. He was as assiduous about his business as his assets. It's a shame that trait has been diluted with each subsequent generation, but he had the foresight to prepare for this by establishing the foundation and laying down strict ground rules for its operation.'

'Is that the matter you need my assistance with?'

Charles ignored the question. 'The president is recruited for his adherence to these values. I made my name in the investment arm. Our strategy is ruthless. We aim to maximise profits through aggressive investment.'

'In keeping with the foundation's philanthropic objectives, I assume?'

Charles appeared taken aback by this question. 'Elucidate.'

'Well, the foundation supports nonprofits working to reduce the impact of climate change or to campaign governments to reduce their military arsenals. I assume that it's not at the same time investing in fossil fuels or the arms trade?'

Trent chuckled as he said this, hoping it would make his question less pointed.

Charles breathed in deeply through his regal nostrils. Then he breathed out equally slowly. Then, he placed his hands on his desk, knotting his fingers together firmly.

'We don't give out information on our investments.'

Their gazes met. Trent had no desire to get into this battle. He wanted to be sure he was working for the good guys, but at this point, his situation was desperate enough that a bit of strategic ignorance was justifiable. He looked away.

With his authority confirmed, Charles turned to a different matter. 'I'd like to discuss your brief here. Let me start by showing you this.'

Charles took a piece of paper from his top drawer and pushed it across the desk to Trent. On it were various line charts. The scale had so many zeroes that they were abbreviated.

'This represents our budget actuals versus targets over the past twenty-four months,' Charles said. 'As you can see, we have lagged behind targets in funds distributed by more than twenty-five per cent.'

It took Trent a moment to adjust to the idea of a target

being to give money away rather than earn it. Truly, he was in a different world now.

'Staff morale is in the doldrums,' Charles continued. 'Worse still, productivity is at an all-time low!'

'Do you have any idea what the issue is?' Trent said.

'None at all! We've asked the staff repeatedly, but they never give us any sensible answers.'

Trent pondered this. 'What answers do you get?'

'Well, they go on about bureaucracy and paperwork.' Charles brushed the back of his hand across his desk as though clearing it of a troublesome cat. 'Inequality and all that. I need you to get to the bottom of what the real problem is. I want you to interview staff and get to know these people. You will report directly to me.'

Trent realised that, whether he liked it or not, the discussion was drawing to a close. One trick he had learned to exude an air of competence was to make sure it was always him that ended a conversation. Only the powerless got dismissed.

He stood. 'Mr Bingham, I want to thank you for your time today. You can leave this to me. I realise that some of my questions have been direct, but it's important to be honest and frank with each other in these matters. Wouldn't you agree?'

'I couldn't agree more,' Charles said. 'Go get 'em!'

The door was ajar, but Hobbs rang the bell anyway. He didn't know who had buzzed him in downstairs. With the traffic noise behind him and the tinniness of speakers, he hadn't even been able to work out if the voice over the intercom was male or female. There was no name beside the buzzer, so he hoped he'd pressed the right button.

Bong's new apartment was in Eaux-Vives, a trendy part of town where many expats lived, which was troubled by household burglaries (many had conjectured that these facts might be connected).

A blonde woman opened the door. She must have been in her twenties, but she looked rough. Her face was smudged with the remnants of the previous night's makeup. She was wearing a leather jacket and carrying her handbag.

'I'll see you later at Apathy,' she called back into the apartment.

'Sure.' It was Bong's voice.

Hobbs knew exactly what they were talking about. Geneva's principal nightclubs were called Apathy, Inui and Pathos. They were all owned by the same person, who presumably thought those words sounded exotic. Geneva's nightlife was a thing of legend.

The woman stepped past Hobbs, leaving the door wide for him to enter. Hobbs peered in, but he couldn't see his friend. He entered, closing the door behind him.

Bong had rented his apartment fully furnished. The unpacking mustn't have taken long, given that he had few possessions, so it already looked well lived in. The front room was spacious enough, with a parquet floor and sand-paper walls painted white, as was the custom in Geneva. There was a dining table in one corner, cluttered with empty bottles and various paraphernalia, which Hobbs didn't investigate too closely. A man was lying on the sofa. It was small, and the cushions were worn flat, but he was sound asleep.

The toilet flushed. Hobbs waited patiently for Bong to emerge, but the door remained closed.

'Bong?' he called.

Hobbs looked around the rest of the place. A small window opened onto the street, affording an excellent view of the yoga studio in the building opposite, which he imagined provided Bong with entertainment if he couldn't find anything to watch on Netflix. The widescreen television was covered with clothing: a T-shirt, a jacket, and was that a bra? A pinball machine stood in the other corner. In the time that Hobbs had known Bong, he had never once heard him express any interest in pinball. Hobbs assumed he had bought it simply because it was essential gear in the pad of any aspiring bachelor.

He detected a faint smell of marijuana.

The toilet flushed again. Still, no Bong. Hobbs called his name again but received no response.

He sat on one of the dining room chairs. He didn't dare venture further into the apartment. He wondered if he should leave.

Eventually, Bong came out of the bedroom, closing the door behind him carefully. His eyes were wild, but Hobbs didn't read anything into this at first. It was an expression he'd seen often on his friend's face during the months they'd lived together. Some people are not designed to fend for themselves.

'Hobbs?' Bong said. He sounded surprised.

'You asked me to come,' Hobbs replied.

'Yes, yes,' Bong said. 'Thank you.'

He walked over to the kitchen and rinsed a couple of pint-sized glasses. Hobbs watched him but said nothing. Once they were vaguely clean, Bong filled the glasses with water and handed one to Hobbs.

This guy truly had all the mod cons. Fresh water on tap! After months of living on a campsite, this was a luxury.

The toilet flushed again.

'I can't believe it's only been two weeks,' Bong said. 'It feels like ages.'

'A lot can happen in a couple of weeks,' Hobbs replied. 'Trent's left, you know?'

'Yeah, he messaged me. His job in Paris worked out, then?'

'Apparently. Some people have all the luck.' Hobbs pushed aside an ashtray and put down his pint of water. 'Why did you invite me here, Bong?'

Bong shrugged. 'I wanted you to see the place. I've really made it, haven't I?'

'Like I said, some people have all the luck.'

'It doesn't feel lucky.'

'I'm sorry, I didn't mean to imply you haven't worked for it,' Hobbs said carefully. 'Those Instagram posts must take planning. And I assume your new employer works you hard?'

Bong slumped on one of the other dining room chairs. 'They fly me everywhere. It's exhausting. Who would have thought saving the climate would involve so much international flight? And we barely see the countries when we get there. We're straight from the airport to the hotel, to the meeting room, and then back to the airport.'

'Sounds terrible,' Hobbs said.

'The worst is the bit in between, when I'm here. People are always onto me, wanting to come around or go out. I don't have time to think.'

Hobbs had never regarded Bong as one of life's big thinkers, but he cold understand where he was coming from. Some people thrive on nonstop activity. Bong, evidently, did not.

The toilet flushed again. This time, someone came out: a man in his forties with greasy black hair and a Guns'n'Roses T-shirt.

'You've got a problem with your toilet,' he said.

'Thanks, man,' Bong replied.

The man grabbed his coat from on top of the television and let himself out of the front door. Hobbs' gaze returned to Bong.

'Bong, who *are* these people?'

Bong wiped his hand across his nose. 'You'd be surprised how much your social life takes off after you stop sleeping under a bridge.'

'You astound me.'

'I can't trust any of them, though. I need you.'

Hobbs paused at that one. He hadn't seen it coming. His friend was living the high life, and Hobbs was still homeless. Who needed who?

'What do you mean?' he said.

'I can feel things getting out of hand. Everything moves too fast. Back in Finland, my schoolteachers used to say I needed a compass. I'd latch onto the wrong people, you know? I think I've done that again. I need you. You're my compass.'

Hobbs regarded his friend with pity. Bong had got everything he wanted, but it had brought him a fresh set of problems.

'We can fit a sofa-bed in here,' Bong suggested.

'What about all these other people?' Hobbs gestured towards the guy still sleeping on the sofa.

'We kick them out.'

Hobbs stood. On the face of it, Bong's offer was a blessing. Hobbs badly needed to get off that campsite before winter arrived, and it was already October. Sharing an apartment with his friend couldn't be a bad thing, could it? They already knew each other's eccentricities.

So, why did this feel like a failure? This was Bong's path, not Hobbs'. He hadn't gone to Geneva to live off someone else's coattails. He could imagine the months ahead, with him stuck in that room searching for employment whilst somehow trying to act as an anchor for Bong and his various schemes. He couldn't be Bong's plus one – the one who stayed home and made sure the fridge was stocked and dinner was on the table.

It would have been the easy option, but it was not Hobbs' path. It wasn't that he didn't want to help Bong – the idea of being someone's "compass" was quite flattering, actually – but he had to look out for himself. He had quit his internship with the International Refugee Agency to care for Trent, and look where that had got him. It was hardly as though Bong had made his offer when he'd moved out of the campsite, either. It had taken him getting in over his head before that happened.

Why should Hobbs be the only one to put others first?

'I'll think about it,' he said.

He left Bong slumped there as he let himself out.

Trent had considered calling an all-staff meeting, but that would have put people on edge. Nobody wants to put themselves on the line in front of others. The best way to get to the truth was to earn their trust, one by one.

He started with those who scored the foundation the lowest on the recent staff survey (advertised as anonymous, but it had been anything but). He hadn't booked to see them together, but three arrived at the same time, announcing themselves as the foundation's "Unofficial Staff Council".

They assembled in Trent's office like a collection of lesser-known supervillains, each distrustful of the other and wrapped up in their own worlds. Trent checked his notes. There was Christoph from IT, who had been with the foundation for eleven years and whose primary achievement, reportedly, was updating everyone's computers to the latest version of Windows. He looked to be in his early forties, although his hairline added a decade to his age. His scalp was a battlefield. According to management's account of him, it had seen more action than the grey matter beneath. They accused him of not being able to organise a piss-up in a server room. His response (that this was only because they had moved to the cloud) had fallen on deaf ears.

Then, there was Henri, a project manager. He and Christoph had been working together on a modernisation project, the details of which remained sketchy. Henri was a wisp of a man who looked like a heavy wind would have knocked him over. He was clearly a worrier; it had seeped into his bones, distorting his facial structure into an expression of permanent concern.

The third was Wilma, a receptionist who appeared to be of African origin. Now, there was someone who kept her thoughts to herself. She spoke flatly, without moving her lips, rarely betraying a hint of her feelings.

'We wanted to welcome the John R. Percival Foundation's latest Happiness Officer,' Wilma said as they sat.

Trent fought back the tears of emotion at such a warm welcome. He found it interesting that they had used the word "latest", but this was not the time to investigate.

'It's good to be here,' he said. 'You mentioned you're the "Unofficial Staff Council". What happened to the official one?'

'It doesn't exist. The president doesn't support the idea of a staff council. He sees it as undermining his authority. The higher-ups think we're planning to rise up and take over the foundation's assets. We're just here to listen to people.'

Trent doubted that Wilma was one of the world's great listeners. Certainly not if sympathetic body language was a precondition.

'And what are people telling you?'

'Ah, no,' Wilma said, 'we won't give that one up that easily.'

Trent tapped a pen on his desk. 'What's the point of being a staff council if you don't communicate what you hear?'

'The point, Mr Argent, is to protect people.'

'Protect them from what?'

'If you haven't worked that out yet, you'll fit in very well here, Mr Argent.'

Trent glanced across to Christoph and Henri, who so far had been silent. He didn't get a sense that there was anything in particular they wanted to say, although he felt confident he would be able to extract something from them if he could get them to open up.

'It's my second day here. I'm very much on the learning curve.' Trent rustled his papers. 'Let's start with what you each do here. Christoph, I understand you're working on a long-term IT project?'

Christoph was sitting on his hands for some reason. 'It

shouldn't be long-term. I've been trying to implement a new grant database. They tell me that the foundation needs to move with the times. It needs to embrace the new technology. And yet, whenever I propose something, they regard it with fear.'

'Change isn't easy,' Trent said.

'Then why ask for it? It's exhausting banging your head up against a brick wall. I tell you, this project has aged me ten years.'

Henri chuckled at that. 'That's because you've been working on it for ten years!'

It was well known that things moved slowly in the world of philanthropy. Whole generations of children were named after various modernisation projects, with middle names like "Intranet", "Database", and "Equality and Diversity".

'I understand you've been working on a long-term project, too, Henri?' Trent said.

Henri crossed his arms. 'I've been tasked with re-evaluating our relationship with grantees. Partnership, that's the new buzzword.'

'I've heard that one before,' Trent said understandingly.

'What no one seems to get is that there's an innate power imbalance. If you give people money, they're beholden to you. They'll do whatever you say. Say whatever they think you want to hear.'

'That's not always been my experience.'

'Okay, and how did that work out? If they don't sign the contract, they don't get the money. If they don't respond adequately to requests, they're a bad partner. After a while, they come to expect certain demands. They try to stay one step ahead. Then, you don't need to ask for anything. They just assume.'

'That's true,' Trent mused. 'And it means you need to keep one step ahead of them.'

Henri frowned. 'One step ahead of them being one step ahead of us?'

'Exactly. Two steps ahead of ourselves. When we have time, I'll share with you some of my experiences in the UK. You might find them illustrative.'

Trent could feel himself relaxing. He felt at home doing this. It was almost as if the previous five years hadn't happened. He knew this game. Yes, the look of the pieces may have changed – maybe it was *Star Wars* chess, or *Lord of the Rings*, to stretch the analogy, but it was still chess. He felt confident he would get to the bottom of whatever was happening there.

'I work reception,' Wilma said out of nowhere.

Trent didn't recall having asked her anything, but evidently, she was feeling left out. He turned his attention to her reluctantly. He had a strong suspicion it would be a waste to spend any length of time questioning her. She was a brick wall.

'An important role,' Trent said. 'Receptionists know everything about everyone. And if they don't want something to happen, it doesn't.'

Wilma appeared unfazed by the acknowledgement of her power. 'Do you speak from personal experience, Mr Argent?'

'I'm sure we've all had the experience of getting on the wrong side of reception,' Trent said, winking to Henri and Christoph, who looked rueful. 'But let's discuss that another time. Right now, I need your help. I'm sure you know the remit of my role. Something's going wrong in this organisation. Can any of you tell me what the problem is here exactly?'

The three of them glanced at each other. Henri and Christoph appeared beholden to Wilma, but they would have to wait a long time for any direction from her. Wilma gripped her handbag on her lap as though concerned Trent might try to snatch it from her.

Eventually, she took pity on him and tossed a few breadcrumbs, as one might do to a persistent duck.

'You assume there is just one problem here,' she said. 'Okay, if you want to play it that way, let me give you a hint. Our president probably indicated to you that this foundation adheres closely to its founder's values. That's probably the most relevant thing he said. I suggest you take a closer look into the life of our dear John R. Percival.'

CHAPTER 13
IN PURSUIT OF HAPPINESS

'I warned you about them,' Amara said.

'Yes, you were right,' Trent replied. He knew that simple statement would please her.

Amara had indeed uttered words of caution when Trent had accepted the job. She'd told him that the John R. Percival Foundation had a questionable reputation. Trent had brushed this aside, pointing out that this was probably why they needed a Happiness Officer. At the time, he hadn't fully appreciated the truth of this statement.

The exchange stuck with him, though, so he'd called Amara shortly after meeting with Christoph, Henri and Wilma. She'd sounded decidedly smug about him asking for her help and was even more so now, calling back to tell him what she'd uncovered.

'Let's just savour this moment,' Amara said, 'I'd also like to mention how I love it that you think we reporters have access to secret information beyond the reach of common people. It's called the *internet*, Trent.'

'I appreciate your research skills,' Trent said patiently. 'What did you find?'

'Well, you're in with a great bunch there, Trent. All slick and high powered on the outside, but with so many skeletons in their closet, they've had to upgrade at Ikea.'

'The same could be said of most politicians.'

'John R. Percival wasn't a politician. He was a businessman. A product of his time, if you're feeling charitable; a highly unpleasant individual if you're not. Either way, the term "of his time" is pertinent here.'

Trent tapped his fingers on his desk. Amara was stringing this out a bit.

'It wasn't easy to find out about him,' Amara said. 'It was almost as though someone had made a concerted effort to scrub all the nasty details off the internet. But you can never get rid of everything.'

'Tell me,' Trent said.

'Well, it turns out this guy made his fortune at the tail end of the American domestic slave trade. Then he turned oil baron. In his later years, he was a wily investor. Wars, they're always profitable, aren't they? He owned stakes in a rifle manufacturer in Poland, amongst others. In his personal life, he was suspected of beating his first wife to death before marrying a teenager.'

Trent coughed. 'He ticked all the boxes, didn't he?'

'Well, at least he avoided bigamy. Anyway, what did you say were the objectives of his foundation?'

'The environment, women's rights and disarmament.'

'He must have been trying to make amends. Of course, they had no idea about climate change then, but he'd have been able to see the impact. The smog; the destruction of landscapes; the extinction of whole species...'

'He doesn't sound like the sort of individual who would have a revelation like that.'

'It's a wonder what impending death can do to you.'

Trent could sense the truth in that. Most legacies were made as people faced their declining years, weighing up the probability of an afterlife and whether they wanted to spend it in heaven or hell. Only then did they consider what they wanted to leave behind.

'Thank you, Amara,' he said.

'You're welcome. Does it explain a few things?'

'Maybe.'

An awkward moment followed, in which neither knew what to say. Amara spoke first:

'Well, I guess I'd better get going. Hobbs wants me to help him prepare for an interview this evening.'

'Really?' Trent said. 'That's good news.'

'It's something like his forty-seventh. He's got to be doing something wrong in there.'

'I'm sure you'll get to the bottom of it.'

'I'll try,' Amara said. 'See you.'

Trent paused for a moment after they hung up. Something about Amara's voice felt off. Admittedly, this was Amara – specifically, Amara speaking to Trent – so her voice was hardly likely to be full of joy. Still, something wasn't right.

Then, his phone pinged, and he checked the messages. It wasn't Zoe.

Amara packed up her belongings inside her tent before she told Hobbs. It felt like she was quitting a live-in relationship: you get everything ready first so you can leave immediately after telling them. She'd used the same tactic when leaving her parents behind in India.

Now she thought back to it, that had been pretty heartless.

Anyway, Hobbs must have had his suspicions. Ever since Trent had left, he'd been making comments about their little group falling apart, hinting that it was only a matter of time. She doubted he'd been trying to soften the blow of his own plans to leave; no, it was her he was worried about. And with good reason.

'I've got to tell you something,' she said, deciding to rip it off like a plaster. 'I've had good news from work. They're going to put me on the payroll. The only catch is, I have to move to Zurich.'

Hobbs had just finished starting the fire. It was early evening, a couple of hours before Amara was due to catch her train. She should have booked an earlier train but had promised to help Hobbs with his interview preparation. She hadn't been about to let him down over that, too. With that out of the way, she had no more excuses to put off sharing her news with him.

'Congratulations,' Hobbs said. His voice was wooden.

'It's a terrific opportunity,' Amara said. If she kept saying so, it had to be true. 'They'll provide me with temporary accommodation while I'm looking for something. And they'll pay for me to learn German. So, all those French lessons were for nothing!'

'That's good.'

Amara handed Hobbs a tin of spaghetti to heat over the fire. She had no intention of sharing it with him. She would grab a sandwich at the station.

Hobbs set about opening it. His movements were jagged and uncoordinated. Amara wondered if she should offer to take over before he hurt himself, not that she was in a much better state.

Everything felt wrong. This opportunity was all she wanted, yet it didn't feel like it. She had moved to Geneva to escape being put in a box in India. Why did it feel like the only thing she had succeeded in doing was getting put in a box somewhere else? Hers would be a life of the 9 to 5 grind, forever aspiring to something more, to a title that promised something greater.

Amara knew she would look back at her time at the campsite as a moment of freedom. Her life there may have lacked the basic amenities, yet its possibilities had been endless. The attraction of not knowing what came next. Now, she could see her whole life planned out for her, as surely as it would have been had she accepted her family's traditions, strategic marriage, and all that entailed.

She got up and started to get her things from her tent.

'You're leaving *now*?' Hobbs said.

'I'm sorry,' Amara said, 'I wanted to tell you before. I just couldn't.'

'Why not?'

They looked into each other's eyes. Amara had always sensed something needy in Hobbs. She had tried not to let that put her off him, but it took effort. She felt sure that, if challenged about it, Hobbs would point out that what he needed was a job, but it was more than that. He needed a family.

There was something off-putting about someone needing you like that. She thought back to the various suitors she'd had in India, some sweet, some arrogant. The sweet ones had fallen first because she'd wanted her boyfriend to desire her, not need her.

She considered using the "It's not you, it's me" line, but that felt crass. She had witnessed Hobbs' world crumble around him in slow motion the past few weeks as his campmates had left one by one.

'I'm sorry,' she repeated.

And so it was with a heavy heart that Amara left the campsite for what she firmly believed would be the final time.

Of all the staff Trent had met so far, Henri seemed the most likely to help. Most were cagey – not to the extremes of Wilma, but it was still challenging to get much information out of them. A pall of fear hung over everyone. Trent hadn't yet delved deeply into the foundation's human resources principles, but he suspected a somewhat traditional approach (i.e. involving frequent use of the phrases "get back to work" and "you're replaceable").

It was pretty much in Henri's job description that he be open to outside ideas. He had been recruited specifically to help modernise the foundation's operations with respect to grantees. Trent only hoped he'd not been working there so long that he'd given up that fight.

He would only know for sure if he could get Henri alone, without Christoph and Wilma. So, he hung out by the water cooler until he came to fill his glass.

'How's it going?' Trent said, trying to sound casual.

'Not bad, not bad,' Henri said as the water poured. 'There's a big spread in this month's *Philanthropy Now* that looks quite relevant to us.'

'You'll be sharing it with Charles?'

'Probably.'

Trent sensed that his short window of opportunity was

coming to an end. Henri's glass had filled, and he didn't seem the type to hang around chatting.

'I found out the truth about our beloved founder,' Trent said.

Henri glanced from side to side. 'Keep your voice down!'

'Just five minutes of your time, that's all I ask.'

Henri's eyes grew distant. He appeared to be grappling with several things. Fear, certainly, but Trent also hoped for a reassessment of why he was there and what he hoped to achieve.

'Okay.' His voice was resigned.

They stepped into Trent's office. It was the only place where they could talk privately, as most of the staff worked in a sizeable open-planned area, and the meeting rooms were far from soundproof.

'What did you find out?' Henri whispered. Was he worried this place was bugged?

'Only confirmation that this foundation adheres closely to its founder's values.' Trent spoke softly, too. 'It's just that those values were somewhat questionable. As is where the money came from.'

'Well, that's a general issue with the sector. Something a lot of foundations are grappling with at the moment.'

'I have a feeling it's more pronounced here.'

Henri regarded Trent for a few moments. 'What do you want from me?'

Trent moved in close. 'You've been here for a little while now. You've seen the problems, and if I've read you right, you're someone who likes to think about solutions. I want to hear your ideas. They don't have to be big. Just one thing might help turn the tide.'

Henri swayed as though battling concussion. 'I'm not sure I can do this. I don't know you.'

'You don't need to know me. And you don't need to tell me anything. Just point me in the right direction.'

'Be careful what you ask for.'

'I'm here to make a difference, Henri. If they don't like it, I've got nothing to lose.'

Henri's eyes darted around Trent's office, no doubt searching for hidden cameras. Once satisfied that they weren't being watched, he said, 'Let's take a tour of the offices.'

'They gave me the tour on my first day,' Trent said without thinking. Upon realising that he had spoken rather too quickly, he added, 'But of course, I may have missed something.'

Henri smiled weakly. 'Yes, I think you probably did.'

The John R. Percival Foundation was based in the La Defense area of Paris – a bit out of town, but as with most major cities, most of Pais was "out of town". Its offices shared a skyscraper with banks, commodity traders, insurance brokers and various other financial institutions. The top floors offered a commanding view of France's capital, its sand-grey buildings and landmarks that were famous the world over. The foundation was quite a bit lower down, on the third floor.

This area had played host to a crucial battle in the siege of Paris, and it was now a bulwark of the city's economy. As far as Trent was concerned, it was the place to be. Just a few storeys higher up, maybe.

The foundation operated an open-plan hot-desking policy. Only the president, a few senior managers, and (somehow) Trent had been afforded the luxury of their own space. In the event, the concept of hot-desking was meaningless. There were fewer desks than employees, but the foundation's work-from-home policy had been quickly curtailed in the aftermath of COVID-19, so everyone had to be in the office. The poor unfortunate who'd lost the morning game of musical chairs had to work in the cafeteria.

But that wasn't the foundation's underlying issue.

The tour didn't take long. The open-plan area was surrounded by the offices of the "higher-ups" and a couple of meeting rooms, with the cafeteria tucked in one corner. A reception desk guarded the entrance, with Wilma on unblinking lookout.

They stopped outside one of the meeting rooms, and Henri instructed Trent to tell him what looked wrong in the open-plan area. Trent peered across the space, trying to pinpoint whatever Henri was referring to. Trent peered across the space, trying to pinpoint whatever Henri was referring to. All heads were down. Keyboards tapped constantly, emitting a gentle dystopian breeze. The sound-proof panels around each work cubicle were meaningless, as they were only high enough to reach people's shoulders as they sat.

'Do you see it?' Henri said.

Was it the lack of any form of collegiate conversation? Or the anonymity of the desks kept bare by hot-desking? Or the fact that their computer monitors appeared about ten years out of date?

'You're seeing, but you're not seeing,' Henri said. 'Forget about those things we program ourselves to look beyond. Just see.'

Trent cast aside his irritation about having apparently ended up in a *Matrix* movie. He did as Henri instructed, trying to take in every detail. There was Wilma at reception. Someone got up to go to the water cooler. The machine bubbled contentedly. And there was the janitor, returned from fetching the morning post. He began distributing it.

Trent studied everyone's faces. He tried to see, unblinkered. All those people were glued to their screens. Were they working hard, or was it the illusion of working? Certainly, it seemed as though they spent the majority of their lives there, and it had taken its toll. Their skin was pallid from a lack of sunlight.

His eyes narrowed. He understood the problem.

'You spoke with the staff?' Charles said. He wore a pristinely cut navy blue suit that day, but Trent didn't like it as much as the black one.

'I did,' Trent said.

'Christoph and Henri, our prime naysayers?'

The foundation's president looked pleased with himself for remembering their names. Trent couldn't imagine this was a good thing for them.

'It was very illuminating,' he said carefully.

'I'm sure it was. If I were you, I wouldn't read too much into whatever they told you. Those two have been here so long that they're part of the furniture, a part we need to send to the *déchetterie*, probably.'

Trent nodded as though he was considering Charles' words carefully. 'It seemed to me they were trying to move the foundation on.'

'That was your impression, was it?'

'And their job descriptions.'

'Ah,' Charles sighed. 'We're going to have another conversation like this, are we? Be careful, Mr Argent. Our

Happiness Officer is supposed to make everyone happy, including myself.'

Trent wondered if he would ever get a job whose title couldn't provide fodder for such comments.

'Have you ever considered doing a demographic audit of the foundation?' he said.

Charles stuck out his bottom lip. Now was his turn to pretend to be considering the other man's words. 'Sounds like an excuse for paperwork, if you ask me. An excuse to hire expensive consultants to tell us what we already know.'

'Which is?'

Charles looked away. 'That we need to move with the times.'

Why did he sound like a sulky child when he said that?

'Mr Bingham,' Trent said, 'have you ever considered this foundation might have a diversity problem?'

'"A diversity problem?"' Charles laughed mockingly.

'Nonsense! We've got plenty of women on the payroll. And blacks, too.'

'In the worse-paid jobs. Seriously, you can't tell me that having a black janitor or a woman working reception is the best you can do for diversity?'

'Our reception is the face of the organisation. It's the first thing most people see when they contact us.'

Then God help us all, Trent thought. *Having Wilma greet you would be enough to send anyone running.*

But that wasn't the problem Trent had been assigned to resolve. Not yet, anyway.

'I took a look at the organigram,' he said. 'All the senior management are white males. The non-Caucasian staff make up less than seven per cent of the total, and none of them are in positions of authority. Does that sound right to you?'

Charles knotted his fingers together on his desk. 'Are you asking me if your statistics seem accurate or if I agree with how we're structured?'

'Come now, you've got to admit that the optics don't look great.'

'I didn't hire you to tell me about optics,' Charles retorted. 'We're trying to do good in the world, and you're talking to me about optics!'

Trent was experienced enough to see that he was hurtling toward a brick wall at high speed and had neglected to buckle his seat belt. He sat back and breathed out, forcing himself to slow down.

He wasn't the foundation's first Happiness Officer; he had to remember that. Wilma had hinted at it, and it had taken Trent only a little research to confirm that he was, in fact, the third in that post. It didn't take much guessing to work out why his predecessors had left or been pushed out. In more than one area, the foundation had displayed a tendency to recruit someone to take an initiative forward and then ardently resist it as though the change was being imposed from the outside. Christoph's database, Henri's grantee partnerships, Trent's happiness. By filling a post and lumbering someone with the issue at hand, the management counted their part as done.

'May I ask, Mr Bingham, who gave me this remit?'

'The board, of course,' Charles said huffily.

'Can't live with 'em, can't live without 'em,' Trent said sympathetically.

It was a cheap ploy, trying to strike a note of under-standing at the edge of conflict, but if Trent knew one thing about presidents (of organisations or countries), it was that their power was rarely absolute, and that could often be a sticking point. So, he made his comment, and the two of them sat there like two fighters after an hour slugging away at each other, now questioning if it was all worth it.

Astoundingly, Charles took the bait. It must have been lonely at the top. He must have needed someone to talk to.

'They won't shut up about it. Between you and me, the problem is that we attract the biggest and brightest in philanthropy. Being on the board is a position of prestige. Why can't they leave it at that? They insist on having opinions.'

'Terrible,' Trent said.

'These things perpetuate. Everything has to be an innovation, and once you've done that one, the race is on to find the next. It's endless.'

'It's progress.' Trent couldn't help himself.

Charles flashed him a warning glare, and the walls were up again. 'The world has been turning well enough without innovation. Now, now, Mr Argent, settle down. Why don't you go off again and try to find out what the real problem is?'

CHAPTER 14

THE TURNING POINT

I t was easy enough for Hobbs to identify the exact moment he hit rock bottom. It happened in the aftermath of another failed interview.

Hobbs plodded his way back to the campsite. What was it that Trent said once about the aimless walk of the unemployed? That was the way Hobbs moved now, with nowhere to go and nothing to do except watch his feet step one in front of the other. If the interview he had just come from was anything to go by, he would be walking like that for the foreseeable future.

They hadn't said "no", but Hobbs knew he wasn't getting the job. As the ordeal had drawn to an inevitable close, there had been no enthusiasm in anyone's voice, certainly not at the levels of, "I really like this guy and can't wait to work with him", anyway. To get a job offer, you need to excite them and to do that, you have to be excited yourself. After so many failed interviews, the only thing Hobbs felt excited about was his bed, and he didn't even have one.

Hobbs faced indifference all the time. He tried and tried,

putting it all out there until nothing was left inside him. No one cared.

One of the downsides of the efficiency with which the Swiss kept their streets clean was that there was no rubbish for him to kick. What he'd have given to have an empty beer can to take it out on right then. The dents he would have made in it, the jangle as it skidded across the concrete, the way it would have crumpled when he eventually crushed it under his heel.

That's what humans did, wasn't it? When they were finished with something and it was no longer of use to them, they discarded it. What a plague on the world humanity was!

Hobbs rounded the corner of the Saint Georges cemetery. The Route de Pont Butin, an arterial route on the south side of the city, was busy. He let the rush of traffic overtake his thoughts and only realised a few minutes later that he had stopped walking.

Why was he going back to the campsite? There was nothing for him there – just his tent, sleeping bag and the journal he had stopped writing in. He could see the afternoon stretch ahead of him with nothing to do, no one to talk with and nothing to look forward to.

Well, it couldn't last forever. Even setting aside work permit issues, it was out of the question that Hobbs pass the winter in Geneva. He wasn't built for the cold, nor was his temporary accommodation. Soon enough, he would have to return home to an "I told you so" from his father and spend the rest of his life consigned to the periphery of the world. That was Hobbs' fate.

He was still standing in the same spot, just like the unemployed man Trent had described, with nowhere he wanted to be.

How did the others do it? Amara's success, at least, he could understand. She had been plugging away at her internship for months, treating it like a prolonged job interview – and her organisation had held up their end of the unwritten contract and offered her employment. But Trent, all he'd done was kick up so much of a stink that he'd been forced to look elsewhere. And Bong, well, what could be said? He hadn't even been trying to get a job; he was too focused on his burgeoning career as an influencer.

Was that the secret? Not to bother? Hobbs was unconvinced that such reverse psychology worked in the job market. He had, after all, scuppered the one opportunity he'd had by quitting his internship with the International Refugee Agency to tend to Trent. That hadn't exactly led to some wonderful reward. His friends had all moved on and left him behind.

Whatever the truth of it, Hobbs had no choice but to change his approach. He couldn't be the nice guy anymore – that path led nowhere. It was no use trying to do good in the world if you couldn't even put a roof over your own head.

This was about survival now.

But what next? That sort of resolution was of little help if it wasn't accompanied by a plan. Hobbs spent the next few minutes scrambling around for an idea. This country was about money, wasn't it? Who had it, who didn't, tax breaks, investments, credit, amortisation and net worth; how you could get it and make it grow.

Hobbs pulled out his phone and searched for the fundraising company Trent used to work for. 'They'll take anyone,' Trent had said when telling him about it. Hobbs wasn't proud to be in the same category as "anyone", but his priority now was to ensure he didn't get labelled as "no one".

The zombie on the pavement outside the Cimetière de Saint Georges animated. It had a purpose.

Trent's phone pinged. It wasn't Zoe.

He was eating a baguette in one of the concrete squares between the skyscrapers of La Defense. He had turned his nose up at the small room designated as the foundation's cafeteria – no one took their lunch there – but more than that, Trent needed to get away from that place, from his colleague's faces. He ended up on a bench overlooking a concrete fountain – because nothing said lunch break like concrete.

France was fabled for its cuisine, fine bread and cheese, so why was his baguette dry and tasteless? Trent set it down on the bench next to him.

Many things were clear for him now.

He understood the John R. Percival Foundation's problems – many of which were deeply ingrained and personified by its current president, Charles Bingham – but it would be too easy to pin them on one man. There was, equally, no simple solution.

He understood, too, why his interview had been so easy. They didn't care who got the job. The less competent, the better. He was supposed to fail. All those things he was so proud of about himself, they must have viewed them in the same way as all the interviewers who passed on him: they were provincial, significant only in a small country on the edge of Europe, whose glory days were long past.

But they were something. He had helped people. The

people of Ramstead and all those other communities where he'd worked were better off for his actions. They might not believe it, but Trent knew in his heart of hearts that they were.

This organisation didn't deserve him. If they wanted his help, they needed to embrace it. He would find another job, somehow.

Would he let people down if he quit? Probably not. Henri, Christoph and Wilma hadn't dared pin their hopes on him. They'd seen this before. He could imagine their "Unofficial Staff Council" reconvening to lament his departure. 'Another Happiness Officer down the drain,' they'd say. 'I wonder what idiot they'll recruit next.'

It was this thought that snagged in Trent's brain. He couldn't file it away with the rest of his self-pity. He was no idiot. He wasn't just another sucker who'd give up at the first sign of difficulty. He couldn't bear the idea of being replaced by someone who might succeed where he had failed. He was Trent Argent. This stuff was supposed to be a walk in the park for him.

It wasn't as if any of his initiatives had succeeded the first time around. They required persistence, and if Trent had one defining trait, it was persistence. He would not allow his only achievement in Paris to be that he'd become more adept at avoiding dogshit.

Trent stood, leaving his baguette behind on the bench. He wouldn't give up.

It was easy enough to look up the board members. The foundation register listed them for all to see, and LinkedIn did the rest.

There were ten of them, a manageable number to contact individually, especially if he discounted the founder's family and other long-standing members. He needed the new blood, those with the fresh ideas the foundation's president found bothersome.

It was careful work. Sometimes, he put a foot wrong. He was unprepared for Gordon Taylor's reaction, for example, when he visited him at his Paris office.

'We leave staff matters to the president,' Gordon said flatly after the pleasantries were completed and Trent had explained the reason for his visit.

Trent shifted in his impossibly soft leather chair. 'But surely you agree that organisational culture is relevant to the board?'

Norman stared at him as though "culture" was a dirty word.

Trent shouldn't have been surprised. He hadn't met many people called Gordon who were open to innovation. He excused himself quickly after that, aware that he probably now had little time to contact the others before word got back to Charles.

Another board member kept referring to his connections with the royal family, reminiscing at tangents about his service to "Her Majesty". Trent had never had a particular issue with the royal family, although being born into wealth and power did seem like cheating. Still, the whole conversation was so stuffy that to broach a subject like staff morale would have felt like farting loudly at a banquet.

He had more success with Leticia Gray, who had made her fortune in startups. Her LinkedIn profile was a shining example of how to collect titles and accolades, and she even had her own website. It didn't get much more modern than that! Trent sensed that there was substance behind the polish.

'How can I help you, Mr Argent?' she said after he had introduced himself.

He had taken the daring move of making this call from his office, forcing himself to overcome any paranoia Henri might have transmitted that his phone might be bugged. She was based in Hamburg, so visiting her personally wasn't an option.

'I'm speaking with all the board members,' Trent said. 'Kind of a getting-to-know-you session.'

'Oh, really? I hadn't heard about that.'

'You're one of the first.'

'Lucky me.'

Trent sat forward at his desk, pressing the receiver closer to his ear. 'Ms Gray, I wonder, are you aware of my remit at the foundation?'

'Aware? I insisted on the post! With all those negative reviews on Glassdoor, it doesn't pay to sit around doing nothing!'

Trent was aware of the reviews. The Glassdoor website allowed professionals to share their experiences working in an organisation. Until recently, he had written off the complaints listed there, assuming they were from millennials disgruntled with the foundation's insistence that they do unreasonable things like turn up to work on time and complete their assignments.

'In that case,' he said, 'I think you'll want to hear about some of the peculiarities I've discovered at this foundation.'

'They do say, "If you've met one foundation, you've met one foundation".'

She didn't trust him yet. Trent considered spending more time probing around the edges, but he had a feeling

Leticia was practised at this sort of conversation. She wouldn't give anything away before he did. He had little choice but to lay his cards on the table.

'I've met one foundation,' he said, 'and I'm not sure I want to meet any more.'

Leticia didn't respond.

'What would you say,' Trent pressed, 'if I told you that this organisation is suffering from a pronounced lack of diversity?'

Leticia scoffed at that. 'I'd say, "Welcome to philanthropy, Mr Argent!"'

'But seriously. This foundation has forty-five employees and makes thirty per cent of its grants in the global south. Does it sound right that only three staff are of non-white European origin? And in the lowest-ranked jobs?'

'Of course, it doesn't sound right! It's a topic close to my heart. Whenever I've proposed something to deal with it, I've been blocked. There's just no interest in pursuing it.'

'But you have ideas, though?'

'Plenty.'

Finally!

Trent leaned back in his chair. 'Let me help you with them.'

His mobile phone pinged on the desk next to where his elbow was resting. He put it on silent mode.

Trent's rebellion picked up speed once he had Leticia onboard. She knew the other board members well and could direct Trent on who to target next. She was aware of four others who were similarly minded. Not enough for a majority vote, but perhaps that didn't matter.

The next board meeting was due in a few days. They took place by Zoom every other month. It was the only way to bring together regularly a group spread across Europe

and the United States. This made matters more complicated. Trent couldn't manipulate things to have the
meeting take place somewhere inaccessible for those he
didn't want there. Still, he was experienced at stacking the
deck. He re-contacted Gordon to inform him he planned to
attend the next meeting and outline his recommendations
relating to staff culture. It was a sure-fire way to put him off
attending.

Fortunately, he didn't need to worry about the family
trustees. Leticia informed him they only attended the in-
person meetings, where dinner was provided, and the lofty
matter of budgets was discussed. That was a few more
crossed off the list.

One initiative alone would not solve all the foundation's issues, but it would be a signal, a beacon light. If it
went through, they might start attracting others with new
ideas and a different way of thinking. Gradually, and with
no small amount of pain and discomfort, things might
change.

Hobbs had never felt so hated.

To be a fundraiser was to be a leper, shoved to the
corner of society and ignored by all but the least wary.

How did they do it, those that thrived in this job? Was it
a game to them? Did they just let it all slide off them, all the
ignorance, all the rudeness, while they kept pick, pick,
picking away at their targets? Could they call upon some
untapped energy reserve to push potential donors over the
line, even as they floundered? How could they sound so
passionate about the plight of the rainforests one day and
domestic abuse the next, without ever missing a beat?

His manager, Jenny, was a bitch. Hobbs would never have imagined himself referring to a woman in that way. His mother, God rest her soul, would have been ashamed, but there were no other words to describe Jenny. She was hard-nosed, foul-mouthed, and respected nobody, least of all Hobbs.

'You can't afford to be timid,' she'd told him. 'No one gives as shit if you're a nice person. You've got to grab them by the balls and not let them go until they've signed a standing order. Show me you're man enough for it.'

Hobbs fought back the tears as he hurried down the stairs out of the building. They weren't tears of self-pity, though, but anger. He was just a commodity to her, something to be used. Hobbs was tired of being used. These people in their minor empires got their kicks from trampling on everyone else.

He saw now that it had always been this way. He'd been wrong to think the world of kings and emperors had been consigned to history. Society still played by the same rules; just the words had changed. Where once they'd called themselves rulers, now they called themselves leaders. Their desires were just the same.

Hobbs was on the street now. He wiped his eyes roughly, self-conscious about strangers' stares. Grown men weren't supposed to cry. He put his hands on his knees, breathing deeply until his heart slowed.

He resolved to take Jenny's advice. He hated himself for it, but he had no choice. Adapt to survive, that was his new mantra. He would lose bits of pieces of himself as he did it, but it was the only way. The Hobbs of old was not made for this world.

A hand grabbed his shoulder. He spun around. This man looked familiar. It took Hobbs a few moments to place him. He had seen him upstairs, in the front room of Fundraising Services AG. It was the receptionist, always on his Facebook feed.

'You're fast!' he said. 'I didn't think I'd catch you.'

'Well, you have,' Hobbs said. 'What is it? Did I forget something?'

This organisation placed massive value on its clipboards. To be safe, Hobbs always kept his safely in his backpack. It couldn't be that.

'I heard what Jenny said to you inside. A few of us have been playing around with some ideas. We could do with someone like you to join our ranks.'

Hobbs stared at this man. He was plain in every way, as though his years in that tobacco-stained office had gradually muted him. His hair was brown, and his eyes were brown; this man was so uninteresting that the only way Hobbs could think to describe him sounded like a ten-year-old writing their first work of fiction.

But maybe that was the secret. Maybe there was another way to get on in this world: don't get noticed.

'I'm Tony.' The man stuck out his hand.

Hobbs regarded it for a second before taking it.

Tony smiled a joyless smile. 'Come with me, my friend.'

'I suppose you're proud of yourself!'

Charles had stormed into Trent's office. He flung the latest copy of *Philanthropy Now* magazine across his desk. It was open on page 54, a full-page spread about the John R. Percival Foundation's board launching an internal investigation into the source of its funds. Trent had read it earlier that morning. It was the idea that he had been looking for.

Perhaps it marked the beginning of the end for the foundation; certainly, it heralded change.

'They get a hold of news quickly,' Trent said.

'Little doubt aided by a well-timed press release!'

Trent leaned forward in his chair. He was not afraid of Charles, not anymore. 'The board has spoken.'

Charles growled. Trent hadn't heard many men his age make animal noises before, but there it was, innate and primal.

'Just wait until our annual meeting,' Charles said. 'We'll have all the right-minded people there, and they'll strike this down in an instant.'

'I don't think so.'

Trent knew for a fact that the family trustees had already come around. If that wasn't clear enough from the fact that he hadn't been fired yet, it was cemented by that article. The foundation was being lauded for its bold move. Direct quote: "A shining example of what the sector should be doing right now". It was ego-boosting enough to ensure that a U-turn would not be quickly forthcoming.

'It's an internal investigation,' Charles said. 'There's no obligation for us to publish the results. Or even to hire someone that will do a thorough job.'

Trent smiled thinly. 'That's why the board has tasked me with managing the recruitment of the consultant. They see me as a neutral party, fresh to the foundation.'

Charles hammered his fist on Trent's desk but said nothing.

Trent stood. 'Am I dismissed?'

This phrase was otherwise known as "Please get out of my office." He was playing with Charles now.

Charles fixed Trent with a glare. It was an expression that had served him throughout his career. For years, it had ensured discipline in the ranks, occasionally reducing underlings him to tears. It just bounced off Trent.

'The board wants you to stay on, against my express wishes,' Charles said. 'I bow to their infinite wisdom, but I tell you this: if you go over my head behind my back again, I will destroy you.'

Trent considered questioning what kind of gymnastics Charles believed he had done, but he didn't want to push him too far. Instead, he said, 'That doesn't sound very philanthropic.' It was not much better.

'Fuck philanthropic!' Charles barked, and he stormed out.

Bong looked around his apartment and tried to remember who he was.

He was alone. It was mid-afternoon. His new acquaintances (he couldn't call them friends, as he couldn't remember half of their names) had woken up, helped themselves to what little food he had, and abandoned him until the next time they needed somewhere to crash.

His apartment was a mess. Fast food packaging covered the table, the bin overflowed, and the kitchen worktops were burdened with dirty dishes and glasses accumulated over days. He hated washing up. He had managed to wheedle out of it at the campsite. Not in his own place.

He couldn't live like this.

The state of his home was a representation of his brain. The second life he lived through his phone and computer had clogged everything up. The stuff he read on the internet and the hundreds of reels he scrolled through had all left a trace, overloading the neural pathways he used for thought. He needed to be creative; his livelihood depended on it. It wasn't enough just to share others' posts; he had to create content. And to do that required that he had something left in him to share. Only, he had nothing. It wasn't easy to consistently come up with clickbait. It took imagination. People didn't appreciate that enough.

The worst part was that this was his dream come true. He was employed, doing a job he could fool himself was for the wider good, even though, in reality, he was just publicising the successes of colleagues at the Ellipsis Foundation. Outside of that, people followed his various social media streams in search of a distraction from their mundane lives. He was a celebrity of sorts.

Bong had the perfect job and the perfect apartment, but all he could see was the mess.

Whatever he did, it always ended up like this. Disappointment.

The youngest of three brothers, Bong had spent his life in others' shadows. Back in Finland, everything he'd done had already been done better by one of his siblings. They were already both established in the family business, managing the butcheries with which their family had made its name. He didn't have their acumen and could never live up to their example. It had taken a move to another country to pursue a career in a very different field to feel like he was a person in himself. Yet, away from others, it was easy to forget who he was.

If only Hobbs had agreed to move in. Bong should have offered it from the start, but he'd been too swept up in his own success. Then, when he'd made the suggestion, he hadn't been able to hide that it was because he needed Hobbs rather than that he wanted to share his fortune. It was hardly surprising Hobbs had turned him down.

No, it was up to him now. Bong needed to find that part of him that took things in hand. He knew he had it in him: without it, he wouldn't have moved to Geneva in the first place. He had found that job. He could do things for himself.

Bong rummaged under the kitchen sink for a black plastic bag. It was time for a clear-out.

Trent took a brush to his new suit. Somehow, it had got cat hair on it. He had never owned a cat and avoided them whenever possible, so it was a mystery how it had got there. He'd had his apartment professionally cleaned before moving, too, although he supposed that one person's "professional" is another's "botch job". He wouldn't put in a complaint, though. It was well-known that new suits attract all the loose cat hair in the neighbourhood. Besides, it gave Trent an opportunity to check out his new suit in detail as he brushed it admiringly.

It was magnificent.

Trent hadn't asked Charles for his tailor, although he would have loved to see the look on his face had he done so. Unsurprisingly, Paris offered plenty of options. It had simply been a case of seeking out one in the higher price bracket range.

It was quite an extravagance for Trent's first paycheque – and had eaten up a good chunk of his disposable income – but he had deemed it necessary. It was a statement that he was planning to stick around. The Trent of old had favoured the quick-fix solution; he had been none-too-keen on follow-up. The new one would see things through.

Trent felt sure his continued tenure at the John R.

Percival Foundation would be fraught with challenges, not least of which was the idea of working for someone else (especially Charles). For most of his career, he'd been his own boss. The jobs in Geneva had been just means to an end, so he'd accepted being managed by someone else. This was more permanent. Still, it was the path he had chosen. He had to make sacrifices.

Who knows, he might end up as president himself in a few years.

Trent pushed that thought down. It was ridiculous, it was folly, it was a remnant of the power-hungry Trent of old. His rehabilitation was not yet complete.

Trent's phone rang. He went for it more slowly than he might have done a few weeks earlier. He had stopped checking his messages so regularly, too.

It was Bong. The two had been communicating via sporadic text for a while, mainly updates on what they were each up to. Trent had always found it useful to cultivate relationships with up-and-coming people, as one never knew what positions of power they might end up occupying.

Bong had never called before. It was odd to have someone phone out of the blue, too. Text or arrange a time before you call; that was the unwritten rule. You have no idea what someone's doing when they pick up their mobile, nor who they're with.

Bong sounded out of breath when he said, 'Trent, is that you?'

'Bong?' Trent said. 'Are you alright?'

'You've got to come back! We need you! Hobbs has lost the plot!'

STEP 6 – SAVE SOMEONE

CHAPTER 15

REUNION

Amara watched the rain streak across the train windows. A Switzerland badly in need of moisture passed by outside. The summer had turned the grass yellow, and autumn had been dragging its heels the past few weeks. Still, it was a beautiful view – not of mountains and chalets, for which the country was famous, but of rolling farmland and small outcrops of buildings. A little way off, the land curved down to Lac Neuchâtel. On the other side, villages clung to the water that nourished them.

The train would pass through the city of Neuchâtel shortly.

Amara hadn't imagined she would be travelling back to Geneva so soon. She'd had grand plans to visit the country by rail but hadn't yet bought her demi-pass, so she was travelling full price. She would be sure to mention this to Bong when she got there.

What had made her respond to his call for help so quickly? It hadn't been the panic in his voice: Bong panicked at the slightest inconvenience; he was not one of life's copers. It hadn't been the mention of Hobbs, either. When she'd left Geneva, it had been with a strong suspicion that she'd hear from him again soon. Admittedly, she hadn't expected the news to come via an intermediary, but who knew where neediness could take you?

She was returning because Trent was flying back, which elevated matters. If Trent was coming back, something serious was happening.

At that time of day on a Saturday, Switzerland's trains were full of people going about their weekend activities, be they family excursions, trips out with friends, or people travelling to a sporting event. Amara had always viewed the Swiss as an active, outdoors sort. With a country as beautiful as this, it made sense that they would spend their time out and about.

Was this the life she wanted? Certainly, it was hers for now, and all things considered, it wasn't bad at all. She was in full employment, doing a job she loved, with her own apartment and enough money to get by. She thought about her friends in India. Would they be jealous of her if they saw her enjoying the comforts of Western society? Or would it be like she had travelled to an alien world where everything was unfathomable and incomparable to home? That was how she had felt when she'd first arrived. But she was settling in now. Some would say she was making a success of it.

So why did she feel that every day she lived added another bar to her cage?

This must have been why she felt a sense of joy an hour or so later when they announced they were coming into Geneva.

～

Bong's apartment was how bachelor pads were presented on 80's TV: neat, clean and completely lacking evidence that a young man with no housekeeping skills lived there. Trent suspected that Bong had spent the morning cleaning.

Trent kicked off his shoes and put them next to his overnight bag because this was the sort of place where one removes one's shoes. Bong watched and didn't correct him.

'Nice place you've got here,' Trent said.

'Thanks,' Bong replied. 'I've tried to turn over a new leaf.'

It was Trent's first time there, but it didn't take much imagination to picture the state the place had been in a few hours earlier.

'I can see that,' he said. 'You get by, then?'

'Ellipsis Foundation pays a Swiss salary. Between that and my sponsorship as an influencer, I get by.'

'That's good to hear.'

'What about you? How's it going?'

Trent shrugged. 'Okay, thanks. It's early days, but you know...'

The doorbell rang, causing them both to jump out of their skins. This building had been constructed before the invention of the volume control.

'That must be Amara,' Bong said. 'She said she'd get here around now.'

'You called Amara?'

'I called everyone.'

Sure enough, it was Amara's voice over the intercom. Bong buzzed her into the building and left the door ajar so she wouldn't have to ring again.

The Amara that arrived looked far happier than Trent remembered. He knew she'd got a job but wasn't expecting a transformation like that, at least so soon. Some people relied on their careers to confirm their identity at a fundamental level. It was as though a huge weight had been lifted from her shoulders.

Having somewhere other than a tent to live couldn't have hurt, either.

She hugged Bong as soon as she got through the door. Trent thought he had been spared when she paused to remove her shoes, but she hugged him afterwards, too. It was the long, warm embrace of old friends reuniting. It had only been a few weeks.

'Are you alright?' Trent couldn't disguise the concern in his voice. If Amara was now comfortable with physical contact, they had more to worry about than Hobbs.

'I'm just pleased to see you,' Amara said. 'And I confess I miss *la bise*. The handshakes in the German part of the country don't quite cut it.'

Trent backed off a little, afraid she might move in to kiss him three times on the cheeks.

'Nice place you've got here,' she said, turning to Bong.

'Thanks,' Bong said. 'I've tried to turn over a new leaf.'

Trent waited patiently while they had an exchange almost identical to the one he'd had with Bong a few minutes earlier.

'So anyway,' he said when they were done. 'Now we're here, why don't you tell us what's up with Hobbs?'

Bong nodded in acknowledgement that they could put off no longer the grave matter for which he had summoned them. 'How about I show you?'

He opened the laptop on his dining table and tapped in his password. A website was already loaded. Trent and Amara moved in to get a closer look.

Six Steps to Salvation

*The revolutionary new donation platform launches on 7th
November
Join us here at 13h00 for our launch stream
Hosted by Michael Hobson.*

'That's Hobbs, you know,' Bong said, as if an explanation was needed.

'He's getting his name out there,' Amara said. 'That's great.'

'Scroll down.'

*Every franc raised will be matched by donations from the Ellipsis
Foundation and the John R. Percival Foundation.*

This was news to Trent. The idea of the John R. Percival Foundation supporting something that touted itself as revolutionary was laughable. He looked to Bong.

'It was a surprise for me, too,' Bong said. 'Even more so for my boss when I asked him about it. He tagged you and me on pretty much every social media platform out there. Seems to think we'll get our foundations to go along with this.'

Trent had a social media presence, but he only checked it periodically. Such tools had only proven important to him when he had a scheme on the go.

'You didn't know about it?' Amara said.

Trent shook his head. 'This is madness.'

'Or desperation,' Amara said. 'What is he thinking?'

'Probably that we have more influence in our foundations than we actually do.'

'That's why I brought us here,' Bong said. 'I can't be associated with fundraising, not on social media. It's totally against my image!'

'There are worse things for your image,' Amara told him. 'Believe me, I'm a journalist. I know.'

'You don't understand. My whole profile is built on taking the piss out of people. The public wants scandal. They want to be able to laugh at other people's expense and be glad they're not them. They don't want to hear about charity. It's a total turn-off.' He turned to Trent. 'What do we do?'

Evidently, Bong believed that his responsibility to come up with solutions ended with getting Trent and Amara to return. Given some of the ridiculous things he came out with in the past, it was probably for the best.

Trent paced around the apartment, gripping his chin. He hoped that imitating a great detective on the verge of an epiphany would trigger something. Unfortunately, it did not.

'We should speak with him,' Trent said eventually. 'Find out what's going on, in his own words.'

There was a lone tent at the campsite. The dust around it was still flattened from where another three once stood. There was no grass to regrow, and the bridge sheltered this place from rain, so the traces of the community that once lived here were preserved as if in volcanic ash.

Amara folded up her umbrella. They didn't bother calling for Hobbs. If he'd been there, he wouldn't have been hidden away in his tent, not at that time in the afternoon. He had zipped it up tight when heading out that morning.

Trent, Amara and Bong rolled the three tree stumps that had been kicked to one side of the clearing back to their usual positions around the fire's ashes. They sat down but said nothing.

Trent hadn't imagined that he would miss this place, but as he sat there, he remembered the meals they'd shared, the laughter, and the singing accompanied by gentle plucking from Bong's guitar. He wished Bong had brought it with him. He didn't think about the sleepless nights, the chill morning baths in the river and certainly not the many, many weak cups of tea.

The passing dog walkers must have thought they were sitting a vigil; such was the sombreness that descended on them over the next hour. They didn't look at each other, didn't talk. Each was caught up in their thoughts and recollections. They had moved on, but a part of them still lived there with the friend they'd left behind.

A few metres away from the shelter afforded by the Pont Butin, rain pattered on leaves that were slowly turning yellow. It started tentatively but gained confidence quickly until it was clear they would be drenched the moment they left that place. So, they kept on waiting.

Hobbs returned when the sun appeared momentarily from the blanket of clouds. He didn't have an umbrella. His blonde hair clung to his forehead, but it lacked the wild element it had the last time Trent saw him. He had visited the barber recently.

He paused when he saw them there, but only for a moment. Then, he smiled to himself before walking the rest of the way to his tent and dumping down his bag.

'Well, that was one way to get the gang back together, wasn't it?' he said.

'You could have sent us a postcard,' Trent replied.

Hobbs sat down on the fourth tree stump, the one

they'd not had to return to its place. He studied Trent's suit admiringly. 'Moving up in the world, are we?'

'I try,' Trent said.

'Well, congratulations. How does it look up there, above the rest of us?' Before Trent could answer, Hobbs turned to Bong. 'And it's nice of you to make the trip, too. They always say those who live the closest are the last to turn up to a meeting.'

'I'm not the one that stopped answering my calls,' Bong retorted.

'I might have picked up if they hadn't all been about you. But who wants to hear, "Bong's done this, Bong needs that" all the time? It hardly makes for riveting listening.'

'I know, I know,' Bong said. 'I'm sorry. I've been trying to turn over a new leaf.'

'Well, keep on trying.' Hobbs glanced at each of them in turn. 'Well, look at our merry little group back together again. I'll bet that in a few years, we'll look back at this like it was our golden days. Romanticising being young, free and single, living under a bridge in fucking Geneva. God, I'm already getting misty-eyed about it. What is this *life*?'

'I know exactly what you mean,' Amara said.

Trent did, too, apart from the "young" bit.

'Why don't we talk about why you called us all here?' Amara said.

'Technically, I didn't call anyone here,' Hobbs said. 'Definitely not you, anyway, unless you've come into some money – in which case, let's talk!'

'We're worried about you.'

'Worried about me?' Hobbs scoffed. 'Bong and Trent came out of self-interest. They want to protect your names – or those of their new employers. Much as I'd like to, I can't bring myself to believe you're much better. I've been thinking about something you said once about it being a selfish male thing to want to save the world. I agree with you about that now. You all went off to save the world and left me behind here. You've got that trait in you, too, Amara.'

'I'm sorry, Hobbs,' Amara said. 'Sometimes you have to put yourself first.'

'I couldn't agree more. That's exactly what I've started doing. The people I work with want me to be the face of something. And I have to pull all the strings I can to make it work.'

'They want you to be the fall guy,' Trent said. 'They're using you.'

'That's what you'd like to think, isn't it?' Hobbs said. 'Naive old Hobbs couldn't be behind anything like this. You're wrong. For the first time in my life, I'm not being used.'

'Then what's behind this clumsy attempt to get our foundations on board? That can't have come from you.'

'Why? Because I'm too honest? Just look where honesty got me! No, Trent, it was me who put this ball in your court. Either follow through on it and get me what I need, or let me fall flat on my face live on the internet. That's your choice. Sounds like a real test of what you think of me.'

It was this that confirmed for Trent that Hobbs was not the mastermind here. It was him in the firing line, with his reputation at risk. Blinded by bitterness, he couldn't see that whoever was pulling his strings had dangled this "amazing" opportunity before him, knowing he'd take full ownership of it. If it succeeded, they'd share in the glory and cut him loose just as quickly if it failed.

'Let's not pretend that helping me is beyond your abilities,' Hobbs said. 'You're a master at manipulating people. I looked you up, Trent. Should have done it months ago. You've had plenty of bad press over the years. Direct quote: "The biggest lying schemer and general bastard I have ever met." That's quite an accolade! There are a whole lot of lying schemers out there. And let's not get started on the bastards.'

'If you do anything in life, you're going to piss a few people off.'

'Wouldn't you know?'

Amara cut in. 'We're not here to talk about Trent. We want to help you. Plenty of people have gone to prison for dodgy fundraising schemes.'

'Who says my scheme's dodgy?' Hobbs snapped back. 'Is it so hard for you to believe I can make a success of myself without you?'

'Then why lie about Bong and Trent's foundations being on board?'

'You have to take risks to get things started!'

Trent let Amara and Hobbs argue for a few more minutes. He had already given up. This discussion had become too circular for his liking, and he had learned everything he was likely to from Hobbs. The man was drowning, and in that state, instinct took over. Gasping for breath and fighting for life, he would pull down anyone who tried to save him.

Trent studied Bong, who had kept quiet through most of the exchange. The young man's face had always been an easy read. His forehead was furrowed with concern, and his eyes twitched, betraying guilt. They had all failed Hobbs.

Trent didn't hear the comment that ended the debate, only an infuriated groan from Amara. Hobbs got up and set about getting the stove ready for dinner.

'Now, if you don't mind,' he said, 'this isn't your home anymore. I'd appreciate it if you'd see yourselves out.'

～

Hobbs stared into the flames. His friends had gone.

It was a strange feeling, burning bridges. He had always avoided it, taking to heart the notion that you don't know which paths you might need to retread. His internship with the International Refugee Agency had further reinforced the idea that you shouldn't offend people you might later rely on. Many of the people he'd met there, who occupied positions of power, had started off as interns. They still harboured grudges against those who had trampled over them at the start of their careers, people who now reported to them and spent their days suffering the consequences.

Despite this, it felt liberating to sever his connection to Trent, Amara and Bong. At his lowest point, Hobbs had made an express decision that his "nice guy" approach wasn't working. Things had to change, and jettisoning his useless friendship with his former campmates was a way to solidify that. He would burn to the ground everything he'd once held sacred, and that fire would light the way to something new, a world in which Hobbs was a success.

They had made it easy for him by assuming that what he was doing was wrong, that he was a pawn in somebody else's game. Hobbs could still feel the rush of indignation at that. Of all people, he'd hoped his Geneva family might see him as something more. They were wrong, and he would prove it to them.

He prodded the fire with a stick. The flames darkened the lines in his face. He wasn't sure whether he liked the new him, but he was beginning to respect him.

They congregated outside the nearby cemetery. It was still raining, so Trent and Bong joined Amara under her umbrella.

'I've never been chucked off a campsite before,' Amara said.

Trent considered whether the same was true for him. He had been driven out of village halls, scout huts, and even whole towns, but no, never a campsite.

'Why did he contact us if he wants to treat us like that?' Bong said.

'I sense great hostility towards us,' Amara said.

'Why, thank you, Deanna Troi!'

'He tagged us,' Trent said, 'because he wants us to help him.'

'Yes,' Bong said. 'Help him make money!'

'No, to get him out of that mess. He may not realise it himself, but that's why he did it. There was no other reason to bring us into this, not really.'

Bong looked doubtful. 'Not everybody wants saving.'

'You've known Hobbs longer than I have,' Trent said. 'If anybody wants to be saved, it's him.'

Amara lowered her umbrella. All three got showered with rain, and the discussion abruptly terminated.

'Sorry,' she said as she raised it again. 'It was just getting a little stuffy, huddled together under there. How about we find a café or something and get some food?'

There was a little *crêperie* down the road, with paper tablecloths chequered red and white. They took a table by the window, from which they could watch the rain and appreciate not being out in it. It was a comparatively cheap meal for Geneva, which was good because none of them had any great desire to blow a chunk of their paycheque on dinner.

'We should have invited Hobbs,' Amara said.

'He'd have refused,' Trent said. 'He's making a statement.'

'Eating tinned spaghetti to make a statement. Whatever next?'

The waiter came over and took their orders. Bong raised his eyebrows when Trent asked for a *Gourmande Suisse*.

'Gruyère cheese, potatoes, onions and lardons?' he said, referring to the menu. 'We're really pushing the boat out, aren't we?'

'I've been told I need to bulk out,' Trent said.

'You need your brain food. I'm expecting you to come up with one of those schemes of yours.'

There it was again: Bong's anticipation that someone other than him had the solution. He felt it from Amara, too, although she hadn't been so explicit.

'They don't happen just like that.' Trent clicked his fingers. 'They take planning.'

'Well, we have until Wednesday, when his stupid scheme launches. Four days.'

Trent usually had unwavering confidence in himself to devise a plan, and that confidence was usually half the battle: things tended to fall in place if he acted as though they would. But now, all he felt was pressure. This would be far harder than the other schemes he thwarted. He needed to do it without destroying Hobbs.

'I need time to think.'

As he saw it, there were two predicaments. The first was that Hobbs' website made a commitment it couldn't live up to. There was no way Trent and Bong could persuade their foundations to support an untested fundraising initiative developed by a nobody. If they didn't deliver the goods, how would that make Hobbs look, preserved for eternity on the internet?

Then, there was the fundraising platform itself. Trent hadn't had much time to investigate, but he doubted it was legitimate. In his experience, people whose arsenal contains emotional blackmail don't tend to be entirely above the board in their other business dealings. At best, any money raised would be passed on minus a hefty deduction for "administrative expenses". At worst, they were looking at fake charities, simple conduits to pass the funds to whoever was behind this.

How much did Hobbs know about that? Trent was only too aware of the depths of guile that humankind can stoop to, but he found it hard to view Hobbs as anything less than genuine. It was like all the grime in the world just slid off him. His display at the campsite had brought this into question, but charity fraud still seemed beyond him.

'We need to find out more about this Six Steps to Salvation initiative,' Trent said. 'Let's scour that website and any press releases and read the small print. We can't dismantle it if we don't know what it is. And we need to find a way to get to whoever Hobbs is working with.'

'I have an idea for that,' Amara said.

The crêpes arrived, so they had to wait patiently and pretend they were not in the middle of the conversation while the waiter delivered the dishes and wished them, *'Bon appétit!'*

'What was that organisation you used to work for, Trent?' Amara said. 'Fundraising Services, or something?'

'Yes,' Trent said. 'Why?'

'If I know Hobbs, he won't have searched far after

deciding to go into fundraising. He'd have wanted to follow in your footsteps.'

Trent's brow knitted, but he didn't question her further.

'I'll try to follow Hobbs' path.' Amara rubbed her hands together. 'Nothing like a bit of undercover journalism to get you going!'

Bong appeared to be even more confused than Trent, although for different reasons.

'Are you sure you're the right person for this?' he said.

'Why wouldn't I be?'

'If you're trying to follow Hobbs' path, you'll need to act nice.'

'I AM nice!'

'Okay, children,' Trent said. 'Amara, you go ahead with your idea. Bong, I need you to help with the research. I need to know everything you can learn about "Six Steps to Salvation."'

'How come she gets to go undercover, and I get stuck doing research?' Bong said. 'She's the journalist here!'

'Setting aside how adept you might each be at undercover work,' Trent said diplomatically, 'the fact is that you were tagged in the publicity for this launch. It's pretty likely whoever's behind this knows who you are. Amara's less likely to get caught out.'

Bong looked unconvinced, but he had no other argument.

'What will you be doing?' Amara asked.

Trent cut into his crêpe and raised a large slice of pancake, cheese and meat to his lips. 'I'm going to catch up with some old acquaintances.'

CHAPTER 16
THE SIX STEPS

Serena looked just as gorgeous as Trent remembered. Blonde, well-dressed and vibrant with an easy-going energy, he could tell why he had fallen for her. Fortunately, he could right see through it all now. It was like looking back at a teenage crush and asking yourself, "What the hell was I thinking?"

Not that Trent ever had a teenage crush.

He watched her from the classroom door as she chatted with one of the male students. She had pulled up a chair to his desk. A few months had passed, and she still hadn't advanced to the next class. Someone needed to concentrate more on her studies.

As Trent watched them, he paid close attention to her body language, and it was there that the illusion truly fell apart. Her moves were so practised; she flicked back her hair and touched his arm at strategic moments. It was a sad, formulaic kind of flirting, flirting because there was no one else around and nothing else to do.

When Trent heard Serena suggest to the young man

that they study together, he took the opportunity to cough loudly. Serena looked towards him, and her smile faded.

'I wonder if you could help me,' Trent said. 'I'm looking for someone to help me with my linguistic skills. I can't seem to control my tongue in the heat of the moment.'

Serena made her excuses to her classmate, grabbed Trent by the arm and pulled him into the corridor. He noted that her touch was less tender than the last time they'd been together.

'What are you doing here, Trent?' she whispered between clenched teeth. 'We're not supposed to see each other again. It's kind of the definition of a one-night stand.'

'You'll have to excuse me,' Trent said in his normal voice. 'I'm not as well-versed in those things as you are. Care to get a drink somewhere? I have a proposition for you.'

'I don't think that's a very good idea.' Serena started for the exit.

'Come on, now,' Trent said, following her. 'I'm not a stalker.'

'They all say that. Either that, or they're here to reform me. I don't need saving. Hunter's very aware of what I do. It doesn't mean he has to like the other men, though.'

'He tried to destroy me.'

Serena shrugged. 'A gesture of his love.'

'Come one, Serena, listen to me. I've moved on. I've got a new job in France now.' Trent was careful not to mention exactly where, not wanting to risk Hunter messing up his career there too.

'"I've moved on." How many times have I heard that one!'

Serena was at the building's exit now. She pushed open

the door and made her way down the stairs to the street. Trent had hoped to speak to her more before she got there.

'Okay, okay,' he said as his other old acquaintance approached. 'Let's get straight to the point. There's someone I'd like you to meet.'

Amara sat in the waiting room of Fundraising Services AG. Her induction session wasn't due to start for another twenty minutes. She had arrived a little early to give her a chance to scout out the place.

Not that there was much to explore. The reception area was a soulless room; every minute she spent there drained her a little further. The receptionist, who must have spent his whole life there, appeared to have fallen foul of its spell. He was a husk of a man, plain and pallid. His mute cream shirt matched the jaded walls.

'New recruit, eh?' he said after a few minutes.

Amara nodded. 'A friend of mine sent me here. Hobbs. Um, Michael Hobson.'

She didn't ask whether he knew him. It would have been too obvious, and the question was implicit, anyway.

'We get a lot of people come through here. Some hopeful, some depressed, some ambitious, some desperate. Your Hobbs may have been here, but who knows if he still is?'

'You sound like a jailer.'

'Heh, heh, I suppose I do.'

Amara didn't know what to say after that. Maybe Bong would have made a better undercover detective than her, after all. There was more to it than that, though. Something about this man made her want the conversation to end. He wasn't repulsive, not by any means, but just so relentlessly ordinary that the very essence of her being yearned for a distraction. Perhaps he was the source of the energy drain in that place.

'Well, good luck to you, Miss Lakhani,' the receptionist said after a few seconds. 'I hope you survive your onboarding in one piece.'

His attention returned to his computer. Amara tried to think up ways to extend the conversation. This man must know more; receptionists know everything that happens in places like that. But how would she pierce through the tedium and get to the useful bits? He seemed the sort of man whose idea of small talk was to read aloud the week's obituaries from the newspaper.

A few minutes later, the other recruits began arriving, and the opportunity passed. She was relieved at the disturbance. She tried to determine which of them was hopeful or ambitious; they all looked desperate and depressed.

Eventually, they were called into the training room by a woman who introduced herself as Jenny. She issued them clipboards and abrupt instructions. Amara didn't listen closely. She was too busy studying Jenny, her mannerisms, her body language. Was this the sort of person that would rope Hobbs into something illicit? Certainly, she gave no sign of it, so focused was she on rattling through a checklist of things she was supposed to tell them. She had done this a million times before.

Amara wondered how far she would have to take her subterfuge before picking up Hobbs' trail. Would she actually have to go out on the street and fundraise? This shit was getting real. Was this even the right place? Amara had been pretty sure Hobbs would have tried to emulate Trent's fundraising "success" (at least, that which he'd had before his extra-curricular activities sleeping with a married woman had been exposed); now, she was beginning to doubt herself.

Jenny sent them off with their clipboards and a stern warning that they had better not lose them. Amara had been paired with a middle-aged man named Steve. He had a beer belly and exuded a stench of urine. They had been assigned to the promenade between the Gare Cornavin and the lake. Amara could barely contain her excitement.

As she headed out through the reception, the receptionist called to her:

'If you were one of Hobbs' friends, you'd be nicer.'

Amara wheeled and stamped her foot. Her response was more extreme than she would have liked. 'I AM nice!'

The receptionist stepped out from the desk. 'If you were nice, you'd have treated me better earlier. But no, you found me boring. You couldn't wait for our conversation to finish so you could get back to sitting around doing nothing.'

Amara smiled. She couldn't help herself. 'Does that happen to you much?'

He led her outside, explaining that they'd have less chance of being overheard. The street was busy, but people passed by quickly, engrossed in private (but very loud) conversations.

'The name's Tony,' he said, getting out a vaping device. 'I suppose you're here because of Six Steps to Salvation?'

'I want in,' Amara said.

Tony laughed a measured laugh. 'You don't want in. You want to get Hobbs out. This isn't a cult, you know? He joined of his own free will. And we're going to make a lot of money.'

'Explain that.'

Tony took a deep breath from his e-cigarette and exhaled a sickly-smelling cloud. 'People like you are complete hypocrites. You go about your little lives like they're the most important thing in the world and only pay attention to others if they can do something for you. A few minutes ago, I was nothing to you. Now, you expect me to spill the beans. Well, if you're that interested, we're doing a livestream in a few days. You're very welcome to tune in.'

'I'd rather hear it from the horse's mouth,' Amara said, positioning herself upwind of him. The second-hand vapour wasn't as harmful as cigarette smoke, but she had no desire to breathe something that had been in his lungs.

'"Horse's mouth", heh, heh, "horse's mouth!" Trying to appeal to my sense of self-importance, are we? Let me tell you something, little girl: I'm proud of being unimportant. It's my superpower. "Don't stand out, don't show off," that's what my parents drilled into me. My teachers, too. "Fit in with the crowd," they said. They thought they were setting me up for success, but if you want to get anywhere in life, you need to stand out. In the workplace, you're up against people prepped to succeed since birth, people who've been told they're important and believe it to the depth of their being. Humility's not a word in their language. That's why people like me end up here.'

'Humility's not a bad thing,' Amara said.

'Truer words have never been spoken! It's the in thing these days, isn't it? Everybody wants to be thought of as humble. We should blame the Bible, I guess. "The meek will inherit the Earth" and all that. I think most people are more interested in the inheriting the Earth bit than the meek bit, though.'

Amara was losing patience. That tended to happen whenever someone started quoting the Bible to her. 'What's the point of all this?'

'"What's the point?" heh, heh. The point is that you

have no power over me. Whatever you say, whatever you do, you can't change what's going to happen. It's time for the people you've forgotten about to rise up. You'll remember us then!'

~

It was Monday evening, two days before the livestream. Trent, Bong and Amara had reconvened at Bong's place. They hadn't seen each other much over the past couple of days. Bong had offered his sofa for an overnight stay, but Trent and Amara had turned their noses up at the idea. Amara had bunked with a friend instead, and Trent had forked out for a few nights at a (relatively) cheap hotel. He would add that to Hobbs' bill when this was all over.

He and Amara had taken the week off work. Usually, this would have been reserved for rest and recuperation, but Trent suspected that wasn't on the programme. He needed it, though. He was tired. The past few years were catching up with him: the alcohol, his time sleeping rough, and the deep ache of ageing. Trent didn't know how to relax, but for the first time in his life, he felt like he needed to.

It would have to wait.

'Okay, Bong,' he said. 'Tell us what you dug up.'

Bong looked tired, too. There were dark circles under his eyes, making him look even more than usual like a member of a boy band caught red-handed doing something naughty. This thing called hard work wasn't for him. Not many people would call surfing the web hard work, but compared with uploading video clips to social media, it must have been a real slog.

'Okay,' Bong said. 'Well, there were two things. I looked

into the charities this Six Steps to Salvation initiative says it's supporting. There are some big names in there: WWF, Greenpeace, the Red Cross, but there are a lot of others. Some of them look to be legitimate smaller charities, but others, I don't know...'

'Something didn't look right?'

'There are a load of tiny associations, mainly Swiss. They don't have much presence on the internet, and they're not mentioned by anyone else. If you look at their websites, they're very basic, and they were all set up this year.'

Bong pulled one up on his laptop – an animal charity. Trent was no expert in these matters, but he spotted several telltale signs of a dummy charity. The pictures were too good. What small association would have the funds to invest in professionally edited photos? They were stock images, surely. And there were too many of them. Every page was splurged with pictures of animals in various stages of distress, being rescued, or on the path to recovery. They say a picture speaks a thousand words, but there had to be some substance behind it. There was hardly any written material – nothing about what exactly the organisation did to help these creatures. Whoever created this website had focused on style over content.

'So,' Trent concluded, 'they use well-known nonprofits as a screen of legitimacy and slip in a bunch of fake charities. They'll probably skim a bit off the money for the big ones but pass it on – no point in getting on the wrong side of them – but the donations to the unknowns they get to keep all for themselves.'

'Do you think Hobbs knows this?' Amara said.

'I can't imagine,' Trent said. 'He may be at crisis point, but he's still Hobbs. He must believe those charities are real.'

'There's something else,' Bong said, and they returned to his computer. 'Something didn't add up about this livestream they're planning. Just because you put something on the internet doesn't mean anyone will look at it. Why do they think people will tune in? Shall I tell you why?'

'Tell us why,' Trent said, affording Bong his moment in the limelight. After all, he had followed through well on a task he'd had no desire to undertake.

'Because they tag people. Not just you and me: hundreds of people. They call them "founding donors".'

'I'll bet you that's the first that most of them have heard about it,' Trent said. 'Clever.'

'Why's it clever?' Amara asked.

'If you announce people as donors, they won't back down,' Trent said. 'No one wants to give to charity, but that's preferable to getting known as someone who refuses to give to charity.'

This couldn't have been Hobbs' idea. As they learned more, Trent grew increasingly convinced that someone else was behind this, someone as devious and cynical as he'd once been. Yes, Hobbs might be angry and disillusioned, but that was very different. It takes years to develop a distrust of human nature deep enough to come up with something like this.

'The only thing I couldn't work out,' Bong said, 'is who these people are. I can't seem to find any connection between them. A lot of them are in Geneva, but other than that, it seems pretty random.'

'I think I can help with that,' Amara said.

And the floor was hers.

'I met our mastermind,' she said. 'His name's Tony, and he's the receptionist at Trent's old fundraising organisation.'

'The receptionist?' Trent said. He didn't have any recollection of them even having a receptionist.

'They must hold a tonne of data there. All the people their operators have ensnared over the years. He'd be in the perfect position to access it.'

'... and if they fall for street fundraising,' Trent said, 'it's a fair bet they'd fall for Hobbs' website.'

'I got the very clear impression this scheme isn't the only one Tony's got up his sleeve. He gave me serious supervillain vibes.'

Trent took a moment to enjoy the fact that, for once, he wasn't the villain of the piece.

'If we don't do something,' Amara continued, 'he's going to get Hobbs put away for a long time.'

Trent felt the two pairs of eyes looking at him expectantly. They had done their jobs gathering information. Now, it was his turn to deliver.

'We have to tackle these things one at a time,' he said. 'I don't go for all this "cut the head off the snake" business. It's always felt more like using a sledgehammer to crack a nut.'

The gazes continued, more bewildered than before. Trent had never been great at metaphor.

'We don't need to go head-to-head with this Tony guy to get Hobbs out,' Trent said slowly. 'That's not the easy answer. And judging by our last conversation with Hobbs, it'll be just as difficult to persuade him to take a different path. That leaves us with one real option.'

'Denounce the whole thing with a coordinated media campaign?' Amara guessed.

'Launch an attack against that website with a load of spam bots?' Bong suggested.

Trent was glad they had put him in charge.

'We need to disrupt that live stream,' he said.

They regarded him as though his proposal was even more ridiculous than theirs.

'I'm good with computers,' Bong said, 'but not *that* good. If you think I can hack them, you've got another thing coming.'

'No,' Trent said, 'we go to where they're streaming from, and we shut them down.'

'How the hell are we going to find out where that is?'

'I have an iron in the fire.'

They waited on the Pont Butin, at the top of the steps. Serena had refused even to attempt descending the embankment to the campsite in her heels.

They must have looked ridiculous standing there, Trent in his suit and Serena wearing something approximating a cocktail dress, red and silky, hardly appropriate attire for a stroll. Drivers gawped at her as they passed by. Trent felt relieved she didn't cause any traffic accidents. Had the barriers not been there, he'd have expected someone to slow down and proposition her.

He *had* asked her to dress up. Perhaps he should have been more specific.

At least it had stopped raining,

They spent the best part of an hour there before Hobbs returned. Serena passed the time on her mobile phone. She had no desire to speak with Trent. This was a business transaction, pure and simple.

'Hello?' Hobbs said as he approached. He did not have any other words.

'You remember Serena?' Trent said.

Serena smiled and reached out her hand. Hobbs stood there, unsure whether he was supposed to shake it or kiss it.

'What's going on, Trent?' he said. 'You know women aren't really my-'

'We can't get you your money,' Trent said quickly. 'We're nobodies in our organisations. I'm a bloody Happiness Officer, for Christ's sake! If you don't believe me, I'm sure the people you're working with will.'

'What's this got to do with her?'

'Trent and I have made a deal,' Serena said. 'I move in wealthy circles. My husband's a powerful man.'

'Is this a threat?' Hobbs said.

'No, silly!' Serena patted his hand playfully. 'We want to commit to Six Steps to Salvation. Five thousand dollars.'

Hobbs glanced at Trent. 'Why would she agree to this?'

Serena's performance had been spot-on, but the question was inevitable.

'She asked me exactly the same thing,' Trent said.

One day earlier

'Okay, okay,' Trent said to Serena as she descended the stairs from the French college. 'Let's get straight to the point. There's someone I'd like you to meet.'

Serena looked around, and Trent could tell she was thinking, "Who, exactly?" No one was there unless you counted the tramp lounging on the nearby bench. Trent hadn't brought a friend to threaten her or a priest to reform her. They were all alone.

As she turned to Trent, a mocking grin began to form. It halted when she saw that Trent looked utterly unfazed.

'Let me introduce you to Vincent, a friend of mine,' he said.

And the homeless man got up and docked his hat to her. It

was a beret, a hat designed to look mocking. Serena regarded him as though that was only one of many repugnant things about him – which, honestly, it was. Vincent was filthy, from his mismatched clothes to the smear of dirt down his cheek. He badly needed a shave, as his facial hair loitered between overgrown stubble and scraggly beard. It was a level of unkemptness only achievable through careful cultivation.

'All I want is a short-term favour,' Trent said. 'My friend, on the other hand, has signed up for a long-term commitment if necessary. He's got a lot of time on his hands and is very keen to learn French. He'll make sure to sit next to you in all your classes. I told him you'd be a perfect buddy.'

For people like Serena, the greatest threat was to sully the food supply.

'Je ne comprends pas bien le français,' Vincent said. It was a nice touch.

'This is ridiculous!' Serena snapped. 'Anyone can see he's French!'

Vincent puffed himself up then, standing straight and sticking his chest out. He looked just like a cockerel. 'How dare you!'

Serena glared at Vincent. She seemed to be trying to decide whether to enter a screaming match with him. The more worked up she appeared, the wider Vincent's grin grew.

'What do you want, Trent?' she said, her shoulders slumping.

'Very good,' Trent said. 'Let's get a coffee and discuss it like sensible adults.'

He gestured for Serena to lead the way to the Starbucks down the road. He waited for Serena to advance a few metres before taking Vincent to one side. He fished out his wallet and pulled out a fifty-franc note.

'Thank you,' he said.

'No need, my friend. An opportunity to piss off an American is payment enough.' Vincent paused, thinking better of it and snatching the note from Trent's hand. 'All the same, I'm sure I can find a use for it.'

'I have a deep commitment to doing good,' Serena said. 'Call it the guilt inherent with privilege, if you will.'

'Serena's well aware that humanity can't carry on living the way it is,' Trent added. 'We have to take responsibility. We can't leave this legacy for future generations.'

Hobbs glanced back and forth between the two of them, his eyes bulging with incredulity. But he needed a break. Trent could sense the hunger in him. For a moment, he dared to hope that Hobbs might take the bait.

'Why would I accept five thousand dollars,' Hobbs said, 'when I've got two foundations that'll give us tens of thousands?'

That was an easy one.

'Because they won't,' Trent replied. 'Bong and I haven't a hope of getting our foundations to cough up. Serena's money is real. And she's got plenty of friends. She can spread the word. Who knows where that might take you?'

'Like I said, I move in wealthy circles,' Serena added, gesturing towards her dress as proof of it.

'I'm offering you another way, Hobbs,' Trent said before Serena could do a twirl. 'If you go ahead with our foundations on your initiative's banner, it'll be an embarrassment. Let's not even think about the legal consequences. Serena offers you a way to save face.'

'I'll be your founding donor,' Serena said. 'You can tell everyone about me. I've got one condition, though: I want to be there. I want to appear in your livestream. Some people don't like the publicity. I'm not one of them.'

Hobbs still appeared doubtful. This offer must have seemed too good to be true. But what did he have to lose?

'I'll need to speak with the others about this,' he said.

Trent pushed the advantage. 'I thought you were in charge. Are you telling me now that you have to check with someone before making a decision like this?'

'Alright, Trent, alright. I understand your play. Let me get back to you.'

It was an old photo studio in the *Pâquis* area, not far from the train station. The area was known for its red-light district and colourful collection of restaurants (Trent would leave the connection between the two to the sociologists). The buildings were close together, and the streets were narrow. Traffic was calmed by speed bumps and a bewildering one-way system.

They entered the door code Hobbs had given Trent. The lights were on, but there didn't seem to be anyone around yet. That was the first warning sign. The live stream was due to start at 1 pm, and they had arrived a little over ten minutes earlier (delayed due to Serena touching up her makeup at the last minute in the glass of the tram stop). Trent had thought they were cutting it fine, but if none of the crew for the livestream had turned up yet, that was taking it to the extreme.

While the others looked around, Serena perched herself on the stool in front of the white backdrop where the photo shoots were taken. She wore a dark blue dress because Hobbs had told her that red didn't work well on screen.

Amara went around the back to see if anyone was there amongst the stacked chairs and ladders. Bong sat at the computer terminal by the front window and frowned at the screen. Trent just stood, his stomach churning with a sense of doom.

When Amara reappeared, she was shaking her head. 'Well, that's a wrap.'

Against his better judgment, Trent still hoped that Hobbs and company would show up. He turned to Bong, who was at the keyboard.

'How's it looking?'

Bong scratched his head. 'Well, it's all password-protected, locked on this screen.'

Trent looked closer. It was the homepage of Six Steps to Salvation. Well, at least there could be no doubt they were in the right place.

'If all else fails,' he said, 'just pull out the plug. The old-fashioned way.'

Then, he noticed the letter.

It was a plain white envelope with a transparent plastic window for the address, the type that only the most old-fashioned of administrators still used. Just above the address window, someone had written "Trent".

Trent's stomach churned louder as he picked it up. He already knew what it contained.

He pulled out the letter and unfolded it. It was hand-written. He had no idea if it was Hobbs' writing – he had only ever seen him type, never handle a pen – but the content left little doubt:

You didn't seriously think I'd fall for it, did you? Appealing to someone's ego, that's the oldest trick in the book!

Enjoy the show!

Hobbs

The website came alive. The screen displayed a picture of a child starving somewhere, behind the words "Six Steps to Salvation. Livestream begins in one minute." And the countdown began.

'We're in the wrong place,' Trent said.

'What?' Amara said.

Fifty seconds. The image changed to an iceberg photographed fracturing into the sea.

'He saw right through my plan. He or they. Who knows where they're streaming from? Not here.'

Every second that ticked past on the screen hammered home Trent's failure.

Forty seconds. A rainforest lizard with large, orange eyes.

Trent couldn't take his eyes off the screen. If he willed it enough, could he make the counter stop? That was what it had come to, just blind hope. He had no clever scheme to save him from the countdown to the inevitable.

Thirty seconds. People out protesting in the streets to "Save our hospitals".

Amara went to fetch chairs for her, Trent and Serena. If they couldn't stop this thing, they would watch it. They had no responsibility to do anything about this now; they were mere spectators.

Twenty seconds. A homeless man in a makeshift cardboard shelter.

Trent looked at Bong and saw that his hands were shaking. Of all of them, he had known Hobbs the longest. What must it have been like to watch his friend create this fate for himself?

Ten seconds. A woman in rags outside a building decimated by missile fire.

Trent, Bong and Amara barely breathed throughout the final countdown. Trent wanted to storm out but succumbed to the basic human fascination of watching a disaster unfold. He wasn't one of those bottle-necked drivers that slowed down when passing a traffic accident, but this he couldn't resist, even though it was an outcome he'd tried desperately to avert.

Only Serena appeared unmoved by what was going on. Hobbs meant nothing to her. She would soon be released from her part in this.

The countdown ended, and there was Hobbs, in a shirt and tie, sitting behind a desk. He gripped a bundle of papers and looked straight into the camera. He looked exactly like a newsreader. Behind him, a montage of the images they had just shown formed the background to a logo: Six Steps to Salvation, with the same "S" shared between the three words.

'A very warm welcome to everyone who's tuned in,' Hobbs said, *'to this inaugural livestream celebrating the launch of the new initiative, Six Steps to Salvation. I'm Michael Hobson, and I'm here to tell you about the different ways you can interact with our site and give you a glimpse of what we have planned for the future.*

'People have asked me, "What's unique about Six Steps to Salvation?" There are many things: the technology, the reach, the ambition, but I want to focus on just one. One word: trust. It's a word that's used too often, but it's at the heart of what we do. We want to celebrate the inherent goodness of humanity and the good we can do to each other. A key part of that is trust. Trust in our fellow man.'

'Can I go now?' Serena said.

It was as if Hobbs was in the same room as them because the next thing Hobbs said was:

'I would like to thank our founding donors, the Ellipsis Foundation and the John R. Percival Foundation, who have agreed to match any donations this week. But that's not all. We've already had many individuals place their trust in us. And now I'd like to turn to one of them. Please allow me to introduce one of our founding donors, Serena Pickering.'

A red light turned on above the computer monitor. It was the first time any of them had noticed the webcam. Serena's image appeared on the screen, along with Trent's and the left half of Bong's head.

Serena's eyes widened. 'Turn it off, turn it off!'

'A little camera shy, that one. Well, I'll tell viewers for her. Serena has agreed to donate $5,000 to Six Steps to Salvation. Truly, a remarkable commitment, and the first, I'm sure, of many. Let's turn instead to the man next to her. Trent Argent is representing the John R. Percival Foundation, which, as I mentioned, will be matching all donations raised this week. Trent, would you care to say a few words?'

Trent floundered. He was never much good with recorded media at the best of times, and this was certainly not the best of times. He knew he should disavow all knowledge but couldn't do that to Hobbs. He couldn't hang him out to dry like that.

'I, um, the John R. Percival Foundation supports a host of good causes,' he said, trying to be as neutral as possible. 'We all, um, know that the sector is badly in need of funding at the moment. New initiatives such as this-'

The light on the webcam switched off, and the screen went blank for a second. Trent let out a sigh. Bong was holding a severed cable and some wire clippers in his hands.

'The old-fashioned way,' he said.

The livestream switched back to Hobbs, who had been thrown temporarily off his game, but he recovered quickly.

'We seem to be having some technical issues with the stream. Let's pass on to the next part of today's programme. A lot of people ask us, "What are the six Steps to Salvation?" Well, here they are...'

'Can I go now?' Serena said again, more resignedly this time.

Trent looked at her, uncomprehending. He was still recovering from his moment in the spotlight. 'Yes, sure.'

'Step 1,' Hobbs said in the background, *'Tell us your interests. We'll direct you to charities working in your chosen field.'*

Serena got up but paused on her way out. 'You'll call off your goon? I held up my end of the bargain. It's not my fault that-'

'I'll call him off,' Trent said.

'And that five thousand? That's not coming out of my pocket.'

'I'll find the money. Just, please, leave.'

'Step 2,' Hobbs continued. *'Select your cause. Our website contains a comprehensive database, including some of the biggest names in the sector.'*

'What do we do now?' Bong said, once Serena had gone. Of course, he expected Trent to have a fallback plan. But Trent was all out of ideas. Sooner or later, Hobbs' scheme would crash and burn, taking him down with it. Trent couldn't think of another thing they could do to save him.

'Step 3: Navigate to your pledge page. You'll have an opportunity to indicate whether you want to make a one-off donation or set up a regular commitment.'

'Come on,' Amara said. 'There's no point in sitting around here listening to this.'

They never found out about steps 4, 5 and 6.

CHAPTER 17
NEW BEGINNINGS

They hung out at Bong's the rest of the afternoon without really doing anything. Nobody wanted to talk, but neither did any of them feel like being alone. Bong checked his social media feeds, and Trent looked to see if he could get a flight back to Paris a few days early. There didn't seem to be much point in hanging around longer, and soon into his job, the fewer days of holiday he took, the better.

Amara seemed to have the same thought. 'I suppose I'd better head back to Zurich. I need to hand back my clipboard first, though. I don't want Jenny sending people after me.'

Trent agreed that Jenny would probably go to such extremes.

He kept telling himself he shouldn't give up. The old Trent wouldn't have done so as easily. But he wasn't the old Trent: he was the outsmarted Trent, the Trent all out of ideas, the tired Trent.

'If I come up with something, I'll let you know,' he kept saying, as though that would somehow make that happen.

Nobody seemed convinced. The fact was that Hobbs had chosen this path for himself and thrown himself down it, knocking all of them aside. When someone is so intent on self-destruction, there's precious little anyone can do about it. Hobbs didn't want to hear from them. Had they still been living together, that might have been a different story, but Trent, Bong and Amara were to blame for severing those cords, not Hobbs.

Trent knew that to get on in this world, you must be prepared to leave people behind. Stay still, and you stagnate. They all knew that. It was tough, but they had to steel themselves to it. Everyone must find their place, and although people might share a road for a short time, it rarely lasted for long. That was the understanding.

So why did this feel like defeat? An old mantra of Trent's was that in business, most schemes fail. Think of Silicon Valley, touted as a hotbed of innovation and success. The "startup mentality", that was a buzzword these days. Nobody talked about the failed ventures there, but they far outnumbered the successes. It brought little comfort when he reminded himself of this. Hobbs meant too much to him.

He surprised himself when he realised this. Setting aside his obsession with Zoe, he had never felt any great attachment to anyone. But these people, they were his family now.

The psychologist in Trent conjectured that Hobbs represented his younger self. By saving him, he was saving himself. It was a neat enough theory, but it couldn't be true: Trent had never been that innocent. But maybe, maybe Hobbs represented how Trent hoped the world could be. If Hobbs could succeed, there was hope for them all.

As the hours passed, his resolve deepened to speak with Hobbs one final time.

It was getting dark when Trent arrived at the campsite. He lit the way with the torch function of his phone, but he still stumbled and slipped a few times on his way down the embankment. He told himself this was due to the past few days' rain, but it was more than that. This wasn't his home anymore.

Trent continued down towards the orange glow under the bridge, a sign that Hobbs was there. It was clear that it would become less and less tenable for him to live there in the coming weeks, as the days shortened and the weather worsened. He understood why Hobbs had been driven to desperate measures. Treading water and keeping trying the same thing just wasn't an option, not with winter coming.

As he approached, he saw that Hobbs was alone at the campfire. He turned off his phone's torch. He wasn't sure why – it was hardly as if he was planning an ambush. No matter: Hobbs had already seen him coming.

'Trent?' Hobbs said as Trent emerged from the shadows. 'Phew! To be honest, I'm quite relieved it's you. Not too many people come down here this time of day.'

'Even less of them with good intentions, I'll bet,' Trent said. Camping alone must have been a very different experience to being in a group.

'Could be the police,' Hobbs said, 'but more likely someone coming to ask if I have any weed. I haven't been raped yet.'

'Well, that's a positive.'

Trent sat on the tree stump, still in the same spot he'd left it a few days earlier. Hobbs hadn't kicked it away. A good sign? Trent was wary about reading too much into it.

'I understand why you did what you did,' Trent said. 'In

325

the same position, I'd have probably done the same. Or worse.'

'Is this the old Trent speaking or the reformed one?'

'That's an interesting question.'

'So, you're not here to lecture me?'

'No.'

'Well, that's a relief!'

Hobbs returned to preparing his meal, pouring tinned vegetables into a pan and balancing it above the fire.

'I'm here,' Trent said, 'because I didn't want to leave it like this between us.'

'You don't have to leave it like this. You can get your foundation to stump up the money. We had quite a good opening night, by the way. It's funny how much people donate when you name and shame.'

Trent nodded slowly, as though he was considering an interesting proposition. 'You must know I can't do that.'

'So, why are you here, then?'

Trent stared into the flames. He still didn't have a plan. Even when down and out, wallowing in his misery before coming to Geneva, Trent used to have a plan – albeit that was usually to drink more alcohol.

'I think you probably pissed off a lot of people last night,' he said. 'Some of them won't hesitate to hire a lawyer.'

'The rich, you mean?' And there was Hobbs' wild side again. 'Why are you trying to defend the billionaires? They're the ones that fucked up the planet!'

'I'm trying to protect you.'

'Wasn't it you who always said about taking advantage of niches?'

Trent didn't have a response to that one. Even if there were a good answer, Hobbs wouldn't hear it.

'This isn't you,' Trent said.

'No, it wasn't me,' Hobbs said. 'And that was exactly the problem. I've changed, and I'm not going back.'

'You'll be going to jail when they catch up with you. We looked into the charities on your website. Some of them are clear fakes. You're promoting a vehicle for fraud.'

'Here we go again! Next thing, you'll tell me Amnesty International isn't a charity! Just give it up, Trent, I'm not going to listen to someone who screwed his way to the top.'

Trent coughed. 'That's not exactly how it happened.'

This "no plan" approach wasn't working. Trent considered himself adept at thinking on his feet, but that was usually only when he had a specific end in mind. Without it, he had reverted to his former position and Hobbs to his.

'Why do you have so much hostility towards me?' Trent said, trying the touchy-feely approach. He wouldn't normally condone it, but he had to try everything.

Hobbs had been stirring the pot. He threw down the wooden spoon in disgust. 'Why? You ask me why? You were supposed to be my role model, you idiot!'

Trent didn't recall signing up for that, and he certainly hadn't announced his candidacy for the job by turning up drunk.

'You need to choose better role models.'

'Apparently.'

Trent sighed, and it was as though all his strength departed with that breath. 'I let you down, I know. I screwed you over without even intending to. You quit that internship because of me, and then I just moved on.'

'Yup.'

'I underestimated you. I blundered into that trap because I equated smart with cynical. I should have known better.'

Trent stared into the flames. He tried not to think. Thinking got in the way sometimes, making things too complicated and over-analysing them. He breathed in deeply, and as he continued to speak, it felt like something released inside him, something that had been pushing down a part of him for most of his life.

'There's another way. You showed me it for a while. You can be something different from me and still be a success. I'm not a good man. Never was, never wanted to be, not until I hit the bottom. But even then, it was all about me. It was me I wanted to save, and all those things I did, I did for myself, not others. That's where you're different. You *care*, Hobbs. Other people have to talk themselves into it, but it comes to you naturally. Yes, you might fall foul of the world every now and then, but that's its fault, not yours.'

Hobbs rolled his eyes. Trent had been hoping for a different reaction.

'That's a lovely speech,' Hobbs said, 'but where's the substance? The world's not going to change for us, and you can't just keep me in a bubble.'

'I know, I know.' Trent felt exhausted from saying all that. 'To be honest with you, I don't have an answer. Everyone keeps expecting me to come up with a plan, and I'm all out of ideas.'

The last of Trent's strength was deserting him. There was a good reason he had rarely been truthful with people in his life: it was tiring. Mixed with a sense of defeat, it was a potent combination.

It occurred to him that he had experienced defeat more often in his new life than in his old. This was what it must have felt like to be Hobbs.

'Will you let me stay here tonight?' he said. 'I don't think I'd make it back up the hill in one piece.'

Hobbs regarded Trent for a long time. At first, he was clearly searching for signs that Trent was having him on. Gradually, his expression turned from doubt to kindness.

'We wouldn't want you breaking a leg, would we? But I don't have any spare bedding I can share with you. It gets pretty cold out here these nights.'

'That's okay. I'll find a few logs to put on the fire. There's got to be something around here that isn't damp.'

Hobbs raised his eyebrows. 'As you wish.'

Hobbs went into his tent shortly after that. Trent set about clearing a space to lie. He knew it would be sensible to clamber back up to the bridge and the hotel, but he couldn't face it. He gathered what dry wood he could and put most of it on the fire, then lay down and waited for sleep.

Hobbs' tent unzipped. The young man emerged, dragging a sleeping bag and an inflatable mattress behind him.

'Alright, old man,' he said. 'I've got my tent, and I can bed down in towels and clothing for one night. It won't be the most comfortable, but it'll do. You can have these.'

He dropped the mattress and sleeping bag beside Trent and returned to his tent. He had already zipped up again when Trent's mumbled objections turned to a 'Thank you.'

Trent slept fitfully, drifting in and out of consciousness like a shaman in a fever dream. It was in this state that the idea came to him.

The fire was well out when Hobbs rose, and Trent was shivering. Hobbs set about lighting it with the efficiency that comes with practice. Trent warmed himself with a tea

– one teabag between two, a definite improvement on old times.

The night spent outside hadn't improved Trent's fatigue. Hobbs didn't look much better.

'I'm sorry about what I said to you last night,' Hobbs said.

'Me too,' Trent said. 'I'm in no position to lecture you.'

'No hard feelings, then?'

'No hard feelings.'

They sat for a while, drinking their tea. Hobbs offered Trent some toast, but Trent refused, even though he was hungry. It seemed wrong to take anything from Hobbs now.

'How much longer will you be living out here?' Trent said.

'I'll be moving soon, I hope,' Hobbs said. 'A lot depends on how things fall after the first week of fundraising. I'm not on a contract. I'll get a percentage.'

No contract, hmm? Trent thought, but he knew better than to say anything. Best to skip straight to his proposal. 'How about if I gave you a contract?'

Trent was cautious in his tone. He tried to make it sound like he was making a joke, to save the embarrassment of Hobbs rejecting the idea. Why he cared about such things, he didn't know.

Fortunately, Hobbs recognised the seriousness of his intention. It was a sign, if ever there was one, that he was looking for a way out, just as much as was Trent.

'What do you mean?'

Trent put down his tea and pressed his hands together, looking Hobbs square in the eye.

'We could go into business together.'

'Doing what?'

'Definitely not fundraising,' Trent said, and he coughed out a chuckle. 'But seriously, there are opportunities here. I'm not talking about exploiting people. Helping them. There are so many nonprofits, and they all need something. You could play a part in it if you like. I need someone like you. Someone people can trust.'

'Don't you think I've blown that now?'

'Maybe not. You were just the host. Where would we be if we punished every actor advertising a dodgy brand? You might come out of this clean if you get out quickly enough. Don't take any money. Just play it like you were doing it out of the good of your heart.'

Avoiding Trent's gaze, Hobbs glanced around the campsite. He took a long time about it, as though the river or the trees would offer him an answer about what to do next. They didn't care. Or maybe he was savouring this moment, taking in the last impressions of a place he had no intention of returning to.

'I need that money,' he muttered. 'You're asking me to take a big risk.'

'Yes,' Trent said. 'I suppose I am.'

They were in Bong's place. Well, it was Bong and Hobbs' now. It hadn't taken Hobbs long to move his stuff across town. It had already been packed, awaiting his ticket out from under the bridge, a ticket he had never imagined would come from Trent.

Hobbs got the frozen pizza out of the oven. It felt like quite a treat, as it wasn't an easy dish to cook over a campfire. Bong was on the sofa, picking away on his guitar. Trent and Amara had pulled up chairs at the table. It felt like old times, only with a roof, rather than a bridge, over their heads.

'Hobbs will be the face of it,' Trent explained, regarding the business plan they'd scribbled on a bit of paper. 'He's much better with people than me, and the more I stay in the background at the moment, the better. If we need other expertise, we know who we can reach out to. If it's a public relations issue, it'll be you, Amara. If it's social media, there's Bong.'

'That's not his real name, you know?' Amara said.

'I know.'

Hobbs carried the two pizzas from the kitchen, and they made room for them on the table, sweeping aside the crumpled pages that bore witness to their failed attempts to devise a strategy. Bong abandoned his guitar to join them.

'You forgot to mention the most important thing,' Hobbs said. 'We keep each other on the straight and narrow. The moment one of us starts straying, we tell them. We all need a compass.'

'I'll drink to that,' Bong said, pouring them each a glass of lemonade.

They toasted their new venture, and the deal was done.

'I never would have imagined it,' Bong said, 'us going into business together.'

'And a consultancy, too,' Amara said. 'Who'd have thought that forming a consultancy would solve our problems? It's the answer to *no one's* problems!'

'It's up to us,' Trent said, 'to find a better way.'

This all still felt surreal to Hobbs. A day earlier, when he had woken up on a makeshift mattress of clothes in a tent he had grown to detest, his ambitions had been tied with a very different group of characters. He couldn't say he particularly liked Tony and his associates, but that was hardly the point: they had offered hope. Perhaps he had been influenced by the respect they'd shown him by asking him to head up their new initiative (a lesson that Trent appeared now to have learned), but it had been more than that. Six Steps to Salvation represented everything Hobbs hoped humanity could be: generous and trusting but professional. How could he abandon that? Why would he give it up for a business plan that hadn't yet been written by a man he had come to resent?

The answer was doubt. That niggling doubt in Hobbs' mind that Six Steps to Salvation was too good to be true. Much as he wanted to, it was hard to believe that people were wandering around eager to give their money away, prevented from doing so only by not knowing who to give it to. If that was the case, why shine the spotlight on them and announce them as donors before they even knew it? No amount of self-deception could fully erase the logical flaw in that.

The more he had pressed this with Tony, the further his doubts had intensified. Tony had responded to every question with emotion. Whenever Hobbs had tried to pin him down to a response, he'd been met with expressions of disappointment. Why did Hobbs need to know all the details? Didn't he trust them?

Hobbs had known for sure that he was making the right choice when breaking the news to Tony, who immediately told him he'd regret it if he backed out. It hadn't been phrased as a threat, but the underlying menace had been unmistakable. People rarely make statements like that unless they've got no other cards to play.

Hobbs now felt like he had been freed from a cage of his own making. Granted, the bars had been forged from society's expectations, but he had fixed them in place. He had tried to turn himself into a different person, but it hadn't stuck. He had betrayed his friends, just as they had abandoned him, but they were together again. They would give each other another chance. And this time, with a bit of luck, they would succeed together.

The train started moving, leaving the platform behind, and Amara prepared to say goodbye again to Geneva. This time, it would be a proper farewell. She hugged her friends without feeling like she was abandoning them. She wasn't slinking away.

She knew she'd be back, too. You can only do so much with a video call. She'd need to meet with Hobbs and Bong if their venture took off. More than that, she'd *want* to meet them because they were a part of her now. She'd be able to look Hobbs in the eye without feeling ashamed.

The train accelerated, leaving the buildings behind and piercing fields that rolled down to the Lac Leman and the mountains beyond. She would invest in that demi-pass soon and get out to see the rest of the country. Not long after that, maybe, she'd be able to afford a trip back to India. She hoped that would be in time.

She'd got the news of her father's illness earlier that morning. She'd tucked her phone away immediately after reading it and had allowed herself to get swept up in the excitement of Hobbs' and Trent's reconciliation. She'd smiled, laughed and made sarcastic comments as they plotted their new course. That was the Amara everyone knew. None of them would have suspected that beneath that, she was digesting the news that she would soon lose the person dearest to her in the whole world – a man she aspired to, not because of where he'd ended up in life, but because of who he was and who he wanted her to be.

Now that she was alone, it came back to the surface. Her throat swelled, making it difficult to swallow.

She dug her phone out of her handbag and scanned through the follow-up messages from her mum, checking she was alright. She didn't make a very good daughter, not by Indian or Western standards. That was something else she would need to work on.

She put the phone to her ear. It only rang three times before someone picked up.

'Hi, Mum...'

A month after the lemonade toast, Trent looked at himself in the mirror. He was in the bathroom of the Airbnb he had rented in Paris. He remained the John R. Percival Foundation's Happiness Officer. The Trent of quick-fix solutions had been consigned to the past; he still had work to do there. Plus, until their new venture was on solid ground, it was best to retain a regular source of income. But there was hope.

Back in Geneva, New Beginnings Consultancy was doing rather well. He couldn't remember who came up with that name (it was corny, so it had probably been Hobbs). They already had three contracts, leveraged through contacts he'd made through the foundation.

Trent had never been one to admire himself in the mirror, at least not topless. With his shirt and suit on, he was ready for battle, but with nothing on, he was vulnerable. He had never liked feeling vulnerable.

This felt different, though. Trent reached up and touched the transparent bandage over his inked skin. The tattoo was on Trent's chest, just above his heart. It was a part of his body that had never known muscle, but it housed strength, nevertheless. Trent's old suit, the one with a scuff on the knee, was beside a bin outside. In a short while, there would be a very sharply dressed tramp wandering around Paris. Trent was happy to pass it on; he had a different armour now. A magnificent tattoo of a double-arched bridge, very much like the one he had slept under for weeks. The image wasn't big – he hadn't been courageous enough for that – but it was there, and it would stay with him for the rest of his days.

He couldn't pretend it hadn't hurt, though.

Trent finally understood how Zoe used tattoos to say goodbye to periods of her life. He had found it an odd concept, carrying around that memory with you, but it made perfect sense now. She wasn't saying goodbye to people and places that had marked her; they had already left their trace, whether recognised in ink or not. No, she was saying goodbye to the version of herself that had lived those episodes, the one without the tattoo, which she consigned to the past as the ink entered her skin.

And Trent realised when getting his own tattoo that he wasn't saying goodbye to Zoe, either, but the version of life he had lived up until that point. This was truly a new Trent. Finally, he had moved on from the sins he had committed. They had marked him; he carried them with him, but they were not him. Not anymore.

A buzz at the door. Trent turned, curious. He had not been expecting anyone. He slipped his shirt on and did up a few strategic buttons to hold it in place before heading for the intercom.

'Who is it?'

'Marvin Benson.'

It was a voice from the past, from another life. This so took aback Trent that he buzzed open the door to the building without further question. Trent had worked with Benson back in the UK. They had been allies (of sorts) in Trent's final initiative, which had brought him into contact with Zoe and Ramstead, the village that ultimately broke him. Benson was the Head of Community Services at the district council and was partly responsible for Trent's hire.

Given the context, it was questionable whether that made him an ally or an enemy.

Benson huffed and puffed as he climbed the stairs. The elevator was broken. He had already been close to retirement when Trent saw him last. The intervening years had aged him little, but he was a man of the office, not the sports field. His head of grey hair was full, and he, like Trent, tended to wear a suit on every occasion.

Only when Trent laid eyes on Benson did he truly believe it was him.

'You're a hard man to track down,' Benson panted before giving Trent a weird half-hug, half-handshake. 'Don't you answer your phone?'

'Not really,' Trent said.

He had been checking it less and less of late. And he'd always had a policy that if someone doesn't leave a message, you don't call them back. That's how the scammers get you. And as for New Beginnings Consultancy, Hobbs was responsible for public liaison, not him.

'How's it possible to go off-grid?' Benson said. 'With the number of ways people have at their disposal to contact each other these days, I can't believe I had to come to Paris to find you.'

'Me, neither,' Trent said. 'Do you want to come in? It's not my place. I'm just renting it for a little bit.'

He added that last bit because he was concerned about what Benson might read into where he lived, although it was unclear what he might discern from the cream carpets, white walls and Ikea furniture.

'How did you find me?' Trent asked after Benson had collapsed on the sofa. He sat down on a dining room chair to face him.

'Your colleagues at the John R. Percival Foundation gave me your details. Have they never heard of confidentiality over here? I could have been anybody, for all they knew.'

'What did you tell them?' said Trent, sitting on a nearby dining chair.

'I said I was a former client of yours.'

'That's even worse. You could have been someone with a grudge, out for revenge!'

'I can quite imagine,' Benson said, getting out a hand-kerchief and dabbing his brow. 'I take it you have plenty of people after you?'

Trent considered this but didn't answer. 'Is that why you're here?'

'On the contrary. We were all so pleased to hear you fell on your feet. Especially our Leader.'

'Councillor Hope?' said Trent. This seemed the least likely to be true of all the things in Benson's statement. Hope had seen through Trent's plans from almost the start and had tried repeatedly to give him the boot.

Benson shook his head. 'Cllr Hope has been taking more of a backseat role of late. We have a new Leader now. That's what I wanted to see you about.'

'Oh?'

Benson pushed himself forward on the sofa until he was perched on the edge, as close as possible to Trent. He lowered his voice until it was almost a whisper.

'We have a problem.'

THE END

ACKNOWLEDGMENTS

Writing can be a lonely activity. This book felt like it was produced by a community.

I would like to thank the tutors and the other authors I interacted with during the writing courses in which I participated in 2024. Your passion, support and critique have been invaluable. Particular thanks to Pete Norris and Juliana Holzhauer-Barrie, who have been exposed to Trent the most over the months. One day, we'll all be household names!

Thanks also to my work for giving me time off for my writing, and to my lovely wife, Camille, for letting me abandon her with the kids while I go off in a cave somewhere to write. And finally, to William for his proofreading skills. That Big Mac tally is growing rather long...

ABOUT THE AUTHOR

P.J. Murphy writes novels that introduce unusual and humorous twists to established genres. If you pick up one of his books, you're in for an unusual read that rarely loses its sense of fun.

As a writer, P.J. tries to stick to the adage 'write what you know', although with the addition, 'just make sure you exaggerate and distort it beyond all recognition'. He is planning to write a novel about taking a road trip with a parrot. He has never owned a parrot.

Six Steps to Salvation is P.J. Murphy's fourth novel. His second novel, Dead Letters, was selected as genre winner for mystery books in the 2023 Page Turner Awards. His third novel, Yesterday's Shadow, won the same award for contemporary fiction in 2024.

ALSO BY P.J. MURPHY

Troubleshot

Trent Argent, community troubleshooter, has been parachuted into an isolated village identified as a problem area. It's his job to tell the Ramstead locals to eat less sugar and stop getting their teenagers pregnant. He's done this countless times before, but how did he end up so rich?

Dead Letters

A year after the disappearance of bestselling author Richard Debden, the manuscript of his unpublished final novel surfaces. As his closest friends delve into the text, they recognise parallels between fiction and reality. The story contains messages for them and a trail that leads across the country and – dare they hope? – to Richard. Also available as an audiobook.

Yesterday's Shadow

On a frozen night in Cambridge, sixteen-year-old Nick becomes the reluctant saviour of a homeless man named Peter. In the weeks that follow, Peter introduces Nick to his faith. But as Nick learns more about Peter, he begins to doubt the path he has chosen.